# PERENIS

## Soliloquy's Labyrinth Series

## BOOK FOUR

Published in 2023
by Truth Devour
www.truthdevour.com

With thanks to my Beta Readers
Danni Erbs & Suzanne Learmonth

Interior layout and design
by Publicious Book Publishing
www.publicious.com.au

Book cover design by:
Artist: Diana Toma
Email: diana@artbydianatoma.com
Facebook: facebook.com/ArtByDianaToma

Catalogue-in-Publication details available
from the National Library of Australia

ISBN: 978-0-6480905-2-6

Also available in ebook
ebook ISBN: 978-0-6480905-3-3

You are the author of your own story, so dream big,
work hard and make it happen no matter what.
Jared Leto

DIRECT
DEVOUR

## Soliloquy's Labyrinth Series

Adult Contemporary Fantasy / Paranormal
with a psychological edge

**Illuminarium**
(1st Book)

**Insurrection**
(2nd Book)

**Quantum**
(3rd Book)

**Perenis**
(4th Book)

**Optional:** Read Enigma Series at this
point before Dualities Reign

**Dualities Reign**
(5th Book)

## Enigma Series

**Readers Choice:** This is a stand alone series
or you can read it straight after Book 4
in the Soliloquy's Labyrinth Series.

Adult Contemporary Fantasy Trilogy
with sensual erotic undertones and a dash of paranormal.

**Wantin**
(1st book)

**Unrequited**
(2nd book)

**Sated**
(3rd book)

# Treaty

Aimlessly I wandered through countless villages within the Toyama prefecture located in the southeast district of Japan. I was a lone gaijin traveling by foot to onlookers, mainly in a state of self-imposed silence. Inside I felt the sum of my experiences causing an emotional storm that fractured my mind into a myriad of distinct voices. Their persistent demand for my attention was draining me lifeforce. I could only muster the strength to place one foot in front of the other as I drew shallow breaths. A certainty came with the pain in my chest that I knew stemmed from my heart metaphorically crystalizing with the shards of a stabbing reality that I would eventually have to face. For now, my focus was consumed by my desire to no longer live while accepting the knowledge that the peace of mind I so profoundly craved could not be granted if I chose at this juncture to allow myself to die, the perfect juxtaposition.

Time no longer seemed to hold any relevance. The only aspect of my life that altered now was the scenery, as I continued to roam from place to place. Occasionally I would catch a glimpse of what I assumed was my sadness reflected in stranger's eyes. It felt as though they held a relatable truth that allowed them to connect to my pain. It was all I could see. It felt excruciating to sense it thriving within them. I wanted to carry the burden alone. One foot in front of the other, step by step, I wander.

Violent waves of hunger pangs surged through my malnourished body. Flashcard images of my father being orally pleasured by Libertine while my mother sadistically laughs in the background with her boyfriend Devon displaying a menacing grimace floods my aching mind. A knotted pit begins to form as I fight against another cramp. Forced to enact the purging of my empty stomach involuntarily, I bent over at the side of the road and began to dry wretch. The rush of discomfort surged to the back of my eyes, invoking a spark of white tendrils to appear. Shades of molten grey hues began to glide across my eyelids. Finally, I felt my knees released as I ungracefully collapsed to the ground. My body's weight produced the sound of a dull thud as the granules of dirt formed a light puff of dust. The impact made my body shudder. I reefed my head back to greedily gulp at the filthy air to fill my winded lungs. An electrical shockwave of pain thrust me into a fetal position. The consuming sensation of my entire body in shock dulled the voices to a distant hum as I felt the warmth from the release of my bowels travel along the surface of my skin.

* * * * *

"Wake Miss, you must eat."

I opened my eyes slowly. In front of me was a whisp of a child who championed a smile so bright that it almost made me involuntarily reciprocate. I looked across at the small table where steam was rising from a bowl.

"Water," I whispered in a scratchy voice.

The little girl ran off and just as quickly returned. She was empty handed, but her radiant smile beamed, while her little plaited pig tails swayed as she walked toward me.

"Grandma is coming."

I heard the shuffle of footsteps then saw a hunched, elderly woman enter. Her tired eyes smiled as they greeted mine. She picked up the bowl on her way towards me and then knelt by the futon where I lay. I went to raise my head only to drop it back down at the first greeting of an unpleasant sharp pain.

"Hit your head. KONK." said the little girl waving her arms about while dancing around the room. "Obaachan say you sleeping near the road. Obaachan drag your body home."

I looked at the frail old lady's hand, scooping a portion of the liquid from the bowl into a wooden spoon. My stomach began to grumble when it was hovering near the entrance of my mouth. Admittedly it didn't smell appetizing, but my hunger drove my decision to reluctantly part my lips so she could pour some of it in. There was an earthy, pungent aftertaste that made me scowl.  No sooner had she emptied the first ladle; the elderly woman methodically scooped up some more to feed me. The sensation of the lukewarm liquid gliding down my throat felt good. I wanted to satisfy my craving to greedily guzzle down a gallon of water but held no strength to do more than open my mouth to gratefully receive the portion of food I was given. Ladle after ladle was delivered until I heard it scrape against the bowl.

My eyelids felt heavy as I watched them both exit the room in slow motion. The little girl turned and energetically waved to me as her Grandma slid the door shut. The greeting of a faint breeze on my skin eased the searing heat from my fever. Exhausted, I surrendered to the need to drift off to sleep. I was safe.

* * * * *

"York, is that you?"

Slowly I walked toward the little boy who was kneeling beside the raging riverbed. I could hear him whistling an unremarkable tune. Reaching out to touch his shoulder, I froze midway when I realized I possessed impaired vision. All that there was for me to see was displayed in monochromatic hues. York swiftly turned and shifted to a defensive stance. He stared at me with his hands up before his body softened, and a smile appeared.

He stepped in and wrapped his arms around my waist. "You found me. You finally found me."

"Where am I?" I asked looking down at the top of his sweet little head.

The little boy's grip loosened as he slowly stepped back. "You still don't know do you?"

I paused and thought for a moment. "I think I do. You're York. Isn't that your name? I read your diary. The one you left hidden in the tree." I said feeling disorientated. I glanced around and then looked back at him, "Where is Huckleberry?"

"You ask questions in search for answers that you already know."

The little boy took a step backward. The water was caressing the edge of his right heel. I felt goosebumps rise on the surface of my skin as I watched him take another step back into the ice-cool water. I was involuntarily flinching at the sensation.

"Who am I?" He asked staring directly into my eyes.

"I don't know. I thought you were York. I'm sorry, I'm unsure."

The boy took another step back and then in quick succession did a few more.

"Please stop. Don't go any deeper. Talk to me, tell me who you are."

"Why?" asked the boy as he slowly lowered his body into the river.

A shiver surged up my spine; my chest felt heavy as I began to cough. I gasped for air with a sudden need to open my eyes. My entire body was immersed in water. Scared and confused, my arms flailed as I felt someone pressed up from behind me clasp their hand around my neck to encourage my head to stay above the waterline. With blurred vision, I noticed the little Japanese girl I had met earlier was naked, running along the pool's edge, waving her hands as she leaned over to get my attention.

"It's okay Miss, you in special onsen with Obaachan. She hold you. No scare, Obaachan work hard to break fever. Very sick."

I could feel my heart beating fast within my chest. My mind was completely scrambled. The soothing heat of the water was reducing my body's need to shiver involuntarily. I closed my eyes as I heard the splash from the little girl jumping in. Her Grandma was using the knuckles on her fingers to work up and down the length of my spine. I wasn't sure of precisely what she was trying to achieve, but it certainly hurt enough to make my cramped muscles flinch.

When the little girl came closer, I could feel the movement in the waters flow churning from her little legs treading.

"What is your name?" I whispered.

"Atsuko and Obaachan, Kayoko."

My lips felt dry as I parted them to speak, "I am Harper."

"Harper, Harper, Atsuko and Harper."

"Thank you for helping me." I said, struggling to keep my eyes open.

"Obaachan, say you are broken. She try fix you."

I nod my head slightly. "You speak English so well."

Atsuko raised her hand to cover her mouth as she giggled, "Thank yoooou."

Kayoko adjusted my body's position so she could support my torso from underneath while she migrated to my right. I looked up at the underside of the elderly woman's weathered face as she steered my body toward the edge of the bath. When she emerged from the water, she placed her arms beneath my shoulders while encouraging me to lift myself out partially. I placed my legs down and used what little strength I had to begin to rise.

"Chotto matte kudasai," said Grandma as she raised her hands to indicate I stop.

"Obaachan request stop. Please sit here, no fall."

I turned slightly to see the old lady drag a stool out and then grab a wooden stick. She readjusted a few other stools before returning. The little girl watched intently as her naked grandmother placed the stick upright, leaned in, and took a step. She was demonstrating that it was a walking aid. Upon nodding my head in acknowledgment, she passed it to me. I grasped the top end, using it as leverage to help me slowly swivel around. Focused on the task at hand, I placed all the energy I could muster into getting myself upright. The little girl clapped her hands with happiness. Her Grandma put one hand around my arm while she placed the other on the center of my back, using it to gently encourage me to navigate to the seat.

Step by step we inched closer to the wooden three-legged stool until I was finally standing over it.

"Please sit," said Atsuko gesturing down.

I managed to ungracefully land the center of my bare bony ass on the tiny stool with a single-minded focus. It was so low to the ground it felt like I was squatting. The little girl picked up two blocks of soap, keeping one and passing the other across to me.

"You must wash before and after bath."

They both sat on the matching stools that were positioned on either side of me. I watched the little girl begin to vigorously rub the soap all over as she encouraged me through gestures to do the same. The floral scent had a hint of jasmine. It didn't lather like soaps I've used before. The granular texture was exfoliating and left a chalk-like coating on my skin. When I was finished, the girl picked up a bucket to fill it with water. It was only partially filled when she stood and dumped it on herself to wash the soap away. She did this three times before turning to do the same for me. I watched as she dipped her little hand in the bucket to check the temperature. When it was almost filled to the brim, she closed off the tap and shifted the bucket closer to me before turning to repeat the same with the next bucket.

Kayoko rose to her feet and moved her position so that she stood over me. Without warning, she began rubbing my scalp with zeal. Satisfied with her efforts, she migrated to my back. Using something that felt rather course, she scrubbed every inch of exposed skin raw. As Atsuko placed the third bucket down, her grandmother

Kayoko picked up one and dumped it over my head. The next was thrown at my back, and the final bucket of water was tossed at my front. Once she was satisfied that I was clean, Kayoko followed suit. It didn't take long before they were both grabbing an arm each to help me to rise to a stand. The weakness in my lower limbs caused me to lose my footing slightly. A sense of light headiness struck the base of my neck when a cold shiver rushed up to my spine. Grandma tapped my shoulder to grab my attention as she passed me the stick. I clasped it in my left hand before attempting to take my first step. Kayoko gave me a reassuring look as she squeezed my arm. With her strength, I leveraged an ability to shuffle my feet to walk. Entering into another room, the little girl ran ahead. I watched as she pulled back a curtain that revealed a row of traditional dressing gowns. She jumped on the little stool positioned near the clothing, removed one of the gowns from its hanger, and threw it across to me. My reflexes engaged as I just managed to catch the edge of the fabric then lifted it in the air to avoid having it touch the ground. The old lady took it from my hand, opened it up, and stepped forward. I slowly turned as I felt her drape it across my shoulders. Methodically she worked to help me into the gown, wrapping it tightly around my body and finally securing it tight against my waist. The oriental quilted fabric felt heavy on my bones. I glanced across at the little girl who was struggling to squirm her way into her clothes. The grunting sounds of frustration she released made her grandma laugh. She went across to guide her grandchild's arms through the sleeves and then slipped out of sight to dress.

Feeling exhausted, I stood there in silence while I waited for them. When Atsuko put on her shoes, I realized I was still barefoot. A rustling sound shifted my attention toward the old lady who returned, dragging a bamboo mat to the edge of my feet. She smiled and directed me to it.

"Lay please. We go home now."

I took a slight step forward. "It's okay. I can walk," lifting the stick and pointing to my legs.

Atsuko nodded. "Kanojo wa arukitai."

Grandma shook her head slightly, "Īe, kanojo wa yowa sugiru."

"Grandma say you still weak. She worry you fall. Please sit."

I knew I was in no position to argue, so I crouched down, turned my body, and shuffled across the edge and onto the bamboo mat. When I was centered, Kayoko placed her feet on either side of the mat to secure it to the ground before grabbing my underarms and pulling me up toward her feet. She then walked across to the foot of the mat, flipping it up on both sides to secure the ends, so it was flush against the soles of my feet. Atsuko passed her Grandma a corner of a blanket that they carefully tucked me into. Together they rolled the sides of the mat around my body then Grandma looped and tied them off in the center to make a basket.

Sporting a lovely smile, Atsuko caressed the top of my head with her tiny hand. "You be okay." With the sentiment complete, she stood up and wandered out of sight.

Kayoko walked to the top of the mat, picked up the rope, placed it across her forehead before looping her hands into it on each side. I tried to remain still while wondering how to alleviate the burden I was causing this kind elderly woman. Just as I felt the first jerk of motion occur, Atsuko returned to place the walking stick inside the makeshift cocoon. My body slid down the mat then settled into the momentum measured by Grandma's steady pace.

It didn't take long before we were outside under a spectacular star-filled blackened sky. I had lost all sense of time, so it was hard to ascertain whether it was late evening or early morning. The absence of any audible detection of wildlife led me to assume it was likely late in the evening. The sound of my body being dragged on the dirt pathway was a possible contributor to their absence. I suddenly had a new appreciation for how unwell I had been. The fact that I had no recollection of when I came to be in these people's care highlighted that I was indeed in need of assistance.

* * * * *

The best part of an hour had passed before Atsuko, and Kayoko stopped in front of an ornate wooden gate where the sounds of a dog sniffing and whimpering could be heard. I saw a glimpse of light filter through from a small door within the gate that was unlatched and opened by Kayoko. Quick as a whip, Atsuko jumped through and disappeared, taking the sound of the dog with her. Grandma closed the small opening before releasing the rope from her head and hands. She knelt and began to unravel the bind that held me within the mat. I could hear voices in the distance, and then a flurry of footsteps made their way to the gate. The doors shook from the force of being slid open. A man in his late forties froze for a moment as he looked at me lying there. I wasn't sure what was happening, and by the look on his face, neither did he.

"Tasukete," said Grandma who was pointing at my feet.

The man glanced across at where she gestured then scurried over.

"Hai" He said, now busily undoing the knots.

Atsuko poked her head out. "This my papa and this Aki, family dog. Mama makes food."

Her father raised his head to acknowledge me with a slight bow. Standing up as the mat released, he stepped forward and offered me both his hands. Our clasp became a vice tight grip. Leveraging the strength in his legs he walked backwards to assist me to rise. Grandma placed her hand on my back to support me.

I felt relieved to be upright. Placing my hands together in a mock praying pose I executed a slight bow to them all as a gesture of thanks, "Dōmo arigatōgozaimashita."

"Dōitashimashite," said the man as he bowed again.

Grandma seemed pleased that I said thanks in her native tongue.

"Here you go." Atsuko passed me the walking stick and grabbed my hand to guide me into the house. Her father and grandmother followed suit. I could tell that Aki was wary of me as he took a wide berth to avoid being within proximity. When I entered their home, he stayed outside but maintained a visual of me with his tail upright and perfectly still.

A lady came out from the hall, touching her hair and bowing as she entered.

"Hello, pleased to meet you, I am Kimiko, Atsuko's mother. This my husband Hiro."

"Hello. Yes, I met him outside. I am Harper."

Kimiko smiles as she says, "Welcome to our home."

"Thank you. I feel very grateful for your kindness. I will find a way to repay you."

"Please, no need. I show to room. You must rest."

I turned to look at the others, "Dōmo arigatōgozaimashita. Oyasuminasai."

Grandma who was now sitting down smiled approvingly at my words of thanks and wishing them a good night.

"Oyasuminasai," she said in response.

Atsuko and her father were taking off Kayoko's slippers. Her feet were red and swollen from the taxing journey. I felt terrible knowing she had gone to all this trouble to help me, a stranger. I had to find a way to return the kindness they have bestowed upon me.

"Come, come, this way," said Kimiko who was already headed down the hall.

I followed her to the end of the passage. She opened the door to a small room with no windows, and no pictures hung on the walls. There was just a tiny tatami mat with a rolled-up futon at the end of it.

"Sorry small," she said in a soft voice. "Berry small."

Stepping inside I nodded my head, "This is perfect. Thank you."

Kimiko followed me in and proceeded to unravel the futon. She then lifted the blanket and gestured for me to lie down. As I did, she draped it over me.

"Rest. I prepare food bring after."

"I'm okay, please, you don't need to go to any more trouble."

There was a momentary change in her expression, "No trouble." With this she left the room and slid the door closed behind her.

I recognized that I felt comfort within the darkness as I wrapped my arms around myself and closed my eyes. The last thought I had was about how much I missed the soft cradle of a quality pillow.

* * * * *

The whispers of the voices made it hard to decern precisely what they were saying. I heard the words "Akuma and kamigami," which loosely translates to demons and gods. There was no way for me to know what the time was, but the pressure on my bladder motivated me to leave the confines of my room regardless. Shifting into a position that allowed me to rise, I couldn't help but notice my body was no longer struggling. In the darkness, I stood for a moment listening and wondered how the old lady had acquired such an ability to assist with healing me. It felt great to be in control of my legs. The placement of my footing on the floor's surface was solid again. When I slid the door open, the voices immediately stopped. I stood in the hallway, wondering where the restroom might be.

To the far left I could see movement as someone slid the door open.

"You have awoken," whispered Kimiko.

"Yes, I am sorry to disturb. I need to use a toilet."

"Hai, come."

I followed her into the main room where I had first entered the house, and then walked past the kitchen, which lead to another passage that ventured outside down a path to a small outdoor facility.

Kimiko pulled a chord that switched on a small light that was hanging from the ceiling.

"You must careful. No foot in hole."

I peered in, "Okay."

Kimiko turned and left me to do my business.

The relief from the pressure I felt in my bladder was blissful.

When I returned inside Kimiko was rushing about the kitchen.

"Please, if this is for me, I do not want you to go to any trouble. I am okay."

"You sleep." She mumbled to herself as she counted with her fingers. "Three day. Must eat."

"Three days? Really?"

"Bery sick. Fever. Obaachan tell must not wake. Body heal. Wake when ready. Now food."

The smell of the miso soup heating on the stove made my mouth water. I watched as she orchestrated a mini feast of seaweed, seared salmon on a bed of rice, placed pickled condiments on the side as well as a small serve of soy sauce.

Kimiko slid the plate over to me. "Please, eat."

I picked up the chopsticks and began to consume the meal. The moment the first mouthful hit my tongue, my senses were engaged, and I was hungry. I shoveled that food in, taking sips of the miso between bites to wash it down. Every serving felt like it was the best I had ever had. In minutes I found my feeding frenzy was drawing to a close.

"Please rest now. When morning you eat. Now I bring bucket."

I looked at her quizzically.

"Body need food. May also say no. Bucket for no."

I started to help her clear the bench. "Thank you."

"Okay, okay to leave. I do. Please, rest. I bring bucket." She passed me a freshly filled glass of water.

I looked at her again.

"It okay, please rest Harpersan."

I took the glass and went back to my room, noting there were five sliding doors plus mine along the way. As I entered my quarters, I swiftly turned to survey the hall. The door that was diagonally opposite seemed slightly more ajar than when I had first walked past it. I glared into the blackness while developing a feeling that someone was staring right at me. I began sliding my door closed, getting the sense that something wasn't right. The energy of the whole family felt genuine, but my intuition was alarming me to the presence of imminent danger.

No longer feeling tired, I lay down with my arms folded behind my head, staring up at the wooden ceiling. I thought about Huckleberry and the dream I had with the little boy. His intense deep stare coupled with his words, 'Who am I?' circled about my mind.

In the early hours of the morning, I fumbled about to find the bucket Kimiko had left for me. I spent a solid hour invested in purging the contents of my stomach while rinsing my mouth with water between stints. Sweat poured from my brow as my hands shook. The cramps in my gut seemed to find synchronicity with the pounding of my rapidly developing headache. An endless supply of thick dark green bile oozed out, leaving a disgusting sweet taste in my mouth. Truly thankful when it was finally done, I crawled under the covers and set off to sleep again.

* * * * *

The bustle of the resident's footsteps gently aided my withdrawal from slumber. When I rose to my feet, I was grateful to see that my disgusting bucket of vomit was absent, and there were fresh clothes laid out for me to change into. It was a plain raw cotton loose tunic, some drawstring pants, and slippers. I got dressed and headed out the door feeling more robust than I had in a long time.

I followed the sound of voices and ended up in their rather extraordinary ornate garden. They were sitting down on small mats in a circle around a feast. When they saw me approach, Atsuko shuffled across so that her mother could place a cushion between them. I knelt on it, resting my hands on my lap.

'Thank you, for the kindness you have shown me. I feel much better."

A strange noise came from inside the house that immediately brought tension to their faces. Hiro calmly stood up and disappeared down the hallway.

"What was that?" I asked.

"Must eat. Body need strength. Here," said Kimiko passing me a small serve of rice with pickles and seaweed.

In the background the whaling noises increased in volume. The family continued to eat without appearing to skip a beat, yet I could feel the energy between them silently shift.

I placed my bowl down. "There is something wrong, I can feel it. What is making that noise? It sounds like someone is in a lot of pain."

"My oniichan, Futoshi."

"You have an older brother that needs help?" I asked.

"Atsuko, no speak."

Atsuko grabbed her mother's hand, "But Obaachan tell she help."

I looked at Kimiko, "Trust in Kayoko and tell me what I need to know. If I can assist, I will."

Kimiko looked at her mother.

Kayoko stared straight into her daughter's eyes and softly spoke one word, "Shinrai."

Shinrai translated means trust. I didn't know what was wrong with her grandson, nor could I fathom what she thought I could do to assist, but after all she had done for me, I knew that I needed to try my best to help them.

Atsuko rubbed her mom's leg, "She help."

Kimiko grasped her daughter's hands and feigned a smile. She then bowed her head slightly as she shuffled her body to face and engage me.

"Sorry mother bring you. No help. Danger Futoshi. I mother, no trust, scared. Please eat food, then must leave. Sorry, no stay."

"No, momma, no," said Atsuko.

"Shhh, Atsuko, no."

I placed my bowl down and rose to my feet. "I understand." Slowly I turned and walked back into the house. I could hear Grandma asking her daughter what she had said. Sweet little Atsuko was sobbing.

Instead of heading to my room, I went to the door diagonally opposite and slid it wide open. Inside was Hiro crouched over a heavily chained boy secured to wooden pillars. Horrific scaring covered every inch of the parts of his body that I could see. Fresh deep gouges were dripping blood from his forearms. The room reeked from the dank blood-stained walls that were covered in writing.

"Kimikoooo, Kimikoooo," yelled Hiro.

The boy jerked from his father's arms and ran toward me with his teeth exposed in a menacing display of intent to execute harm. I remained still as I watched him hurl at me. Kimiko came running toward the door & pulled me back as his hands extended in an attempt to secure me within his grasp.

"No, you go. Secreto," she said pleadingly.

My heart was palpitating fast as I tried to make sense of what I was seeing. Their son looked tortured, but they exuded love and acted in a protective manner.

Grandma came from around the corner and was walking toward us calling out in a stern voice to Kimiko and her son Hiro, "Sorera o sa seru."

She was telling them to let us be. There was obviously a strong element of faith that Grandma held for her to risk exposing this secret.

"Why is this child chained?" I asked.

Hiro was clearly angry. He brushed past me as he stepped out of the room, walking straight up to Grandma to challenge her request. Kimiko joined him.

I maintained my distance while observing the boy's active display of ferocious behavior. It seemed to contradict the vacancy in his dilated pupils. He visibly projected anger, but I sensed a deep-seated fear. While the others were distracted by arguing about my presence, I took the opportunity to step forward carefully. As I re-entered the room, I ventured close enough to almost be within his reach. There was drool oozing from his mouth as he snarled. The overpowering stench of his poor hygiene was distracting. Subconsciously I felt weighted by an energy that was guiding me to sit on the ground. I ignored the boy's menacing presence and knelt in front of him. I then placed my palms on my lap, face-up, and closed my eyes. Calming my breath, I focused on exuding serene energy to remove any sense of perceived threat. I could feel the thrusts of air as the boy lunged toward me. His arms were waving about in an attempt to grab hold. It was terrifying, but for some reason, I felt compelled to calm my energy and visualize surrounding the boy with a healing vibration of light. I deepened my breath drowning out the noise of my surroundings. Deeper and deeper, I fell into a hypnotic rhythm where I expanded my energy to flow freely about the room.

"Look," said Atsuko.

I could feel the air stir as the shuffling of footsteps came closer.

"Noto possible," stated Kimiko.

"Shinrai," whispered Grandma.

# Gaijin

The steam was still rising from my freshly boiled pot of green tea. I poured the piping hot liquid into a cup and blew on it as I took some time out to enjoy watching the birds in the garden darting in-between the cherry blossom trees. It had been a while since I had felt this good. My core strength was slowly being reclaimed, but my mind was yet to free itself from the insanity that I had chosen to physically leave behind.

"Harpersan hungry deska?" asked Kimiko as she approached.

"No, I'm okay. Please come sit with me."

Kimiko obliged my request and sat beside me.

"I want you to tell me more about what happened to Futoshi. I believe that I can see glimpses of your son; he is still in there fighting. My instincts tell me that Futoshi is locked in his body. He keeps tearing at his skin. His behavior indicates that he is trying to get something out. Help me understand how he became this way."

"Harpersan offer great kindness, and Futoshi trust. Not possible to help. Futoshi my son. Mother love son.

Even no help," said Kimiko dropping her gaze to stare at her hands. "Futoshi gone."

"Futoshi is in there. I know it. I want to help him and believe that I can, but I need your insight. Please, tell me everything." I placed my finger underneath Kimiko's chin to encourage her to lift her head. "You have nothing to lose and a very real chance to regain your son. I cannot guarantee the outcome, but I promise I will do everything I can to give him the best chance at returning."

A stern voice called out from behind us, "Tell her." Kimiko's husband Hiro stepped forward and placed his right hand on her left shoulder. "Okay. Must tell her."

Kimiko released a huge sigh as she rose to her feet. "Come."

She led me down the passage back toward the kitchen. The rest of the family scattered into various rooms away from us. Kimiko remained quiet as she boiled a fresh pot of green tea, placed it on a tray with two cups and headed out to a secluded section of the ornate garden. She poured a serve of the tea for me, before placing the pot down. I then served a portion in another cup and passed it to her. The light breeze had the steam freely dancing toward the endless blue skies. Using both her hands, Kimiko lifted the cup and took a sip. She paused for a moment, took another sip and then dropped her hands down, while cupping the drink.

"Two year ago, bad men take all children. One boy, all family. So confused. We scream, fight, some die. Berry scary, lights, dogs attack family, bado men break door, come, take our Futoshi. If family no son, take youngest daughter."

Her hands were shaking.

I remained silent.

"Why? Government betray village. Scared to fight no make trouble." Her head lowered. "Village berry fear come take other children." Her teardrops made a splotch on the ground. "Children gone, village no speak, scare. I scream, cry, look for Futoshi. Village angry Hiro, angry me for speak. Village scare to fight. No want lose more children. Atsuko secreto live Kayoko keep safe. Hiro look Futoshi. Long time nothing. Many hundred children taken from province. How children ghost?"

Kimiko paused to take another sip of her tea.

"I home market, listen noise see Futoshi door open. Heart so fast. Drop vegetables run to room. Futoshi no speak. He look me berry anger. I try touch, Futoshi attack. Neck shaking head this way." Kimiko opened her mouth to enact the bite and shook her head left to right. "Run from room close door. I on floor, here me door, him door. Blood here," she moved her hair to reveal a scar on her neck. "Pain no here, pain here." She tapped on her chest near her heart. Kimiko paused for a moment to draw a deep breath. "No Futoshi, not son. Like animal, go crazy dog. Hiro try calm, no trust. Futoshi secreto, no villager, no police. Danger for Futoshi. Here secreto."

"Since his return, has he ever talked?"

"No. Like animal. Groooowl, Hsssssspt. No speak."

"The writing on the walls, I can detect by the smell that he has used his own blood. The section where the kanji repeats, what does it say?"

"Clean, Futoshi again. Clean, Futoshi again. We leave."

"What does it say?"

"Get it out."

"Get it out?" I replied.

"Hai, get it out."

"Did you check his body for surgical scars or needle marks?"

"Hiro think something. He look Futoshi body, see nothing."

"Does he have a normal temperature?"

"Hai."

"Can you get Hiro to check please?"

"Hai."

"When you were bitten," I tapped her neck. "What happened? Blood? Fever?"

"Lot of blood."

"Did the wound heal quickly? Did it get infected?"

"Fever ten day; head hurt. Obaachan put medicine here and here." She was pointing to the scar on her neck and her forehead.

"It doesn't give me much to go on, but it helps. Thank you. I'm going to need to contact a trusted advisor to ask for some help. Would you be okay with me arranging for him to do some tests on your son?"

"Tests? No."

"We will try to learn what we can from a pathology sample of his blood, skin cells, hair, nail, urine and poo. We might need some swabs from the inside of his mouth and nose too. I want to see what type of microbes, parasites and bacteria are living within your son and will compare them to you, your husband and daughters' microbiomes."

"No understand."

"I need my friend to come and help me run some tests on the family to help Futoshi."

"Futoshi sick make crazy?"

I nodded my head, "I honestly don't know, maybe. I want to do tests to see what we can learn. I cannot take

Futoshi to my friend's laboratory, so I will ask him to travel to Japan, to your home. Are you okay with this?"

"I must speak Hiro."

"Of course, I understand. I'll go get ready to head into town to make contact with my friend."

"No disrespecto. Friend, can trust?"

I placed my hand on hers. "Hai. I trust him. If anyone is going to be able to assist me in understanding what is happening to your son, it is him. He is the only person I know that might be able to help. Please speak with Hiro now. It will be useful to find out what Grandmother placed in the medicine she used to heal you." I tapped on Kimiko's neck near the scar. "Also, gather the information on what she used on me to help heal my sickness. We may need to have this available."

"Okay," said Kimiko.

Fueled by a sense of hope, there was a positive shift in our respective energies as we both stood up and made our way inside. I headed across to the bathroom to wash, while Kimiko went in search of her husband.

Using a small towel drenched in cold water, I cleaned my face and then placed the cloth under my clothes to methodically freshened up the rest of my body. The luxury of showers was a distant memory. There were no fancy shampoo's, just a bar of soap made with local ingredients and fragranced with seasonal dried flowers.

"Will you save my brother?"

Startled I jumped to the side.

"Obaachan told me you can." Atsuko, laughed. "I scare you."

I smiled, "Yes, you did. Where I come from, people don't walk into the bathroom when it is being used by someone."

"Why?"

"We like to have privacy."

"What is privacy?"

"It is when you leave people alone to do what they want with no-one watching."

Atsuko placed her hand to her mouth, "Oh."

I put the towel in the basin before crouching down in front of her. "It's okay, you didn't do anything wrong."

She smiled as she leaned in, placing her forehead against mine, "I know. Will you help my brother?"

"I'll try," I said as I put both my hands on either side of her face, lightly squeezing her cheeks. I then kissed the top of her head as I stood up.

Pleased with this, Atsuko waved on her way skipping out the door.

* * * * *

"Roman, over here." I said with a wave.

He came toward me, dropped his swag at my feet, bent down as though he was going to collect it again but picked me up with a twirl instead.

"Girl, you look amazing."

I laughed, "You need a shower. Put me down before you drop me."

He rubbed his face into my neck before gently placing me back on the ground.

"Awe, you love it. This is the aroma culminated from a ten-hour flight, complete with a two-hour bus ride from the airport, direct to you. Inhale deep my friend."

I feigned an expression of disgust that made him burst into laughter. "No thanks." I said, then stepped across to pick up his bag. "Is this all you brought with you?"

"God no. I shipped my equipment ahead of my arrival. My secretary confirmed that it is safely stored at the warehouse you arranged for me. I'll head over there once I've checked into the hotel. Is it the same place you are staying at?"

"Secretary? Since when does an underground Bio Hacker have a need for a secretary?"

"Ha! Things have changed, I've gone mainstream. My genetic engineering and epigenetics research has been officially acknowledged. I have write ups in scientific journals and spend nearly half of my time traveling around the globe on speaking engagements. It's been a blast."

"I had no idea. Congratulations."

"I should confess that my secretary is actually my wife, but she was my secretary first, then one thing led to another and you know, now she is my wife."

"Amazing, we clearly have some catching up to do. Are you hungry?"

"Starved."

"Great, just across the road down that lane is this little place that makes the best okonomiyaki." I swung his swag over my shoulder and led the way.

Inside the dimly lit eatery we found a table away from the rest of the patrons dining. We ordered two beers and a couple of house special okonomiyaki's.

"Can you give me a brief on the little boy? Your email just referenced that he was likely infected, but you didn't say with what."

"I'm not sure whether he is infected or not. I have a suspicion that there is something that has been introduced into his system. I haven't got the faintest idea of what it is or what it was supposed to do. I sense him, being present but trapped by something."

"Okay, well let's start with what you do know."

"Prior to him being abducted Futoshi was a healthy, fully functioning child."

"Abducted? You never mentioned anything about an abduction."

"Shhh, try to keep your voice down. I told you I was restricted in what I could tell you until we met in person. I'm not sure who's behind all of this, which is why to keep us safe, I needed to ensure you were unencumbered by the details. In case your presence caused suspicion for the authorities to ask questions."

"Got it." Roman pretended to zip his lips shut.

"When Futoshi returned, he was unable to verbalize anything. He seems to understand what is being said to him, but he fails to reciprocate. Instead of using words, he grunts and growls. I have watched him go into a frenzy scratching his body. Some fevers come and go that appear to synchronize to bursts of uncontrolled rage. He uses his blood to write on the walls over and over, 'Get it out.' I guess that is where my thoughts latched to the idea of implants."

"A microchip?"

"Not hardware as such. I am more inclined to suspect that it is a synthesized virus."

Roman squinted as he gazed into my eyes. "Why?"

"The fevers. The rage. I get the impression it is something biological. That's why I called you."

"Okay sure, but why this little boy? What is the underlying motive?"

"Oh, sorry I get what you mean." I paused as I heard footsteps approach.

"Excuse me, two house okonomiyaki specials and two beru's." The waitress placed the order down on the table. "Thank you for waiting, please enjoy food."

"Dōmo arigatō."

"Thank you," said Roman repositioning his meal to be closer to his chopsticks.

The waitress smiled, gave a slight bow of her head and left us.

"This smells fantastic, what is it?" Asked Roman.

"It's a Japanese savory pancake that is made out of shredded vegetables, bound by some egg and rice flour. Their house specialty is infused with freshly harvested Mozuku seaweed from the coastline waters of Okinawa as well as the purple sweet potato, which is sourced from the same island. The traditional Japanese mayonnaise and tongutsu sauce is served on top, but the absolute hero of this dish that brings the whole experience to another level is this side sauce that you dip into." I lifted my sauce and drizzled it all over my serve. "Alternatively, you can do as I did and drown your meal in it."

Roman picked up his beer. "My mouth is watering, let's dig in. Cheers"

I clinked my glass with his and took a mouthful of the ice-cold beer.

After Roman drank half of his beer in two large gulps, he placed the glass down, picked up the chopsticks in one hand, the sauce with the other and began to devour the meal. I quickly followed suit.

"Oh my, you aren't wrong about this sauce. It's insanely delicious."

I nodded my head as I stuffed another serve of the pancake into my mouth. "It's a combination of a locally made light soya sauce infused with goya."

"What's goya?"

"It's a bitter melon that is used a lot by the Okinawan's. The chef was raised there, which is why the regions gastronomic influences are so prominent in his menu."

"Wow, wow, wow, I can't believe how delicious this is."

There was silence between us as we ate mouthful after glorious mouthful. If speed eating were an occupation, the two of us would qualify as masters. We both consumed our serves in record time and chased it down with the remainder of our beer.

Sitting back in my chair post the culinary indulgence, I looked across at Roman and smiled. "I'm full, but you look like you could smash down another serve. Do you want me to place the order?"

"Seriously, Harp's, I could eat three of them, but I won't. This is no time to get side laid into a food coma." He looked around the restaurant and smiled. "Who would have thought that such an unassuming little place would serve up one of the best meals of my life?"

I chuckled, "I'm glad you liked it."

"Nay, this is true love, my friend." He raised his hand to get the waitress's attention. She quickly scurried across the room toward us. Roman lifted his empty beer glass. "Can we have two more beers, please?"

She nodded, cleared our table and went off to fulfil our order.

With the release of a satisfied sigh, he leaned back in his chair and smiled, "I'm sorry. You were going to explain why this boy was cherry picked as a target."

The waitress returned with the beer. "Would you like to see desserto menu?"

"No, thank you," replied Roman. I shook my head to confirm the same.

When the waitress left, Roman raised his glass in my direction as a gesture before taking a big gulp.

I looked around to ensure that no one was in earshot. "Futoshi wasn't cherry-picked. Six years ago, an unidentified covert military group came at night in full raid gear and took one boy from each lineage. Every home was raided, and hundreds of children were taken. Futoshi, as far as we are aware, is the only one who ever returned home. It is critical that no-one finds out that he is back."

The expression on Roman's face changed as he placed his beer down and lent forward. "I'm sorry. I didn't realize. How have I not heard about this?"

"The whole operation flew under the radar. The villagers were petrified that if they did anything, their other children would be taken too. It seems to have been a clandestine operation executed with uncanny speed and precision."

"How could so many children just disappear?"

"Exactly. How could they? I don't know the answer. Whoever is behind this has clout."

Roman looked around the room then back at me, "What do you think I can do to help the boy?"

"Do you remember in University when you had that condition that always sent you running to the toilet?"

"Yes, IBS. Irritable Bowel Syndrome."

"You told me you cured it with a fecal transplant. Right?"

Roman smiled, "That was the birth of my Bio-Hacking interests. No existing medications provided a cure. I tried many off-the-shelf and prescription products with marginal results. All the signs led toward changing my gut and bowel flora. I believed if I could alter the composition, the severity of my condition would lessen, possibly even get abolished."

"And it was, yes?"

"Yes. It's not perfect, but I am not running to the toilet in pain, cramped, and sweating after every meal. What has this got to do with the boy's condition?"

"I don't know. It's a hunch, but I somehow believe that Futoshi may be imprisoned within his own body. I keep feeling like it is a hostile takeover by something foreign that was introduced into his system. My first instinct when I looked into his eyes was to contact you. His best chance is to have a complete system overhaul, to flush out whatever is in there." I took Romans hand in mine, "I'm talking about the works. A full blood transfusion, an introduction to new gut and bowel flora, along with high doses of immunity-building antioxidants to help strengthen him. What do you think?"

"There are risks to it, Harper. It is not as simple as you think. If the child is already not well and we don't know why I have no idea if what I am doing will help him or further hurt him. Does it have to take place here? I would feel more comfortable doing this in a controlled manner within my lab."

I shook my head, "Impossible. His parents aren't going to let him out of their sight, especially since we have no idea which organization was behind this atrocity. We can't afford to draw any attention to the family or the child. Anything that is to be done must happen with minimal knowledge or assistance from the outside world."

Roman raised an eyebrow. "How are you connected to this?"

I looked down at my hands for a moment. "The boy's Grandmother found me on the side of a road unconscious. She took me in, nursed me back to health, and in return, I want to find a way to help her get Futoshi, her grandson, back."

"What happened to you?"

Roman and I had known each other for a very long time. I trusted him, but I couldn't tell him the truth.

"I didn't know I was sick; it might have been a parasite or something. I just wasn't well, and she came at the right time to save me. I am grateful and want to do what it takes to get Futoshi healthy again."

"We will need a donor."

I looked up at him and smiled, "You are going to help?"

"Harper, of course, I'll try to help. I cannot make any promises, but there are some things that we might be able to do. The blood transfusion without the right equipment is very tricky and increases the risks of complications, so we will do this last to see if it is needed. Worst case, if I can build the trust of the family, I have a friend who can provide papers for a new identity to keep them off the radar. That will allow me to move Futoshi to my lab."

"Good to know. Let's cross that bridge if we need to. Specifically, what kind of a donor do you require?"

"A poop donor." He said with a laugh.

"I know I might regret asking this but explain to me how it works. Whatever the standard procedure is may need to be modified because Futoshi will not be a cooperative patient."

Roman rubbed his hands together. "First we have to identify a donor who is very healthy."

"Do they need to be a related?"

"Not at all. They must be willing, fit, and healthy. Once we have identified suitable candidates, I will run some tests to ensure that there aren't any underlying issues. As part of their preparation, they will be placed on a rigorous raw vegetable-based diet and undergo a full spectrum parasite cleanse."

"What do we need to do with Futoshi to prepare him?"

"I'll have to run some tests on him too. The tricky part will be getting him in a sterile environment where we can clear away his gut and bowel flora, remove all the germs from his mouth, nails, hair, and skin. These steps are important. To give his body a fighting chance to adopt the fecal donor's biosignature, he will need to be completely sterilized." Roman reached into his pocket and pulled out his phone.

"Who are you contacting?"

"No-one yet. I'm just jotting down some notes for possible extra supplies. We will need HAZMAT suits, biohazard containment grade plastic, and sealant. I'll have to go and visit the site to figure out the best approach. I'm not going to lie to you. This will be a hit-and-miss operation. The process is relatively simple in lab conditions, but it's tricky in the absence of this. We may have to do it a few times to get it right."

"I understand. All I care about is that it is doable. Together we can find the safest possible way to make it happen."

Roman reached out and touched my hand. "Anything for you Harp's."

"Thank you. I really am grateful that you dropped everything to come and help."

"An adventure in Japan, with Harper Perelle. It's about time you let me return the favor. I probably wouldn't be alive if it weren't for you."

"Don't say that. You would have been fine with or without me. Regardless I am grateful for your willingness to help."

Roman released a big yawn. "If you don't mind, I might head over to the hotel now to get some sleep. I'm starting to feel a waft of jet lag taking over."

"Of course. Go get some rest, and I'll be in touch."

"When can I meet the boy, Futoshi? Is that how you pronounce it?"

"Yes, that's it. Let's leave it for a couple of days. That will give you some time to reconcile what you have shipped over for your pseudo lab."

Roman reached across to lift his bag. He unzipped a side pocket, rummaged around then retrieved his wallet.

"Don't be silly. This is my treat." I said, pushing his hand back down toward the bag.

"You flew me here first class, the least I can do is pay for our meal."

I stood up and smiled at the waitress, signaling that I was ready to receive the bill.

"Not a chance, Roman. I've got this. You head off to the hotel, get some rest, and I'll arrange to fetch you in a couple of days. Please remember to maintain discretion about what we are doing. I don't want to place this family in jeopardy. Visit a couple of sights, act like a tourist. Post images on your social media platforms. It's important."

Roman stood up and leaned in placing a gentle kiss on my right cheek. "I'll be careful. Are you sure I can't pick up the bill?"

"I'm certain. Go."

He swung his swag over his shoulder, giving me a half salute as he made his way to the door. I felt relieved that my maverick, Roman Air was here.

I settled the bill on my way out.

* * * * *

The whole family was sitting on cushions in a circle, patiently waiting for the first round of testing results. All eyes were on Roman; he had deep furrows appear across his brow. His visible tension made me feel uncertain about what he was going to present. Post the first round of testing, his disposition seemed to change, and he became shut down. Not even I knew what the results had yielded.

"As you are aware, the testing that I arranged to be executed was to ensure we obtained the healthiest donor to give Futoshi the best chance for positive results. It is based on a point system that I created." He paused to clear his throat. "It isn't a medically endorsed system. It"

Kimiko reached out and touched his arm, "Risk, okay. Noto perfecto understand. Please tell who help Futoshi?"

Roman looked at me, then back at Kimiko. "It is Kayoko who is the best suited to become the donor."

Hiro rose to his feet, "No, my mother too old. The test wrong. I am strongest. You must do again."

I followed suit and stood up to gain Hiro's attention. "It is not about your physical strength." I said raising my arms up to flex my biceps. "The testing was executed to establish the best biological match to the donor. If Roman's results say that it is Obaachan who provides the best chance, then that is what we need to honor."

Kayoko, looked at her son and smiled nodding, "Shinrai."

Kimiko immediately shifted closer to Kayoko, placing her hand on her lap as she glared at her husband. "Kayoko must do for Futoshi. Pride, no. Honor, yes. Must help our son. Kayoko give hope. Please, Hiro."

He bowed his head while listening to her words, "Forgive me," he whispered.

Kimiko shifted her gaze to Roman and me, "Please, bring back Futoshi."

"I will do my best," said Roman bowing to them all. "Can I speak with you Harper?"

"Sure, follow me."

I took Roman to the back garden out of sight and earshot of the family.

"You look nervous. What's up?"

Roman shook his head, "I've never seen anything like this. Whatever is in that kid must be a synthesized virus. It is multiplying inside Futoshi's healthy cells at a rate that I've never seen before. He is being invaded. His immune system is triggering off an inflammatory response and trying to fight back, but it's ferocious. I don't understand what's happening or how it hasn't taken over by now. This is one tough kid."

"Man made?"

Roman nodded, "I can't be one hundred percent certain, but I believe so. I've tested his blood sample against every known human virus in the global medico database, and this thing has no recognizable marker. The virus is either a full mutation with new biomarkers or completely synthesized."

"Who has access to this database? Can anyone trace the test results?"

"No, I made sure that it was all executed offline. I deleted the results and uploaded a lab contamination report, then redid the test using generic sample blood and uploaded it. No red flags will be raised."

"Isn't it possible that it's a virus that isn't in the database?"

"Yes, of course, there is a slim chance but unlikely. The moment something new is discovered, the bio-health authorities get notified, and it becomes registered into the system."

I took a deep breath. "What about biowarfare contagion. Do they get registered in this system?"

"Of course not. Anything that is strictly classified is held in a secure database that requires the highest level of clearance. Do you think it is connected to biowarfare?"

"I don't know. I do feel it is possible that it is somehow linked."

"It can't be ruled out that's for sure."

I nodded, "What do we do now?"

"Harper, I'm out of my depth on this. It is one thing executing a bio-hack on myself, but this is more complex than anything I've worked on. I'm scared of this virus. Whoever is behind this created something straight out of a horror film."

"If we do nothing, then Futoshi remains as he is or worsens with time. His body can't keep fighting this thing. Given what you have described, he is doomed to succumb to a complete invasion. Whatever we try to do to help him is his best chance at recovery."

Beads of sweat were forming across Roman's brow. "Kayoko's blood, when introduced to the virus, developed antibodies. Yours did too. In fact, the virus wasn't able to survive in your blood at all. It was obliterated almost immediately leaving no trace. I thought it was an anomaly, so I repeated the same test several times. The outcome for each was the same. This virus cannot live in your blood."

"You're hesitating. What is it?"

"Using the antibodies from Kayoko's blood sample, we might be able to develop a vaccination against this virus. I'm flying solo on this one, making it impossible to predict how long it will take to create. In the meantime, we can get a light transfusion run using her donated blood. I'll pull some of his out while simultaneously replacing it with hers. I don't know if this will have any effect. I believe it is worth trying. Starting small is best. Given Kayoko's age, I need to make sure she is not left at risk. If the first blood swap yield results, then the next time we can do it will be around sixty days. That is providing that Kayoko passes the post donor medical check. I think it's too risky to try to do the fecal transplant. I'd have to place him on antibiotics to wipe out his gut flora. Knowing how lethal this virus is, I think that would leave him vulnerable to attack. Once we do the transfusion, we can reassess the approach. The kid's immune system is strong. He is fighting hard. We need to try anything to bide our time while we work on a vaccine."

I knew that Roman was holding something back. It was the way he was looking at me. His vibe was entirely off.

"This all sounds positive. I agree that doing anything that risks overloading his system or reducing his immune defense would likely be a death sentence. I feel like there is something you aren't telling me. Has someone approached you? Are you in danger?"

Roman used the sleeve of his shirt to wipe his brow. "No, it's nothing like that. The whole situation is complex. I have colleagues I would like to consult. Don't worry. I know that it's out of the question."

I stared at him for a moment.

"Why don't you use my antibodies instead of Kayoke's to develop the vaccine? You said it wasn't able to live in my blood."

"Um, well, Harper, I don't know how to put this."

"Just say it," I said, feeling the heat rise to my chest.

"Your blood, it's peculiar. I'm not sure that it is even human." He blurted as he took a slight step back.

"What?" I said raising an eyebrow and laughing. "Don't be ridiculous."

Roman shook his head. "Your blood type is unknown. It's completely different. I ran the tests over and over. I used my blood as a control executing the same tests to ensure I wasn't doing something wrong. I'm a standard A positive, and yours is, well, unique."

My face went flush.

"Well, let's ignore that and focus on what we need to do for Futoshi," I said.

"Sure, but at some point, I think you need to get a whole series of tests done. This could become serious. If you are the only person carrying this new unknown blood type, then you have no backup if you need a transfusion in an emergency."

"Don't they do a blood panel on newborns? I wonder why this is the first time it has been detected."

"It's got me beat," replied Roman running his fingers through his hair.

"Ha, just another oddity." I shrugged my shoulders. "Don't stress. Let's get to work on trying to cure Futoshi."

"If you just let me take a few more samples of your blood, I can send it off to my colleagues who are hematopathologists. They could do a full spectrum analysis to try to."

"Roman, no. Please don't get distracted and make this about me. I need you to focus on helping this family get back their son. Once he is in a better place you know your attention will need to shift to using what you have learnt about this pathogen to isolate the genetic material of the contagion. It's the only way to start the development of a vaccine. If the people behind this event decide to cause an outbreak it could be catastrophic for children. It's important. Please forget about my blood anomalies. Destroy any remaining samples you have - no more tests. I can't afford to have any attention drawn to me. I need you to forget what you have seen and stop the temptation of deviating from the task at hand."

He could see that I wasn't kidding.

"Okay, sure. I'm sorry. I'll go prepare Kayoko to donate blood and then get to work setting up a sterile environment within one of the rooms in this house before I move Futoshi. Everyone will need to help. The family might think it's awful for me to shackle him in place but given his state of mind I will need to sedate him and secure him to the bed. I'll do my best to reduce the need to calm him chemically. The less negative interference we have on his immune system, the better. I think the stress of being bound will fare better than the alternative of ongoing forced heavy sedation."

"Thank you. Let's go advise the clan of what the next steps will be and how they can assist."

Roman hesitated as if he was going to broach the subject again but then changed his mind. Instead, he gave me a half-smile and turned to head back inside the house. I remained there for a few minutes to allow myself some time to gather my thoughts. The words echoed in my mind, 'I am not human.'

# Xenophobia

Trekking up the mountain was beginning to tax my body. The steep ascent up the Higashizawa route of the Hida Mountains was even more challenging than I had imagined. When I set out to find the plants that Grandma needed for her remedy, I knew that it was going to be somewhat arduous. I had, however, assumed that the path would be far more accessible than this. It was difficult to imagine her traipsing around the mountainous ranges, foraging for these botanicals alone at her age. This experience was providing me with a newfound respect for this remarkable woman.

The harsh developing conditions had my body feeling frozen as the wind cooled the sweat on my skin. There was a battle welling in my mind with each step up. I felt my burning legs protest against my desire to advance. I couldn't control my eyes from wandering about the place, looking for a spot to rest. It was as though a portion of me was lost to this need to survive past the physical pain. I had no intention of stopping. By my calculations, my pace was an hour slower than planned. Ideally, I wanted to be up and over the worst of it before nightfall.

In Grandma's sketch, she had marked the location of a cave where I could rest. I was set on making it there.

A final scramble up a rocky formation revealed the view to the top of the ridge up ahead. The sound of an almighty crack quickly squelched my sense of relief. It felt like something was just behind me to the left. I spun around with my arms up in a defensive mode. There was nothing there. I took a deep breath and returned to continue my slow ascent. Little Atsuko had told me a legend about these mountains that suggests the Japanese gods could shapeshift into a horse. In this form, they moved around undetected by travelers. It made me wonder where all the animals were. Since I had begun the trek, I had seen few living creatures. There was the occasional ant train carrying forest debris, some wasps gathering nectar from tiny flowers, and the tale of something that slithered under a rock as I walked by. Aside from this, I hadn't witnessed anything notable. I wonder where they all were.

Three more boulders stood between the top of the mountain and me. It was impossible to think that Grandma can trek around this terrain with ease. I'm beginning to feel as though I may have gone off the intended path. The further I ventured, the less friendly the access became. There was a sting in my eyes as the salty sweat made its way down from my brow. Wiping it off with my sleeve, I blinked a few times to clear my vision so I could survey the surrounding area. I needed to establish my best option. There were only two ways up that appeared achievable. I pulled out the spare t-shirt from my backpack and wrapped it tightly around my right hand. I needed to wedge my fingers in the crack of the partially split boulder. I took the fact that it was coated in spiderwebs as a sign that spiders were likely close by. I knew it wasn't a complete safeguard from what lurked in the darkness, but it made me feel better.

With my heart pounding a little faster than I am used to, I secured my grip, placed my foot in the first decent hold I could reach, and heaved myself upward. Methodically I climbed the boulders. One after the other, I inched closer to the top. The sweat was pouring, I was heaving for breath, and my arms and legs were burning under the strain, determined I would not stop until I cleared them.

Standing on the flat ground immediately alleviated the stinging sensation that had lived in my calves for the last three hours of the trek. The vista was breathtaking. I found myself unconsciously offloading my backpack onto the ground. Stepping back without a glance, I crouched low until my ass was positioned on top of it. I knew now that there was little chance of making it to the cave. The sun was an hour away from setting at best.

I rummaged around the side of the pack to get a moist towelette and a fresh pair of socks. It felt good to be sitting and even better to take my shoes off. I had a few pressure points that were sore but had managed to escape getting blisters. It had been a long time since I had done a trek as hard as this. I gently wiped down my feet then gave them a pressure massage by squeezing and releasing. After I palpated them a few times, I put on the fresh pair of socks. Just doing this simple switch made me instantly feel better. I loosened the laces on my shoes before slipping my swollen feet into my boots. It was time to set up camp.

Using my cupped hands as a pseudo shovel, I created a tiny hole in the dirt for the fire pit. It didn't take long to gather much dry kindling and fallen branches to use as fuel. I set up the structure in the shape of an A-frame to ensure the oxygen could flow to maintain the embers' heat. Before I lit the fire, I scouted to locate some stones. Once there were enough stacked around the circumference of the pit, I was ready to light it up. The first couple of attempts were a complete failure. On the third try, there was a small section that managed to catch. It took a few more goes before I could get enough heat generated in the center of the pile. I watched the flames steadily grow, with the embers at the base of the source becoming a deep orange. Satisfied with this, I shifted my position and reached for my belongings.

Unpacking the contents of my goody's storage bag in front of me, I sorted the various portions of food into two piles. Edible cold foods versus the ones I could cook. The chill in the air had me craving to have something warm in my belly. I quickly assembled the mini portable stand and placed it directly over the fire. I then poured water into the cauldron-shaped bowl before hanging it on the hook in the center of the frame. While preparing my simple dinner, it felt like I was a forest pheasant from the imperial dynasty era. The water almost instantly started to bubble. Just as it looked like it was close to boiling, I added the fresh herbs, miso paste, dried wakame, dried reishi mushroom pieces, and dehydrated tofu. I used some chopsticks to swirl the ingredients around for a couple of minutes. The intense heat was causing the soup to generate a lot of steam. I added another cup of water, whisked the ingredients into a swirl for a further minute before removing it from the hook. The bottom of the cauldron was releasing a hissing sound as it smoldered against the rock, I had placed it on. The delicious aroma of the soup was making my stomach churn with hunger. I grabbed one of the seaweed-wrapped onigiris from my stash and greedily took large bites. The glutenous goodness of the rice ball immediately helped to abate the hunger pangs. It was a safeguard that prevented me from succumbing to the temptation of trying to drink the scalding hot soup.

After the last bite of onigiri was in my mouth, I shifted my focus to setting up the rest of my camp for the night. I rolled out the thin foam mat, arranged the sleeping bag on top along with the torch and a single toilet roll. I figured it would become a frigid night once the sun disappeared. In preparation for this, I took off my jacket and put on another couple of layers of clothes. When I was done, I placed my coat back on. With the zip-up and hood secured, I was already feeling the difference in my body temperature shift. I quickly stuffed everything else back into the bag and tied it shut. I used a rope to fasten it to a reasonably sized boulder situated just above my head. I didn't want some wild animal sneaking off with it while I'm fast asleep. Once everything was organized, I tapped the edge of the cauldron to see if it had cooled enough for me to pick it up. It was still a little hotter than I would like but manageable. Satisfied that I was ready, I removed the pot stand from the fire, threw on some more fuel to keep it burning hot, and hopped into the sleeping bag. Propping myself up, I felt content watching the remainder of the sunset as I sipped on the soup. The liquid running down my throat had that welcoming feeling of comfort. It was precisely what I needed. My surroundings were eerily silent, except for the crackling from the fire. Quietly I sipped on my soup while memorizing the beauty displayed by the last rays of light reflecting color on the mountains' snowcaps in the distance.

* * * * *

The condensation from the morning dew had trickled down the bridge of my nose. It settled at the tip, forming a singular bead that was swelling in size. I lay still waiting for the moment to come when the mass would be greater than its ability to maintain form. Its time was brief but long enough to trigger my awareness of the need to become more of a cohesive part of life's simplicity. Everything here exists without complexity. I want my mind to stop replaying the sound of my father's groans as Libertine pleasured him. That seething glare from my mom held as she blurted out profanities toward me. It was too much. My life was a compilation of events that were founded on absolute madness. I desperately want to become one with the droplet and follow the path of simplicity.

*CRACK.*

I sat up and twisted my torso toward the direction of the sound. I carefully surveilled the area. There didn't seem to be anything there. Perhaps it was an old branch falling, a noise of the forest catching its breath. Still, I couldn't help but feel that there were eyes on me. I have no idea if it is a human or a wild animal; I know it is something. I looked up into the trees, nothing. A thought flashed through my mind. With a rush of adrenaline, my eyes jutted about in search of my bag.

"No, no, no, no, no," I said as I leapt out of my sleeping bag and began to run around the perimeter of the camp looking for it. How could it have been taken? I picked up the rope to inspect the frayed end. Was it chewed or cut with a blunt knife? What animal would be calculated enough to chew through the cord to take the bag away from where I lay? There were no drag marks. A pack of that size and weight would have to be dragged by an animal unless it was a sizable bear. Still, there are no animal tracks, just footprints. I dropped the end of the rope and began to look for other signs. Anything that would help me nut this out. There were footsteps everywhere. Did I walk around that much yesterday? Then it dawned on me like a sledgehammer. Some of these were made by bare feet. I'd been robbed.

"Shit." I checked my pockets to see what I had with me. I pulled out a stick of gum, some lint, and the map of instructions from Grandma. At least I had that, although it was of little use to me without the dried sample herbs for comparison.

"Fuuuuuuck." I took a deep breath and tried to squelch the frustration that was welling inside. From my current perspective, I only had three options. Return empty-handed, restock, and start again. Try and track the perpetrator down or continue with no supplies and no assurance that the herbs I collect are the right ones. In the short term, not having any food I could live with but no water and no vessel to carry it when I find some was undoubtedly a problem. I turned to look at the firepit. The stand and cauldron were still there. It wasn't practical to use it to carry water, especially without a lid.

The warmth of the morning sun was starting to make me feel overheated. In auto pilot, I took off my jacket, removed the extra layers of clothes until I was down to my tunic. As I threw the clothes in a pile on the sleeping bag, I wondered how I would carry all this stuff without my pack. I guess I could use the sleeping bag as a pseudo pouch. I turned to look at the view. What am I going to do? I was drawing blanks on the best course of action. If I had a coin, I would flip it for a decision. To me, all three options were crap.

It felt like the better part of the morning escaped me as I stared blankly at the remarkable view. Somewhat deflated, I decided the best course of action was to follow their footsteps to see where they might lead. I'm not sure it is the wisest of choices, but I had assumed that if the person wanted to harm me, there was no better opportunity than when I was asleep.

The footsteps seemed to display a pattern that would suggest the individual took an ultra-wide berth around me. They clearly didn't want to be seen. Their prints were easy to identify up to the edge of where the path meets with the ground scrub, and that's it. The trail ends. A total of six yards and then nothing discernible can be seen. I crossed-checked to ensure I wasn't missing another avenue. Each route returned me to the same spot. If I wanted to go any further, I had the direction the person had headed as my only clue. I turned and looked at my sleeping bag and other items. I didn't see a point in packing it all to carry while I searched. If, as a consequence, it got stolen too, would it matter? I decided to proceed forward without it.

The forest floor was littered with leaves, pine needles, and other decomposing matter. I was careful where I placed my footing. It wouldn't take much to roll an ankle or, worse, step on a well-camouflaged snake. The deeper I ventured into the thick of the forest, the atmosphere seemed to blossom into a cacophony of sounds. Frogs were croaking, birds chirping, and there was something distinct that I hadn't heard before. It was making an 'Ah woo, Ah woo' noise. Each time it was a double call and then silence. I surmised it might be some kind of monkey. It certainly projected its voice loud enough to make me feel it might be substantial in size. Tiny swarms of insects arose in pockets when I disturbed the ground. They swirled upward in a whirlwind and then returned down the same way once I passed. Contrary to yesterday's experience, the forest was now teaming with life. It felt nice to be amongst it.

Well, over an hour had passed by. It no longer felt as though there was any purpose to proceed. There were no detectable clues to show which direction the person had taken. I could continue to wander in a straight line, but the probability that the perpetrator's course held true would be slim. Besides that, the terrain was gearing toward a sharp descent, and I had no desire to fumble my way down on the unstable ground and then try to make my way back up again. I needed to accept that my stuff was gone. With this thought in mind, I turned around and headed toward camp.

The hike back seemed to pass quickly. As I approached my campsite, I realized that someone had been there. I walked over to the firepit in disbelief. My sleeping bag & mat were rolled up and positioned right beside my bag. The rope that I had used to secure it was gone. There was a message inscribed into the ground. It was a Japanese word with a singular message: 'Leave.'

Slowly I bent down and began to unpack my bag to ascertain what had been taken. My clothes were all there; the sample herbs Grandma had packed were too. Only the food seemed to be missing. My water container was intact. The stand, cooking utensils, pot, it was all accounted for. While I repacked the bag, I tried to discretely look around to see if I was being watched. I didn't detect anyone the first time I surveyed the area. The person was likely up high or down low and very well camouflaged. The perp took the food, which I understand, but why the rope? Why make an effort to return my things?

*CRACK.*

I jumped up and ran toward the sound. I started flailing my arms, whacking shrubs, yelling, "I know you are still here." I kept stomping my feet on the ground as I scurried from bush to bush, whacking the leaves. Then I saw it from the corner of my eye on the left, situated behind a tall wide tree.

"Hey, you!"

The kid's eyes widened as he lifted his hands to his mouth and called out, "Ah woo, Ah woo, Ah woo, Ah woo."

I started running toward him. He quickly turned and ran in the opposite direction. I called out again, "Stop. I want to talk. Yameru, Yameru." I continued to follow him without success. Soon he was a small indistinguishable aspect in the far distance, moving at a pace I could not match. Just like that, he was gone.

My heart was racing. I crouched down for a moment to catch my breath. It was a child. He didn't look to be any older than ten at best. What is a kid doing out here? Placing my hands on the ground, I propelled myself to an upright position and began to walk back toward the campsite. Four times. The child made that call. Four times. It was the same sound I heard while walking through the forest. He clearly isn't working on his own. That call must be a form of communication, where four times is set to signal an alarm. Whoever left the message ordering me to 'leave' was able to write, so it stands to reason they can read. His clothes were tattered. There were crisscross scars that streaked up both his spindly arms. That look of pure fear in his eyes when he realized I had spotted him was unforgettable. Perhaps there is an impoverished community of people living here that don't want strangers present. Still, why go to all the trouble to return my bag? They could have kept it all and left me no alternative but to go back down the mountain. I don't get it.

Arriving at the campsite, I secured my sleeping bag and mat to the outside of my pack, slung the whole thing onto my back, and went searching for the path that would lead me down to the valley below. I wasn't going to let myself be intimidated by a bunch of nomads. I could live without food for a few days providing everything else goes smoothly. It was a full day to get to the top, so I now had my trek down the other side, do some foraging for herbs that may take a few days, and then the entire return trip. Best case, I estimated five days and worst-case seven. I could water fast that period providing I found fresh springs along the way.

Once I located the path, I immediately increased my pace on the descent. This goose chase had consumed my entire morning. I wanted to get down the mountain to find a safe place to take cover before nightfall. At least with the graduating slope, I could pick up the pace without expending too much energy. On the way down, I was wracking my brain over the details of what happened. Something wasn't sitting right with me about this situation. That child was petrified. Why was he out there on his own? Maybe there were others. I have no way of being sure of anything.

Gravity and momentum proved to be great allies. I'd made it down the mountain with thirty minutes to spare. Thankfully I crossed a creek mid-way and was able to refill my canteen. I now had enough water to get me through to the end of tomorrow. There wasn't much time before I would be left in a cloak of darkness. After being raided last night, I didn't want to feel vulnerable. I surveyed the area and headed for the only tree I thought I might have a chance of climbing. When I reached the base of the trunk, I placed my pack down. Rummaging around inside it, I quickly pulled out a few tops and put on as many layers as possible. The valley might be warmer than the top of the mountain, but there was no doubt it would be cold. I put the pack on my back and began my first of several attempts up the trunk of the tree. It didn't feel like a stupid idea in the moment, but once the bull ants started to make a stance and attack my arms with a sting that felt like fire, I realized this wasn't going to work. It's times such as these that make me appreciate the luxury of insect repellent. If only I had thought to pack some.

The sun had now entirely disappeared from my view. Only a sliver of its shine was spread across the sky. I knew I couldn't lean against the tree in fear of more ant attacks. I already had a mass of searing welts developing. No, I needed a place to rest that afforded me some protection. That child and his posse took the rope for a reason. I didn't want to wake up hog-tied and surrounded by a group of hostile people. Tonight, there wouldn't be a fire. If I wasn't followed, I should be okay to settle here until morning.

Fumbling about in the dark was proving to be hazardous for my ankles. I had stubbed my toes on enough rocks for one evening. Instead of searching for a more secluded position, I wound up settling down in the open field. Once I was in my sleeping bag, I used my pack as a makeshift pillow. This time I would be woken if anyone tried to take it. I stared up at the star-filled sky, wondering what the consequences might be for my choice not to leave. That child was scared. Why would they send a child to spy on me? Perhaps it's because he was quick as a whippet. Honestly, if that kid moved any faster, he would have looked like he was levitating. Under different circumstances, with the right opportunities, he could become a successful athlete. He was so quick.

I don't recall falling asleep, but the insect biting me sure did see to it that I woke up. I jumped up, whacking my neck to make it fall. When I saw a black lump drop to the ground, I mercilessly stomped on it. My hand was on my neck, cupping the painful area. When I lifted my shoe to inspect, I saw an oversized black beetle with giant pincers. I checked the palm of my hand to see if there was any blood. There didn't appear to be. I must have just caught it in time. Crouching down, I poked it with a leaf to see if it was still alive. The armor on its back could probably withstand a proper pounding. No matter how much I pushed and flipped it about, there didn't appear to be any movement. Satisfied with this, I turned to my pack to retrieve some toilet paper and went off to find a spot to relieve myself.

* * * * *

Venturing into the triangular-shaped meadow Grandma had described, I began collecting the wild grasses that were needed. These were the easiest to identify from the dried samples she had provided me to use for comparison. I spent the day walking around, gathering as many of the varieties of herbs she had marked for me as I could find. In between collections, I took a small sip of water to abate the rumble in my stomach. My mission was now starting to be fruitful. I didn't want to give up, nor did I want to spend any more time than required in this place. Between the absence of food, the insane desire to scratch the welts on my arms, and the exposure to the beaming sun, I was feeling deflated. I knew I wasn't going to last too much longer. I needed to get as much of the ingredients as I can, then head back.

The one item that would be challenging was the flower from the Japanese Snake Gourd. They grow tangled to the trees or other plants in the forest and only bloom their spindled white flowers during the night. Grandma had marked the map where her supply was located and said that I might need to camp for days until the right conditions enticed the plant to release its flowers. I was already three full days into this trek and wasn't sure that I would likely last a fourth. What I had collected would have to do. It was going to be a two-day trek back to the village. I rested at dusk for a couple of hours and then mustered up the motivation to begin making my way back up the mountain. This evening I was blessed with the presence of cloud-filtered light from the moon. I figured if I didn't stop, I'd make it back by late afternoon tomorrow. Using two pieces of wood as makeshift walking poles, I held a steady pace up the incline. My mind was focused on the end game of receiving a hot bowl of food as my reward.

# Lost Boys

woken by the sound of a curdling scream, I jumped up in a reactive panic. My mind was foggy from lack of food. I spun clockwise, surveying my surroundings to try to get my bearings. I must have fallen asleep on the trail. I recall sitting down to rest for half an hour. I could hear voices, and someone was screaming in agony. It sounds like they are experiencing an enormous amount of pain.

Reaching into my bag, I rummaged around to retrieve my water canister and then my compact first aid kit. I tucked my backpack and other belongings partially inside the rotten stump hole and covered it with forest litter. I took a couple of sips of the water then closed my eyes to listen. The commotion was coming from the right. I would need to cross into the heart of the forest again if I was to get closer to where the unrest was occurring. Pausing for a moment, I considered whether it was best to mind my own business and continue the remainder of my ascent. The person's screams were still present, but the intensity of the cries was becoming subdued.

"Ah, fuck it," I said as I began a light jog in the direction of the voices. It may not be the smartest option given my previous encounter; however, I didn't want to leave without knowing if they needed help.

The sound of the voices grew louder as I approached. It was hard to discern how many people may be present. Slowing to a walk as I drew near, I carefully considered where I placed my feet to reduce the amount of noise made. When I arrived within visual proximity, I quickly realized they were all children. One boy was lying on the ground holding his left leg crying, and the other four were standing together in a huddle. I couldn't make out what was being said. They were malnourished and disheveled in appearance.

I placed my hands with open palms in front of me as I stepped forward, "Watashi wa tasuketaidesu. (I want to help)."

Two of the boys bent their posture, placing their hands in a defensive mode as they released a growl, exposing their teeth. The other two grabbed the arms of the boy on the ground and began to drag him. He screamed in agony.

"Watashi wa tasuketaidesu. Watashi wa tasuketaidesu." I said, stepping forward. The boy had a massive laceration below his ankle that likely required stitches. If he doesn't get the wound cleaned and sutured, he will almost definitely get an infection.

The boy recoiled his arms and growled at them, causing the others to let go. They tried to grab hold of him again. He folded his arms and wriggled in resistance, snapping his teeth like a rabid animal. I continued to press forward with my hands open and my head nodding in an attempt to reassure them. The closer I came toward the child on the floor, the further the others stepped back. The menacing looks on their faces indicated that they could lunge. It was a volatile situation. Still, I pressed on. It was difficult for me to ascertain whether my eye contact with the boys was aggravating the situation. Even if this is the case, I couldn't trust them enough to remove my gaze.

I slowly crouched down near the little boy's injured foot. He was now propped up partially on his elbows, glaring at me while panting. All his mannerisms showed signs that he was in pain and very distressed. I looked around to see what might have caused the gash. There wasn't anything in my immediate visual range that appeared to be the culprit.

"Watashi wa tasuketaidesu." I said while lowering one hand down to help stabilize my position. I leaned across to see what type of damage he had done. There was a decent amount of blood flowing from the area. The good news was that despite the child being filthy, the wound seemed to be relatively clean.

I held up my first aid kit. "Watashi wa tasuketaidesu." I then lowered it to the ground, unzipped the soft casing, and began to look at what we could use. Given the boy's situation, wrapping the injury in a bandage might cause more complications once it was soiled. His best chance was if I stopped the bleeding, cleaned the wound, and then use something to close it. There was no way I could entertain giving him proper stitches. It had to be something that would bind the skin and allow the cut to breathe.

Slowly I opened a bottle of saline solution and held it just above the child's wound. "Watashi wa tasuketaidesu." I squeezed it over the area, ensuring it poured directly in and around his cut. He watched intently as I got some gauze and placed it gently on his leg. Not knowing what his reaction would be, I chose not to press down. I hoped to draw off as much of the blood as possible to see the extent of the damage more clearly. When the gauze was soaked, I switched it out for another. I did this several times before I realized I was so fixated on the task at hand that I never noticed the other boys had vanished. I turned my head to check that they weren't behind me planning some half-baked ambush. It didn't sit well with me that they suddenly left their friend alone. I was starting to feel on edge. Perhaps they were off arming themselves with weapons.

Once the bleeding subsided, I poured another lot of saline solution to ensure any debris washed away. The little boy had calmed. He watched me intently as I looked inside my first aid kit. The gash needed to be closed. I pulled out a row of six small band aids. They wouldn't be strong enough to close the wound. He needed stitches.

The boy snatched up something in his hand then grabbed it with his other hand holding it between the tips of two fingers. He shuffled back away from me and brought his ankle toward his torso. I watched him try to pinch the wound together. As he winced, I moved forward, staring at him while I reached out my hands to put pressure on either side of the injury. Once I was in position, I pushed the skin together until it sealed and waited to see what he was aiming to do next. He readjusted himself, so he was better balanced before placing his two fingers over the wound. He pressed down, held his hand in position then winced. A quick twist of his wrist revealed the solution he had in lieu of stitches. He used the vice grip of a bull ant's jaw to hold the two pieces together and ripped the body away from its torso to lock it in place. I looked at him and smiled, feeling a sense of amazement. The boy continued the process until he had a neat little row of ant heads holding his wound closed. When I released the pressure on his leg, I was in awe of his ingenious solution. It worked.

Standing up, I offered my hand to the boy. He looked at it before leaning back to release a call, "Ah, whoo, Ah whoo."

It was time for me to leave. I stuffed all my first aid gear unceremoniously back into the satchel. Glancing around to ensure my path was clear, I executed a slight bow to the boy then turned to scurry away. There were some notable crunching sounds made by footsteps walking on the carpet of forest leaves. It appeared to be coming from a distance behind me. I didn't look back. The others were likely returning to claim their friend. I had no business being in the vicinity when they arrived. My instinct was set on having a reasonable amount of distance between myself and all of them.

Returning to the path, I retrieved my pack and began my ascent up the mountain. I knew if I could make it to the top before sunset, then I might have a chance to tackle the boulders before dark. I soldiered on at an advanced pace, ignoring the searing burn in my shins.

There was a welcomed drizzle that formed as I got higher. The tepid breeze that blew was covering my face like a refreshing towelette. My mind found solace in the rhythmic sound of my footsteps. I no longer felt consumed by the pangs of hunger nor feared the possibility of an unwarranted reprisal by the lost boys of the forest. I was confident they would be feeling abated now that I was heading back the way I came.

Nearing the summit, I paused to consider the source of the flickering shadows from a glowing light. It was moving too fast and randomly to be the sun's rays diffused by the forest greenery. With caution, I walked up to the top of the clearing. My heart was pounding as I saw a fire lit in the same place where I camped on my first night. Approaching the campsite, I could see footprints everywhere. Beside the fire was a pile of dried white flowers. I picked one up. It was from the Japanese Snake Gourd. I was sure of it. Dropping my swag to the ground, I rummaged around to find the sample Grandma had given me. I placed them side by side, then turned them to inspect from all angles. I was right. It was the flower. I carefully unfolded a piece of cloth and placed them all on before folding it into a secure bundle. Could it be that the lost boys knew that I was collecting the herbs for Grandma? They must watch her when she comes to do the same. Perhaps they learned from her visits, and they began to build a supply of their own. It's the only plausible explanation. How else could they have some available to share? Why did they share?

The sun was looming over the horizon. It wouldn't be long before it set. I crouched down to place my hands over the fire. As I did, I noticed a single onigiri was sitting on a stone. With little hesitation, I found myself dusting it off while looking to see if it was bug-ridden. I flipped it around to satisfy myself that it was edible. Biting into it, I released a pleasurable sigh. The saltiness of the seaweed complemented the sticky plain rice.

*CRACK*

Jumping up, I quickly spun around, almost choking on my loaded mouthful of onigiri. I spied in the distance the boy I had helped with two of his friends positioned one on either side. His injured foot was hovering, with most of his weight displaced onto a big, smooth wooden stick. The boy on the left had a broken tree branch in his hand. They made that noise intentionally.

I held up the portion of the onigiri that was in my hand above my head, tucked the remaining desiccated food in my mouth to one side, cleared my throat, and said, "Arigato gozaimasu."

The boy tilted his head in a slight bow, then turned and hobbled away slowly with the aid of his friends. I watched them disappear into the bowels of the forest's darkness while I ate the rest of the onigiri.

As the sun danced on the horizon, I found myself unpacking my gear to settle in for the night. I took a couple of sips of water, found a secluded spot to relieve myself before returning to get settled. It was time to surrender to a solid night's sleep.

I heard the calls of a lone owl in the distance as my eyelids became so heavy, I could no longer fight to keep them apprised. Meanwhile, my stomach was happily making a concerto of digestive noises. Smiling, I quietly lay there as I felt myself letting go of consciousness.

* * * * *

The cool frost in the morning breeze greeted my lips like the tingle of the first touch from a long-lost lover. I opened my eyes, stretched my arms out as far as they could reach as I released a big yawn. A single solid day's hike lay between me, a hot bath, and a nutritious bowl of food. With gusto, I collected everything into the backpack and began my return journey to the village.

There were armed men in military uniform at the Mountain's foot near the main road's entrance. They appeared to be taking a break. One of the five butted out his partially smoked cigarette when he noticed me heading toward them. He twisted his foot from left to right several times before he seemed satisfied that it was extinguished. As I was about to pass, he stepped out, raised his hand, and said, "Teishi shite Kudasai."

I stopped as requested.

He did a slight bow as he looked me up and down, "Kon'nichiwa. Nihongo ga hanasemasu ka?"

I return the bow and replied, "Kon'nichiwa. English. I speak English."

"Engurish. Hai, so desu."

He paused for a moment then said, "You," pointing his index finger at me. Then reshifting it to the direction of the mountain path, "Up?"

I looked back, then turned to engage the man's eyes. "Hai, up." He watched my two fingers as I emulated walking up the mountain. I used the palm of my left hand as the mountain. When my fingers reached the top, I released an exaggerated "Phew" and wiped my brow. The men behind him seemed entertained by this.

The soldier nodded his head thoughtfully. "Berry danger, up," he said with a look of concern.

I shook my head and feigned an expression of confusion.

"Bangō? Hai, Berry danger, up," he said with insistence.

I shrugged my shoulders and said, "Okay." I clasped my hands together and gave a slight bow. "Sayōnara." I started to walk by, waving at the others behind him.

"YEMERU" yelled a man from the back. I halted and glanced at a sixth man who appeared from behind the vehicle. The other men stiffened up as he passed by. The soldier I had been speaking to stepped back to clear a path for him. He had a serious expression on his face.

Without any of the graces, he stepped within my personal space and stared into my eyes. "Why in Japan?"

"I am a tourist."

"Go up Mountain? How long?"

"Hai, up Mountain." I raised my hand to depict the number five. "Go days."

"No scared? See, hear strange noise?"

I scrunched my face and shook my head. "Noise? No. No-one. Just ants. Lots and lots of ants." I lifted my sleeve to show him some insect bites.

He executed a token glance at my arm and was straight back to glaring into my eyes. His intimidation technique was solid, but I had the advantage of knowing what he was attempting to do and did not break my expression.

"No see boy's?" he asked, placing his hand down to depict them being little.

Careful not to overreact, I pouted my lip ever so slightly, shook my head, and said, "No. Nothing but ants and an owl. Hoo-ha Hooooo, Hoo-ha Hoooooo." I stretched my arms and flapped like a bird. The others giggled softly, but he was not amused.

He gestured with his hand that I could go.

I bowed slightly and casually went on my way.

Walking down the narrow footpaths, I decided it would be best if I took a detour in case they had me followed. The fact that he asked about the boys had me concerned that I would now become a person of interest. The soldier's poker face made it unclear whether he was satisfied that I didn't know anything more than I had conveyed. In hindsight, I should have asked questions about the boys. It might have seemed odd that I didn't.

My stomach started to growl in anticipation as I turned the corner to walk down the lane where the dimly lit eatery was located. Inside I positioned myself at a table that had a clear view of the entrance. I ordered one beer and a couple of house special okonomiyaki's.

When the food arrived, I made light work of the first serve and paced myself on the second. It was a welcome relief to feel sated. I sipped on my beer and continued to watch the door.

No one had entered the place in over an hour. I grabbed my things, went to the restroom before paying for my meal and exiting the restaurant. I'd continued to meander the streets, walking in and out of stores, buying a few things to keep my cover. Even though I was beginning to feel comfortable that no one had followed me, I decided to withdraw some cash and book a few days in a Western-style inn. Any further investigation into my background would look less suspicious if I had a corroborating financial footprint.

The place was modest for the price. It was an open room with a double bed, two side tables, a freestanding wardrobe, and a small ensuite. I switched into the bathrobe and called room service to collect my clothes to be washed. Once they had been and gone, I unpacked the Kimono and obi I purchased from a quaint little seamstress. When it was laid out on the bed, I ran my fingers across the embroidered silk. The delicate intricacies of the pattern depicting a landscape with mountains in the background, a koi-filled river in the foreground surrounded by a lush Japanese garden during cherry blossom season were divine.

Digesting the food had zapped my energy. I decided it would be best to have a refreshing shower before I made any further decisions. I disrobed, letting the dressing gown fall to the floor. Glancing in the mirror, I smiled at my disheveled appearance. I transferred the small bar of soap along with the complimentary bottle of hair shampoo and conditioner to the little wooden shelf in the shower bay and stepped into the cubicle. It wasn't until the stream of water saturated my body that I realized how much I missed regular showers. A thick coat of dirt and dust changed the water to a murky brown as it glided over my body and swirled down the drain. Tiny particles of the heavier sediment settled on the floor, resisting the water's pull. I was filthy.

It took three washes with the shampoo and then a ten-minute soak with the conditioner to make my hair feel clean. While waiting for the conditioner to penetrate, I crouched in the shower with the water switched off, trying to extract the wedged sediment out from under my nails. I truly underestimated how positively filthy I was.

With my hair dried, my body slathered in moisturizer, and my neck doused in a light fragrant floral perfume, I placed the delicate Kimono and obi on. Next, my feet were shoved into a pair of dainty open-toe sandals. Looking down, I could still see a faint line of dirt deep beneath the nail bed on both my big toes. It would probably require a proper soak in the tub to get them completely clean. Unsure of the time, I glanced outside the window to see where the sun was positioned. It didn't seem to be far offsetting. I might have an hour and a half at best. I quickly repacked the herbs in the cloth then crammed it into a small bag I had also purchased during my afternoon shopping spree. On the way out the door, I grabbed the hotel key fob and my coin.

There was a hive of activity in the streets. Most of the shop owners in the province were preparing themselves for the upcoming annual harvest moon festival. I slinked through the crowd across a few blocks before jumping into a rickshaw to get me the rest of the way. When I was close, I asked the man to stop. Continuing to feel cautious, I wanted to walk the rest of the way to ensure I wasn't followed. Two streets from the Moto family home, I hovered on a corner for a few minutes. I couldn't see anything unusual. Satisfied with this, I quickly made my way to their residence and through the mini door situated at the front gate.

"Kon'nichiwa," I said as I enter the front entrance of the home.

I heard footsteps, the door opened, and I was greeted by Atsuko, who leaped up in good faith that I would be ready to catch and lift her.

"You home," she said, squeezing me with a vice grip.

I laughed and squeezed her back. It felt so good to be greeted with such enthusiasm. Even Aki, who was now bouncing around my feet yapping, was pleased to see me.

I entered the front door with Atsuko still in my arms. Kimiko came from down the hall.

"Welcome. You are safe. We worry. Hiro scared you go alone," she said.

"It was harder than I thought. I am safe. All the herbs are in my bag."

"Atsuko, let go now. Harper needs to rest." Kimiko grabbed her daughter's waist and tried to pry her from me gently.

"No mamma."

"Atsuko." She said once again, gently pulling at her child. "Sorry she miss you. Asks every day when return."

"It's okay." I tickled Atsuko to loosen her grip. She giggled as her mom placed her on the ground.

"Leave her to rest."

"I'm okay. Here, all the herbs are inside," I said passing her the bag.

"Thank you. Obaachan will be pleased. I give to her after I make you something to eat."

"No. It's okay Kimiko. I've already eaten. Is Roman here? How is Futoshi doing?"

Her face lit up, "Come see."

I followed Kimiko down the hall to the last room on the right. She opened the door softly then stepped back, allowing me to enter first.

"Harps you're back. Nice threads."

"Thanks," I said as I opened my arms to accept Roman's hug. "What have I missed?"

Roman kissed my forehead before stepping back. "I'm super glad to see you."

I laughed, "Trust me, I am glad to be back. Now, don't keep me in suspense. How did the transfusion go? Are there any signs of positive change in Futoshi?"

Roman grabbed my hand and led me to the sectioned-off portion of the room. "Are you ready for this?"

"Wait, don't we need to sterilize ourselves first?"

"Nope." He pulled back the curtained wall of plastic. "Ta Daaa."

There inside the room was Futoshi lying on a bed with his grandmother Kayoko sitting beside him. Futoshi's face lit up as I walked toward them.

"Kon'nichiwa Kayoko san. Kon'nichiwa Futoshi chan. Genki desu ka?"

"Genki yo, genki yo," replied Grandma as she squeezed her grandson's hand.

Futoshi smiled and gave a slight bow at my query about how he was feeling. There were no restraints. He had been bathed, and his hair was cut. He looked positively radiant in comparison.

I turned to Roman, "He looks fabulous. What did you do?"

Roman shook his head. "It's not what I did. You are the one who helped to heal him."

I glanced at Futoshi again. "The difference in him is remarkable. What was the bio-hack?"

"Well, I started by extracting a donation from Kayoko's blood then gave that to Futoshi. After a couple of days, even though there wasn't a visible difference, his pathology showed that he was responding to fight off the virus marginally better. That got me thinking about the reaction your blood had when introduced to the virus. It died within minutes, no matter how concentrated the introduced virus sample was. Following a hunch, I did some research around alternate ways to extract plasma safely. You see, AB is the only universal plasma that can be given to patients with any blood type. I wondered if your unique blood was universal too. It took me a few days to get the separation process accurate as I had to go old school, given I don't have any of my equipment here. I then used your plasma in a range of tests using the samples I had collected from the Moto family and my own. The results of all the blood compatibility testing proved my hunch was on the money. Your blood appears to support universal donorship. The best part was that your plasma, when introduced to the samples, significantly increased the resistance to the virus."

"I'm speechless," I said, feeling a great sense of relief.

"Harps, you don't know the half of it. I only introduced a small sample of your plasma into his system early yesterday morning. Right up until then, he was still hyper-aggressive and had to be fully restrained. Now, look at him. It's a miracle." Roman placed his hand on my shoulder and gave it a little squeeze. "Your blood is miraculous."

"I guess so."

"I'd like to take more of your blood so I can give him another dose of plasma to see if we can get him to clear the virus completely from his system. Do you feel up to it?"

"No. I'd like to wait a few days to see how he is before we look at doing anything else. Are there restrictions on how plasma can be introduced to the body? Does it have to be done intravenously to be effective?"

"I'm not sure. I've only ever seen it delivered intravenously. Why do you ask?"

"Hmm, no reason. I'll explain later if there's a need. The less you know, the better."

"That sounds a little concerning. You can trust me, Harp's."

I looked into Roman's eyes, "I know I can, and I do." I turned to look at Grandma. I smiled as I said, "Shinrai."

"Hai, shinrai," she replied.

"Roman, come with me."

I bowed at Grandma and Futoshi and exited the room to return to the kitchen area. The smell of Kimiko's cooking wafted down the hallway. I smiled, knowing she ignored my request not to cook. Entering the room, she immediately pointed to the places she had set.

"Please sit. Eat food."

"Dōmo," I said, sitting down as requested.

Roman sat beside me, "My mouth is watering. It smells wonderful, Kimiko."

"You like smell. Tastes good." She held out a tray that had two steaming bowls of rich black soup. Roman grabbed one and I the other.

"Thank you, this looks amazing. What is it?" I asked.

"Toyama specialty, black ramen soup white shrimp."

Roman already had his chopsticks in position. "Bon appetite."

I picked up mine, swirled the soup, and grabbed a length of thick noodle. My tastebuds were instantly greeted with a light blend of pepper and soy sauce. I sipped a little of the juice next and found it was somewhat overbearingly salty.

Roman was busily fishing around his bowl for the shrimp.

"Thank you, Kimiko, this is delicious."

"You help Futoshi. Thank you."

"Futoshi is the true hero. He has fought the virus, and now with all of our support, his body will win this battle. I am very happy for us all." I turned to Roman, "Thank you for coming to help. We couldn't have done this without you. I truly do appreciate it."

"As I said, Harp's. You saved my life. I was wrapped to get an opportunity to help you in return finally."

"You save his life?"

"It's nothing, Kimiko. Roman is exaggerating."

Roman put his chopsticks down. "I'm not exaggerating. I would have likely died or at the very least been permanently injured. There is no denying that you saved me."

"Save how?" Asked Kimiko.

"The University we attended had a Ski club that we were a part of. This particular year there was a trip planned to Whistlers Blackcomb in Canada. The first couple of days, I was skiing during the day and partying hard all night. We were about a week into the trip when I met a bunch of international travelers who were staying at the same lodge. They were set to party at the peak of Horstman Glacier and invited our club to join them. I ventured out with the foreigners ahead of the club to begin drinking. I drank, I smoked some weed. The music was blaring. We were dancing and having a great time. A couple of hours later, Harper and her two buddies arrived. I wasn't acquainted with them at the time, but these three were inseparable. I'd see them on campus a lot. We knew of each other but never really hung out. Anyway, so, there I was, dancing about like a fool, when Harper came up, grabbed my hand, and coaxed me toward her, saying that I was getting too close to the edge. I wasn't in my right state of mind. I continued dancing about and eventually migrated back closer to the edge. That's when it gave way. I fell off the side of the cliff, smashed my head on some exposed rocks, and was slowly sliding down completely unconscious. What happened next was said to me by her friends who were witnesses to Harper's brave insanity. She was the only one that realized I had fallen. Without hesitating, she passed her drink to her best friend Peppy and said, call for help. He then saw her run and leap off the cliff face. They thought she had just committed suicide. When they ran to the edge, they saw her sliding down toward me. She grabbed my body with her arms and dug her heels into the snow to try to slow us down. The bottom of that ravine was adorned with hundreds of sharp, exposed unforgiving granite rocks. If she didn't manage to stop us from falling, we both would have likely died. Thankfully she did. I was shivering, so Harp's took off her jacket and wrapped it around me. She used her body to press against mine to keep me warm. Meanwhile, she was now in a singlet top with her back exposed to the wind and sleet."

"Oh, come on, you're making it out to be so dramatic."

"You know it's true."

"Yeah, I gave you my jacket and was wearing just a singlet top, but my adrenalin rush was keeping my body warm. It's not as though I was freezing. I knew they would alarm emergency services and get a rescue crew out to us way before any frostbite or hyperthermia set in. It was a calculated risk."

"That's not the point. You jumped off the side of a cliff to save a stranger and then gave me your warm ski jacket when the temperature was below zero. It's huge Harp's. The snow was unstable, and the cliff was so steep that we had to be rescued by a helicopter crew. You risked your life to save me, and I am always going to be grateful."

I leaned into Roman and bumped his shoulder with mine. "Eat your soup. It's getting cold."

"Kayoko insist Harpersan special. I happy we listen. You berry big heart."

"I'm not sure about being special, but I'm glad you let me try to help your son. Perhaps when Futoshi is a little better, we can ask him to tell us what happened. If there are more children still alive, then we need to find them."

"Hai. We must helpu desu."

I looked at Roman, "I'll give you some more of my blood in a couple of days. I'd like you to attempt to put the plasma in a liquid capsule. I know taking it orally will have its own set of challenges. The digestive enzymes will be hard to bypass. If the dose is strong enough, maybe some could get absorbed before gastric juices break it down. We need a simpler, less invasive way to administer an impactful dose. If we find others like Futoshi, they are not going to be co-operative."

"I'll get onto it and see what I can come up with. I'm sure there are experiments already in progress or completed with results published that we could leverage. And um Harp's."

"Yes."

"I'm sorry about what happened to Peppy and Sam. I know that must have been hard on you. I felt torn that I couldn't be there for their funerals. I was on a speaking engagement tour when I heard what had happened. There were binding contracts, a tight schedule. I couldn't break my commitment. I tried but,"

"Stop. It's okay. I'm okay. Let's just leave things in the past where they belong. I've sort of found my way to make peace with the loss." I paused for a moment. "I can't change what happened and miss them both more than I can express. We shared some of the greatest times of my life. I still find it hard to accept that they are gone." I dropped my gaze to stare at my reflection in the black bowl of soup.

"I'm sorry. I guess I shouldn't have brought it up."

"It's okay. Thanks." Picking up my chopsticks, I recommenced eating. I was slowly becoming accustomed to the intense salinity of the stock.

# Origin

Pretending to be a tourist was starting to wear thin. I was sure my room had been searched, so I began switching hotels every couple of days, replaced all my clothes with new items, and ditched the others in random bins behind a string of restaurants in the main drag. It was all a precaution in case micro surveillance devices were planted on my things. I wanted to keep whoever was spying on me on their toes. The most concerning part was that I wasn't able to identify anyone following me. I couldn't afford to assume that it was the Japanese soldiers, although they seemed the obvious choice. When I had pulled the cash out from the ATM days before to make a financial paper trail, I understood I risked alerting the interferons of my whereabouts. With their global reach, they could easily have watchers deployed to track me down.

Today I was headed to the Toyama glass art museum. I was tempted to take Atsuko with me. I'm sure she would have enjoyed a day out of school to wander around the museum, and I most certainly would have appreciated the company. I'd been passing a lot of small dog parks while exploring the prefecture. It made me think about sweet Huckleberry. He's in good hands with Kichiro and my brother. I miss him.

"May I join you?"

A man appeared to my left. His English accent seemed out of sorts for this region.

"Join me for what?"

"Your walk."

"I don't want to come across as ungracious, but I'd prefer to be alone."

"Smile and look ahead, Harper. They are watching."

I did as he suggested.

"What do you want?"

"We know what you are doing."

"Okay?" I replied.

"You need to be careful. There is much at stake if you continue with your current plans."

"Sure."

"I don't think you are taking this seriously. There are serious consequences to interfering. It is a grave matter."

"Yep. Seriously got it."

"Foolish girl. If you don't stop, you will leave us with no choice but to prevent you from causing any further damage. Hope is a fool's plight. People will get hurt because of you."

I switched direction suddenly, then turned to walk back the way we had just come. He followed with a slight delay in his tempo that kept him a step behind.

"I'm not interested in your warnings, cryptic messages, or veiled threats. I have no idea of what you think my plan is or the associated consequences. I'm just trying to enjoy my travels and do a little sightseeing. You need to stop wasting my time and go be a nuisance somewhere else."

"Don't make this difficult on yourself. Leave Toyama. You won't be warned again."

The man stepped off the footpath and veered toward a narrow laneway. I didn't bother to look in his direction. My visit to the glass art museum would need to be postponed. There were more pressing things to do now. First on my agenda would be to return to my room, pack my bags and check out of the hotel. He didn't spook me. His warning purely confirmed I wasn't paranoid. They feel threatened by me and likely know I am friendly with the Moto family. Kimiko said that she and Hiro were outspoken about the disappearance of their son. Perhaps my hike into the Hida mountains fueled their suspicions. That would mean the soldiers waiting at the village entrance wasn't a coincidence at all. If I am right, they don't know about Futoshi. Instead, they would be worried that I'm looking for him and the other children. Still, I couldn't be sure of any of it. Why would they send a pompous Englishman? All I could be sure of is that something was happening around me that could impact our work to restore Futoshi to complete health. I needed a new approach to my plan.

Inside my apartment's room, I quickly got to work packing the few possessions I had into my backpack. I considered indulging in one last shower but decided it was best to leave. I wanted whoever was watching me to think that I was hastily getting out of town. Until I gained some certainty around what was going on, I needed to demonstrate I was taking the warning seriously. If they were watching, then fleeing would give them temporary satisfaction that I was no longer a threat.

The concierge organized a taxi to take me to the local train station. I purchased a one-way ticket to Ishikawa and boarded the carriage just minutes before its scheduled departure. According to the itinerary, it would be a solid two-and-a-half-hour journey. Just as I located my seat, the train started to move. I squashed my bag under my chair and sat down. This trip would give me some time to consider my options.

I leaned into the headrest and began watching the passing scenery as the train picked up speed. The approach of the Englishman has awoken my sense of urgency. There wasn't any more time to wait for Roman to find an alternative way to administer the plasma. I have to find a way to convince the lost boys to let me inject them. Their behavior demonstrated similarities to how Futoshi acted, with the exception of their ability to temper their aggression. The scars are the main clue driving my hunch that there is a plausible link between them. If I'm wrong, and they are a crew of wayward feral children living in the wild, then my plasma won't make a difference.

When the train reached its peak speed, the passing landscape became an animated Claude Monet painting, especially when I squinted my eyes. As much as I enjoyed the effect, it stimulated my thoughts to consider the complexity of determining what is real. The perception of everything could be shifted by a simple introduction of a new view forming an alternate reality. I squint my eyes and see the world differently. The Interferons didn't need magic. They feed perceptions to guide people's beliefs toward their agenda-fueled reality. What if they are behind all of this? Initially, I thought the virus Futoshi had might be a germ warfare experiment. The aggressive response swayed me to consider the idea that it might be an attempt to create a designer armed force of hyper fearless warriors. Taking young children certainly would increase the success in grooming them. Libertine is living proof that influencing a young mind works. What doesn't make sense is the decision to kidnap the eldest boy of each lineage. That is too specific. Targeting them must have stemmed from somewhere. Why else would they go to such lengths?

Hours had passed, there were clear signs we were getting close to arriving in Ishikawa. The conductor's announcements were becoming more frequent. People in the carriages were already gathering their things and forming a lengthy queue at the door. I remained seated. My mind was consumed in a swirl of thoughts. I wondered if I should take up Roman's offer to get new identities for the Moto family and organize to relocate them to the USA. Roman could then escort them out of the country. This would certainly assist with getting access to better facilities to analyze the virus. I'm just not sure if it would be a good move in the long run for the family. If they aren't in any danger, then I don't want to uproot their whole lives. Futoshi's recovery has been astronomical. He still wasn't speaking but is adapting by communicating in other ways. The virus itself was a concern. The last thing I would want to do is cause an accidental spread of the contagion. When Futoshi attacked his mom, she didn't get infected. That could have been because her immune system was robust or there wasn't a big enough exposure to overtake her body. The outcome of every option held potentially dire consequences. There was too much at stake, and not enough was known to make an educated decision. Perhaps what we achieved is all that can be safely done for Futoshi.

"Excuse Miss, please make way to exit."

"Oh, hai. Gomen'nasai." I said, apologizing for not disembarking.

Scooping up my things, I hurried down the narrow aisle and got off the train. There were people everywhere greeting one another. It was a pickpocket's ideal vacation place. I politely excused myself as I brushed past hordes of individuals between me and the gate that led to the exit. There was a true sense of relief present when I made it to the other side. Crowds and I are like oil to water. We can co-exist but don't mix well.

Walking the streets, I scouted for a suitable hotel. At each place, I asked to see the available ground floor rooms. A solid hour and eight establishments later, I booked five nights at a modest little inn with a single room with bath and private courtyard. The first thing I did was unpack my clothes and quickly bathed before getting dressed in my new attire. Strategically I placed the do not disturb sign on my door, switched the TV on, and adjusted the volume to a mid-range setting. It took some time, but I discovered how to program the timer to have the TV switch off and then back on again every few hours. I was ready.

I opened the sliding door to the courtyard, took one last look at the room to ensure I remembered how it was staged, then locked the door behind me. A few minutes went by while I figured out an easy way to get over the courtyard fence. I peered over to confirm the laneway was clear of foot traffic before I made my move. Landing solidly on both feet, I hurried down the length of the stone path until it intersected with the main road. I randomly turned left and began walking for what felt like a mile before I stumbled upon a commercial travel center. Inside I grabbed the schedule for any buses passing through Toyama. Purchasing a ticket for the 3 pm shuttle gave me enough time to get settled and satisfy any watchers that I was here. I returned to my room the way I had left, only to change back into my original clothes and walk out the front door. Venturing into town, I briefly looked around, meandered into a few random shops, and got a bite to eat. Once I was done, I returned to my room to try to get some sleep. It wouldn't be long before I was due to get on my bus back to Toyama. There would be little to no time to sleep tonight.

* * * * *

Hiro paced back and forth as the tension built in the room.

"No, my mother no go. I forbid. Berry danger."

"I understand Hiro, but without her, I am afraid there is no way anything else can be done."

"I come. You, me to boys. I speak for you English and tell what they say."

"It won't work. These boys are wild, like Futoshi. I'm not sure they can speak. They will not respond kindly to a big man such as yourself approaching them. I know they have watched Kayoko gather the herbs in the fields, so they are aware of who she is. The best chance we have of getting them to co-operate is to have her explain what has happened with Futoshi and try convincing them to inject the plasma into their vein. I feel they will trust her."

"How boy's know mother?"

"When I was leaving the forest, they gave me a collection of the white flowers from the Snake Gourd. They could only have known my desire for them because they watched Kayoko collect them."

"This flower?" He pointed to the pile sitting in a small wicker basket.

"Yes. I helped one of the boys who was injured. I believe the flowers were a gift. A way to thank me for helping."

Kimiko stepped closer to us, "Perhaps I go not mother. I can do."

"No, forbid it," said Hiro shaking his head. "No do this."

"We musto help," replied Kimiko. "Look Futoshi. Children need help. Children scaredo. No trust." She grabbed her husband's hand. "Please. We go."

"No. I have forbidden."

"It's okay. The decision has been made. I understand," I said.

"Sorry Harpersan. Risk danger family."

"I understand and respect your decision Hiro," I said, bowing.

I turned to Roman, "Do you have everything packed?"

"Yes. You said there were five of them. I have given you ten doses in syringes ready to go that are equal to the amount we have given Futoshi. I've provided you with a bundle of extra syringes and enough plasma for thirty more doses in case you find that the five know where the others are being held. Are you sure you want to do this?"

"I am."

"Kimiko, I'd like to take some food to the children. Anything you can spare would be greatly appreciated. It needs to be light enough for me to carry."

"Hai. Hai. I make now," she said, heading toward the kitchen.

"Roman, I think it's time for you to go home. Futoshi is doing great. Any further progress he makes will happen over the course of weeks, maybe months. Hiro is right. It's getting dangerous. You should head off."

"No. I can help you with the other children. You said there are more. We need to try and assist them."

"Yes, we do, and you will. Go home. Use your lab to find a way to easily administer the cure. I don't know how many kids are alive, but I am certain the virus these monsters injected into them is still out there. The best thing you can do is help from the other side."

Hiro gently cleared his throat, "Do ask him leave to punish family?"

"No. Futoshi is well. Roman has confirmed the virus no longer exists in his body, and his blood tests show he has now built immunity to it. He is safe. There is no more to do. Futoshi, with the Moto family's love and support, will hopefully regain his speech. The best way Roman can help us further requires access to special equipment. This is why I am asking him to leave."

Hiro acknowledged my words and looked at Roman. "Thank you save our son."

"It has been a pleasure to help. I am grateful that I was able to be a part of Futoshi's recovery."

I interjected, "So, you will go then?"

"Yes. I'm uncomfortable with leaving you here on your own. Why don't you come back with me?"

"I can't. I came to Japan on a quest of sorts to find myself, and I am not yet done with what the journey has to offer. Don't worry about me. I've got to head off soon. Did you want me to help you pack anything from here?"

"Nah, I'll do it. You have enough on your plate."

Atsuko came running toward me and wrapped her little hands around my leg. "I am scared. I don't want you to go on your own."

I leaned down and picked her up. "Where did you come from? I thought you were asleep."

She leaned in and whispered. "I told Grandma. She will come."

I shook my head, "No, sweetie. It is okay. Your father is right. It is dangerous. I'll go alone."

Hiro turned and looked at his daughter. "Atsuko, nani tte itta no?"

"Shinrai Otōsan. Shinrai."

"It's okay. Please don't be angry at Atsuko. She thought she was helping. Kayoko knows about my request."

Hiro grunted as he turned to head to Futoshi's room to speak with his mother.

Kimiko called out from the kitchen, "Atsuko, nerujikan."

I gave her a squeeze and a peck on the cheek before placing her down. "Listen to your momma. It's time to go to bed now." She ran off toward the hallway, turned, gave me a quick wave, and then disappeared.

I could hear Kayoko raising her voice at her son. Hiro was frustrated as he reciprocated the tone. It was out of character for him to do so. He respected his mother immensely.

"Get yourself organized to leave here, Roman. I'm about to do the same."

He gave me a hug and rocked me side to side. "I love you."

"Thank you. I truly couldn't have done this without you."

"Come home soon, okay?"

"I will," I replied.

Roman released me from his embrace. I smiled, mouthed the words *'thank you'* then grabbed the backpack before heading to the kitchen.

"I need to go, Kimiko. Do you have the food ready?"

"Hai." She passed me a big pouch filled to the brim with food. "For you. Eat. Rest for children."

"This is great. Thank you." I resorted the contents of the backpack to fit the satchel in. Kayoko and Hiro were still at it. "Okay, I am ready. Please wait twenty minutes, then go tell them I am gone and for Kayoko not to follow."

"Hai."

I secured the pack on my body.

"Harper. You come home?"

"Yes. I will find a way to send word about my success, and when everything quietens, I will arrange to visit."

"Please yes. Moto family Harpersan."

I bowed. "It is an honor that will never be forsaken."

I exited out the back garden through the side gate. If I hustled, I could try to make it to the peak before the break of dawn.

* * * * *

Pondering how I was to climb the boulders; I took the opportunity to pull out an onigiri as a snack. Knowing what I was up against this time around, I had packed some gloves. Those tiny cracks filled with spiders and other creepy things weren't going to get a chance to nibble on my fingers. I sat on the floor to rest my legs. The trip up the mountain to this point wasn't anywhere near as hard as the first time. The cool of the night tempered my body from overheating, which helped. I had maintained a steady pace and only stopped twice along the way.

Dawn was breaking. I convinced myself if I held out for ten more minutes, it would be easier to tackle the boulders because I could see what I was doing. In reality, it was just a ploy to delay the climb. I found it challenging the first time I had done it, and now with a heavier load, I could only imagine it would take a wad of strength to climb it without falling. I gently rested my head and closed my eyes for ten.

"Harpersan,? Harpersan?"

I opened my glazed eyes, "What are you doing here?"

"We decide. We come. Moto Family."

"And me," said Roman poking his head over Kimiko's left shoulder.

Hiro reached out his hand. I grabbed it and rose to my feet. "Thank you."

"Harpersan bravery, and Moto family bravery. Together help children. We carry food for children. Futoshi too."

Walking up the path, I saw Futoshi, Grandma, and Atsuko were approaching, all holding hands.

"I don't know what to say. I'm speechless."

Hiro grabbing my backpack.

I turned and pointed, "We have to climb up this group of boulders to get to the peak. Maybe if I go first, I can secure the rope and throw it down to help you all make your way."

"Harps, I could climb it. If I follow that lineup, it might be easier than going via the middle," said Roman.

"The last time I was here, I took the line to the left. It was a little scarier because the potential fall is greater, but it had better cracks to hold. I think the same way might be best."

While we continued to banter about the options, Grandma walked past us, releasing a little chuckle. She followed around the circumference of the boulder and disappeared with Futoshi and Atsuko.

"Ne ni shitagatte kudasai." Grandma was calling out for us to follow.

Hiro led the way, and the rest of us fell in line. Behind the rock was a narrow gap. The two boulders formed a tunnel that led into a small cave. When we entered, we could see Grandma coaxing the children to the top of the stairs that were crudely cut into the side of the wall on the far side that led to a small opening. The formation of the stone around us suggested this space was once filled with running water. I could tell by the waves of erosion that it had a faster flow at the bottom. As the last of us climbed to the surface, we were at the top of the peak puffed. The stairs were steep but still a far better route than attempting those boulders again. I realized that the cave on the map that Grandma drew for me was likely this one.

"Where to now?" Asked Roman.

"Now we catch our breath and wait."

"Wait? For how long?"

I turned and pointed to my old campsite. "That's where we can stay. Let's unpack and separate the food that we want to give them."

"How will they know that we are here?" Kimiko asked.

"I'll call them. They communicate using a sound."

Kimiko translated for Kayoko as she directed her and the children to the spot to unpack the food.

"What do you want me to do, Harps?"

"Grab all the medical items from the backpack so that we can reach it easily."

Hiro passed Roman the pack.

"What can I do to help?"

I looked at Hiro. "I'd like Kayoko, myself, and Futoshi to stand when the boys appear. I will have your mother explain what happened to him and how he is now better. She can then tell them that we want to inject them with the cure. I truly believe they will trust her. If anything happens that looks threatening, I will shield them both with my body. If this occurs, I need you to grab and pull them back. Your job will be to get everyone to the cave. Don't hesitate."

"Hai."

"Thank you. Let's see if they are ready."

We walked over to the camping area. Kimiko and Kayoko had almost finished separating the food parcels with Futoshi and Atsuko watching. Roman was starting to unpack the medical bag. While he was doing that, I explained the approach to everyone and had Kimiko translate it to Kayoko, so she knew what to say. Once they were settled, I shifted the food parcels closer to the edge of the forest and made sure one final time that everyone was clear on how to behave. Satisfied with this, I made the call.

"Ah, whoo, Ah whoo."

I re-joined the others. "Now we wait."

* * * * *

I made the call every hour. I was just stood up to head over to make my third call when I heard some slight rustling. I froze in position and waited for a moment.

*CRACK*

"They are here. Be still. Please, no sudden moves."

"I can't see anybody. Are you sure they are here?" whispered Roman.

I placed my hands in the air and stepped forward. "Watashi wa tasuketaidesu. Watashitachiha tabemono to kusuri o motte kimashita."

Kayoko came and stood beside me. She nodded her head approvingly at my statement about the supply of food and medicine. Futoshi squeezed between us and grabbed both our hands to hold.

We stared into the forest as Kayoko explained why we were here, what had happened to her Grandson and how he had been cured. She continued to speak in detail about the ordeal and how this awful tragedy has caused endless grief for the families. This went on for over ten minutes. When she finished, we remained in position.

"Shinrai."

I looked down at Futoshi. "You spoke. Hai, Shinrai. Trust"

He let go of our hands and ran to the edge of the forest. "Shinrai. Shinrai." He shouted.

Kimiko hugged Hiro and Atsuko squeezed her way in between them.

A child stepped out from the shadows, then another and another. There were seven of them. Futoshi took off his shirt and slapped at his scar-filled chest. "Shinrai."

"Futoshi wa koko ni kite kudasai."

While Kimiko was calling her son back, I signaled for Roman to stand and bring me the medical kit. I rolled up Roman's sleeve, put the tourniquet on, and pulled out the syringe. "Kusuri." I wanted to demonstrate what they would need to expect.

Kayoko bowed then offered out her left hand. "Shinrai. Kono kusuri was tasuke ni narimasu."

"Shinrai," Futoshi called out again.

The boy who I had helped popped up from behind a bush. He looked at the others then, without further hesitation, limped directly toward me. He held out his arm while staring into my eyes. I released the tourniquet from Roman's arm and slid it onto the child's skinny right arm. I slowly tightened until it gave enough tension for one of his veins to pop.

All the other boys watched intently.

"Pass me the needle."

"Do you want me to do it?" Asked Roman.

"No. He trusts me. I have to do this. Pass me the needle and step back."

Once, the needle was in my hand. I tapped on the boy's vein. Placed the needle near the insertion point and said, "Shinrai." I inserted the needle and steadily released the plasma directly into his bloodstream. As soon as it was done, I pulled it out, placed pressure on the puncture, and released the tourniquet. Roman passed me a piece of tape with a sterile bud that I put over the wound.

"Kimiko, please explain that it will take twenty-four hours for him to start to feel much better."

While Kimiko explained this to the boy, he continued to stare at me. I intentionally blinked my eyes and smiled at him when she had stopped talking. He responded with a little bow before backing away.

Kayoko pointed to the bags of food, "Tabemono o turu." She re-joined her family while the boys cautiously moved forward to grab the supplies. As each of them secured a bundle, they scurried off.

"Ask them to wait. See if anyone else will take the medicine."

Kimiko called out, but none of them stopped. They got their food and were off. Just the brave boy who I help remained.

"Hiro, Roman, would it be okay if I tell him you will return in two days to give the others their medicine? It's too much of a risk to the boys for me to try to return from Ishikawa. I'm sure if they are watching my hotel room, they would have figured out by now that I'm not there."

"I'm in. If you think they'll come. I can administer the dose."

"Hai. I, too, will come."

"Kimiko, please tell him that when his medicine works, it is important for him to encourage his friends to come and get the same medicine. Let him know Hiro and Roman will return in two days. Tell him to wait until he hears them call. He is then to try to bring all the boys here to get the same help."

As Kimiko translated, the boy never disengaged his lock on me. Once she finished speaking, I placed my hand on my heart and then on Hiro. "Shinrai." I did the same action with Roman. The boy tilted his head to acknowledge the message.

I stepped forward and did a slightly exaggerated bow with my hands clasped. "Go shinrai arigatōgozaimasu. Sugu ni genkininaru watashinotomodachi."

There was a slight smile that surfaced when I thanked him for the trust and referenced him as my friend. He turned and limped his way back into the depth of the forest keeping his arm bent.

Swiveling around pumped with excitement, I let out a quasi-squeal. "We did great. I hoped to do them all, but one is a start. I'm sure when he feels the effects, they will all be lining up to get the injection."

"My heart was beating so fast when they started to appear. I was beginning to freak a little," said Roman shaking his head.

"Hai. Berry scary. All those children need their mother."

"I know Kimiko. Hopefully, after they are free from the virus, we can find a way to have them reunited with their families."

I crouched down in front of Futoshi, "And you speak. Shinrai. Hai, Shinrai." I gently cuddled him. "Watashi wa anata o hokori ni amou." He squeezed me tight as I told him I was proud of him. I truly was.

# Expectation

Indulging my senses with a carefree walk in a Japanese garden was a treat. I was in the capitol city of Kanazawa wandering around the 'perfect garden' of Kenroku-en. It was labeled perfect because of the design. Cleverly the landscape was structured to display the heightened beauty offered by every season. It meant that anytime was the best time to visit this haven. I felt connected to the energetic flow and was awash with a sense of peace. In this sanctuary, I could enjoy nature's display without my mind being clouded by the circumstances that drove me from my home.

Maple trees and old pines extended their branches over a rambling stream of water that bounced against the moss-filled edges of the rock containment walls. Random bridges were placed along the way so tourists could cross to gain a new perspective. The occasional koi fish swam past. At the controlled feeding spots, countless Koi were anticipating their next meal. Queues of eager children and parents waited for their turn to sprinkle some food then take a picture with the feeding frenzy as the backdrop. What a wonderfully simple life they lead.

I sat in the middle of a bridge in a quiet section of the park and took off my shoes to dip my toes in the cool waters. The light breeze created a rustling in the trees. The birds were whistling. Tilting my head back, I closed my eyes to watch the shadow play across my eyelids. How divine it feels to be alive. I breathed in and exhaled with intention. My lungs expanded deeper with each inhale. What a truly glorious day.

Post my walk through the rest of the garden; I stopped by the Higashi Chaya district to book in to attend a tea house. I had seen advertisements that mentioned there were traditional tea ceremonies with Geisha, who provided entertainment. There were several available, with most either exclusive by invitation or by membership. After visiting a few, one of the owners kindly directed me to a place that was open to the public. She had assured me that the entertainment was mostly the same. The main difference was that more junior Geisha called Minarai practiced their skills, whereas the most sought-after Geisha called Maiko and Geiko's attended the exclusive tea houses. I was okay with this, so I located the tea house she had mentioned and made the booking for six pm.

By the time I returned to my room at the modest little inn, I only had a few hours to burn before I would need to return to the Higashi Chaya district. Instead of sitting down, I jumped into the shower for a quick rinse to freshen up, wrapped myself in the complimentary robe, and lay on top of the bed. Setting the alarm for four-thirty gave me just shy of two hours to rest.

Looking forward to getting some sleep, I fluffed up the pillow and put my head directly in the center.

Yawning in anticipation, I smiled as I closed my eyes. Today had been a good day.

* * * * *

I found myself in the unusual position of feeling self-conscious. I was wearing my kimono but somehow still felt underdressed. The brochure I had read outlined what to expect at a ceremony and the etiquette required. Dressing in a Kimono was listed as highly preferred. I entered the Oriental Blossom tea house.

"Engurish?"

"Hai."

"Okayyyy. Welcome to Oriental Blossoom Tea House. Please leave shoes here. Puto-on compli-ment-ary slippa."

I tucked my sandals into the pigeonhole shelving and placed the white terry-toweling slippers on.

"Forow me, please."

She shuffled her feet in a way that made me wonder whether her legs had elastic binds that restricted her movement. It seemed to be a very unnatural gait. When she stopped at what looked like a coffee table, she put a cushion down on the tatami mat aligned to a place setting and gestured for me to sit. I positioned my ass on the pillow with my legs stretched out underneath the short-legged table. The brochure had mentioned the proper seated position would be to sit with bended knees and resting my ass on my heels. That was not going to happen. The lady glanced at my feet, popping out the other side of the table, then, without a word, shuffled back to the reception area to serve the next group of tourists who were waiting. I watched as she shuffled back and forth, showing people to their tables. It was apparent this place catered to tourists and was highly commercialized. Typically, a private room is given to the different patrons rather than an open space such as this. Every group that was seated had the table set for the number of attendees. Mine seemed to be the only one that curiously had two.

The walls of the large room seemed steeped in traditional décor. Large scrolls hung on opposite sides of the room. There were two ink paintings with a dual theme. Both had beautiful details that depicted a single blossom tree in full bloom. One had a man laying his head down on a Geisha's lap under the canopy of the tree, while the other portrayed a man spying on them from behind the blossom tree. Just below the two paintings is a simple yet intriguing flower arrangement composed of twisted dead branches and a single spiked white orchid sprouting from a bright green bed of moss. The room had a lovely ambiance.

A stern-looking elderly lady walked across and stood near the center of the room. She clapped her hands to which a group of ladies entered. They all positioned themselves in front of a table and knelt on a cushion. As the ceremony started, the audience was reminded that the process was to be enjoyed in silence. Traditional music was introduced in the background. I smiled at my host and bowed my head ever so slightly. She seemed shy as she mimicked my gesture.

While the hosts began the ritual with the tradition of cleaning their tools, two sliding doors were pulled apart to reveal the music was produced by Geisha minstrels. Three instruments were in play. A bamboo flute, a seventeen-string koto, and a three-string guitar called the shamisen. Another four Geisha's appeared from behind a side screen. They executed a slow synchronized dance. I found the way they looked to be fascinating. Not a hair was out of place. They carried their heavy white makeup and their perfectly painted redfish lips well. It was incredible to think that these women maintained their appearance to such a high standard and voluntarily devote their lives to mastering the art of being a Geisha.

I was conscious of balancing my attention to ensure my host felt appreciated. In normal circumstances, she would not be competing with Geisha's entertainment in the background. She was using a silk cloth to check on a hot iron pot filled with water before she started grinding the Matcha tea into a fine powder. Tiny particles of green mist rose and landed on her hands. I looked across at the other hosts and could see they were all at the same stage of the ceremony.

One Geisha began to sing. It wasn't the most melodic of tunes to try to sing to. She seemed to be extending the words in the lyrics for dramatic effect. I felt it was out of place, disruptive rather than serene. By the expression on the other patron's faces, we seemed to all be in silent agreement.

Reshuffling my position to relieve the pins and needles in my legs, I alternated between placing pressure on my left ass cheek and then my right. It was rather uncomfortable to be seated on the floor for long periods when an expectation was present to be still and silent. The creature comforts of the Western World had made me soft. The host was maintaining her kneeling position with ease. It made me recall the first time I had to use the squat toilet and almost lost my balance. Everything we repeatedly do becomes a form of conditioning.

I struggled to squat the first few times, feeling unbalanced, whereas now I don't even think about it.

The water being poured into the ceramic cup released hints of the matcha's fragrance. When the host placed the cup in front of me, I claimed a moment to appreciate the process it took to get to this point. This ceremony was filled with tradition connected to Zen Buddhism and the use of tea in spiritual practices.

Picking up the cup in my right hand then supporting its base with my open left palm, I turned it one hundred and eighty degrees before bringing it to my lips to indulge in my first sip. I bowed my head slightly to acknowledge the host, then took a couple more sips of the tea until it was empty.

I executed a final exaggerated bow as I placed the vessel in front of her and whispered, "Oishikatta. Dōmo arigatōgozaimashita." She smiled and nodded, seeming very pleased when I gave thanks and told her the tea was delicious. With a gliding hand gesture, she offered me more. Politely I declined. Activated by the tea, my tummy was rumbling in a request for food. My mouth salivated at the thought of getting something substantial to eat. In truth, the real driving force was my ass. I couldn't bear sitting still for much longer.

It took another ten or so minutes for the host to clean her utensils and pack everything before the ceremony was drawn to a close. I was thankful the singing Geisha had completed her last tune. The shrill of her voice at the latter stages of the final song invoked a desire to block my ears.

People were starting to fumble to their feet to leave. I took this as my queue to do the same. I executed several bows acknowledging the Geisha and then staff at the reception area. The hosts had already left the room through a side panel. Trading my slippers for my sandals, I quickly exited the venue just ahead of the crowd.

"Excuse me."

I felt a tap on my shoulder, so I stopped walking and turned.

"Do you speak any English?"

"Yes."

"Oh great. I'm Martha, and this is my husband Bert and our son Aloysius."

"Hi. I'm Harper. You're clearly from Texas."

"Well, yes indeed. We all are. Texas-born and bred."

"Awesome, how can I assist?"

"I was wandering if you could recommend a restaurant. We're famished."

"Sorry. This is my first time in the district. I'm about to look for somewhere myself."

"Well, we'd love to join you. I noticed your friend didn't show up to the ceremony."

"Martha," said Bert with a disapproving look on his face. "My apologies; sometimes my wife says things that might be offensive without any wrong intentions."

"What? What did I say wrong?"

I smiled, "I believe what Bert is saying is that you assumed that an extra place setting meant that I had a friend that stood me up. That is your creative embellishment. I came alone. There just happened to be an extra setting on the table. Nothing more."

"Oh. So, you don't have a friend? You're all alone. You poor dear. We'd be happy to let you join us." Her face lit up, "We could be your friends."

"Martha. You're doing it again," barked her husband.

"Momma, I'm hungry. Can we go get something to eat, pleeease?"

I smiled at the boy who was now rolling his eyes. "Aloysius is a great name."

"It means famous warrior," he said, correcting his slouched posture and looking proud as punch.

"Wow, impressive."

"Bert had a fascination with history and warriors from different cultures. He's such a smart man, my Bert. We just knew when we had a boy; his name would need to have a connection to warriors. When I found out that Aloysius meant famous warrior, I was sold. I mean, being a warrior is great but being a famous warrior, well, that sets our Aloysius up for the right start in life."

I tried to contain my amusement. "Well, like I said. It's a great name. I think if you head down this way and turn right at the first intersecting road, you will find a variety of restaurants. I'm certain all of them offer quality food. It was lovely meeting you. Enjoy your stay in Japan."

"Are you sure you won't join us? We'd be happy to keep you company."

"I'm sure. I appreciate the offer. Have a good evening."

"Okay then, Bye."

"Bye, Harper, and sorry again."

"It's not a problem," I replied.

Martha whacked Bert on the arm. "Stop making out like I said something wrong."

I intentionally began walking in the opposite direction.

"It's such a shame she didn't want company. She must get awful lonely."

"Well, right now, I'm a might jealous of her."

"Why?"

"Sometimes, I wish you would stop gabbing for a minute and let my eardrums recover."

I chuckled. Bert, Martha, and Aloysius were a long way from home.

* * * * *

It took a bit of patience, but I managed to find a cool little sushi bar to dine at. Inside there were three chefs behind a long wooden bar that had a glass display showcasing all the different types of fish. The waitress sat me at the very end of the bar on a stool that had bicycle pedals to rest my feet on. The width of the restaurant didn't seem to be any bigger than eight feet wide by twenty feet deep. It was filled with locals all dotted along the bar. Empty plates were stacked sky-high. A couple of waitresses were going from person to person, jotting down their orders. Others shouted their requests directly to the chefs. The chef who responded executed the order and then placed a piece of paper in front of them that I assumed was the charge. It all seemed a little hap hazard, but the energy was uplifting. A frazzled-looking waitress came down to my section and passed me a menu.

"Engurishu menu. Raise hand when ready order please."

I accepted the menu, "Dōmo arigatōgozaimashita."

She had already walked off but waved her hand in acknowledgement.

One of the cool things that I liked about eateries in Japan is their menus almost always have photos to reference against the description of the dish. Often shop fronts display plastic models of the types of food they serve to entice people to enter. The food that is produced almost always looks either the same as depicted or better. They pride themselves on quality and presentation.

Just as I finished reading the last item on the menu, I put my hand up to grab her attention. When she looked across, I gave her a little wave. She immediately came scurrying toward me.

"Hai, hai, can I have order, please?"

"Hai." I began pointing at the pictures and using my fingers to demonstrate the amount. "I'd like two of each of these nigiri, one miso soup and one serve of green tea soba, please."

"Any drinku?"

"Hai, Mizu o kudasai."

"Hai, mizu? Et to, no sparkaring?"

I shook my head, "No sparkling."

"Okay." She turned and started yelling out my order to the chefs.

The one closest to me confirmed he would fulfill the request. He raised his cleaver and waved it in my direction. "I make best nigiri. One extra chef special for you. No charge."

I clasped my hands together and gave a slight bow in thanks, such fantastic energy. I loved this place.

The waitress delivered my jug filled with water, a somewhat rustic ceramic earthenware cup, miso soup, and the cold green tea flavored noodles. She provided a napkin then passed across a pair of wooden chopsticks.

"You need western?"

"No thanks." I placed the chopsticks in my right hand and clicked them together. "Chopsticks are good."

"Okay, chef, bring nigiri when ready. You wave more order." Off she went down the narrow aisle again.

I took a sip of my soup then a mouthful of the thick noodles. The flavor fusion and contrast between the warmth of the soup and cold noodles were divine. My head was permanently bent over in the perfect position to accept mouthfuls of the noodles. It tasted so good.

"Nigiri, order and chef berry special for you."

I slurped the tail end of a noodle that was hanging out of my mouth as I lifted my head to acknowledge him.

"Dōmo arigatōgozaimashita," I said, reaching across to bring the tray closer to me.

"You berry welcome," he said with a massive grin on his face. He stood there waiting for me to sample his special.

I picked up the nigiri with my chopsticks, placed the whole thing in my mouth, and chewed. The fish looked like it was a yellowfin. He had carefully decorated the nigiri with roe as the garnish and had some type of light green sauce between it and the bed of rice it neatly sat on. There was a burst of saltiness that stemmed from the row with a lovely peppered citrus flavor I assumed was his signature sauce. I poured some water into the cup and took a sip to clear my throat.

"Totemo oishī." I said, nodding my head at the chef. "Totemo totemo oishī."

He turned and raised both fists in the air and called out, "Totemo oishī."

People responded by lifting their drinks in cheers and yelled, "Totemo oishī."

The chef continued to walk back to his station with his fists pumping in the air and said, "Totemo totemo oishī." The patrons reciprocated.

My spirits felt high. I poured some soy all over my nigiri, spread wasabi on the sides, added a slither of fresh ginger, and began consuming each morsel.

What a great day.

* * * * *

A fortnight had passed since I had been in the Toyoma prefecture. It felt strange to be entering the Moto family residence again, yet the familiarity held a certain comfort. I followed the sound of the voices to the back garden.

"Ohayou-gozaimasu." I said with a big smile.

"Ohayou-gozaimasu Harper san," replied Kimiko

"Ohayou." replied Kayoko

Atsuko ran up and cuddled my legs, "Ohayou. I am happy you return to us."

I seated myself beside them and placed Atsuko on my left knee.

"How is everybody going?"

Kimiko reached out her hand and placed it on my right knee. "We are berry happy you return."

"It is nice to be back. Is Hiro at work?"

"Hai. He working."

"How did he and Roman go with the boys in the forest?"

"Firsto time, six boys. Secondo time, tirty. Many children. Forty-seven total present for cure."

"Forty-seven, that is a lot. How many children were taken from this village?"

"Hundreds, many, many hundreds."

"Maybe there are more boys out there. Where are the children now? Can any of them speak?"

"Yes. They tell Hiro what happened to them. They want to go home too scared. Fear being taken again. Every two day we take more food for them. Clothes too."

I looked across at Futoshi, who was sitting quietly beside his Grandmother.

"Atsuko, can you please take your brother inside so I can speak with your momma?"

She wrapped her arms around my neck and gave a little squeeze, "Okay." Climbing down from my knee, she grabbed Futoshi's hand and coaxed him to follow.

When I saw they were out of view, I refocused on Kimiko.

"Is Futoshi speaking now?"

"He speaks then quiet."

"That sounds more like an issue of emotional trauma rather than a physical issue with speech. He has been through so much. Patience and support will help him. When it is safe to do so, we can get him and all the others the support they need to deal with what had happened."

"I think so. Berry big trauma."

"What did the boys in the forest say happened?"

"No, berry confuse. Big hole in forest. Many boys sleeping. Some wake try to wake up other. Darkness, noises, lights, boys run, they scare. Go back, hole gone."

"A mass grave? They buried the children?"

"Hai, think so. Sound like."

"This is awful. Do they know where the hole is?"

"Hai. Scared to go."

"Do they know who did this to them and why?"

"No, berry confused. No memory." Kimiko paused for a moment. "Harpersan, children need mother, father."

"I know. Let me consider the options on how to make that happen safely."

"I scared, berry danger for children. Futoshi too."

"Yes. We will need to make it impossible for whoever is involved to hurt the children or their families."

Kimiko patted my knee three times with her left hand then return it to rest on her lap.

"Hai," she said in a somber tone.

"We will figure this out Kimiko. Together we will find a way to get those children returned safely to their families. We can do this."

"Thank you."

"You are welcome. Did Roman return to the USA?"

"Eto, no. He stay. Wife come soon. Introduce to Moto family."

"Oh, okay." I was very surprised to hear this and very concerned.

"Harpersan hungry?"

"No. I'm okay. I would appreciate a cup of green tea."

"I make." Kimiko rose to her feet, placed her hand out offering her Grandmother a hand to stand. "Ocha o tsukurou."

"Hai," responded Kayoko.

Together they walked arm in arm inside to prepare some tea.

The birds seemed active this morning, jutting about from branch to branch. I watched them while I considered the options. The conundrum was apparent. How do we retrieve the boys and integrate them back with their families without any heinous repercussions? We don't know who's involved. We have no clue as to what the real motivation for the abduction was. We do know every family in the village was impacted by the loss of a child. A virus was introduced into Futoshi that we believe is synthesized. We can assume for now that all the other children, when tested, will confirm the same.

I could only see three avenues. 1. Entrapment to expose the perpetrators. 2. Expose the story globally to force them underground. 3. Organize a safe haven to relocate the children and eventually find a way to reunite them with their families.

Option three was the hardest to execute. Secrets never remain intact. Those children would always need to be on guard. If they were ever located, they would surely be made to disappear permanently. These monsters already demonstrated that they are willing to discard them when their 'experiment' went south.

Just as with option three, option two allows the perpetrators to remain unhinged and without punishment. This was a rather unpalatable concept. The real focus is to provide these children with an opportunity to mend and have a future. If either option were required to play out, then we would all need to make peace with the imbalance of justice.

Entrapment was my obvious preference. I'd like to reveal all the faces that supported the monster(s) in charge. It had to be a significant operation to coordinate the abduction of so many children. I couldn't imagine how it is possible to convince people to consciously participate in this activity without questioning the act's integrity. Where is their moral compass?

I jumped a little as Kimiko passed me a tray with a pot of green tea, a cup, and some petite sweets on a plate.

"You deep think?"

"Hai. I was. Thank you," I said, taking the tray and placing it beside me.

"Kimiko, do you think that the children can point out where the hole is on a map?"

"Better they show. Map too confuse. May be wrong."

"Hai." I released a deep sigh.

"Kimiko, tonight, when Hiro returns from work, I need you to ask him if he would be willing to help me try and expose the men who did this to the children. I will need some assistance from Hiro, but no one else can know what we are doing. Not even Roman. It must be a secret."

"Oh, secreto from Roman?"

"Hai. It must be only the three of us who know the plan. Okay?"

"I will ask. Hiro will say yes. I already say yes."

"Thank you."

"Thank you, Harper." Kimiko bent down to grab the pot. She poured some tea and passed me the cup.

* * * * *

My underground contacts linked in with their Japanese counterparts to source everything that I had asked for. Given most of it was military-grade surveillance equipment and assorted apparel, I was surprised to have it available within less than a week of the request. It reconfirmed that anything was accessible if you had the right contacts and coin to pay for it. In this space, there was no room for haggling. I supplied the list; the list gets fulfilled, and the cost is non-negotiable. Given most clientele are involved in illegal activities, the fee is ridged because of the closed market and the need for the utmost secrecy. The premium on my transaction was significantly higher due to my insistence on ensuring the equipment was not sourced in-country. It was not to be traceable to any dispatch or specific unit. I needed it to come directly from the manufacturer or distributor, so it had a definite cold trail. The local suppliers fulfilling my order had to ensure everything was shipped. I didn't care from where. It was an extra precaution to reduce the possibility of red flags being raised around the transaction or linked to what we were about to use it for. Nothing is foolproof, but it made me feel better to approach it this way.

I'd taken a risk by going to Roman's hotel to see him. The concierge had assured me that he had checked out days prior and left no forwarding address. It seemed out of character. When I asked if he was with anyone, they confirmed he was on his own. Without any means to contact him locally, there was nothing more to do. All Kimiko had mentioned was his wife was arriving. It was hard to determine if he was showing her around or whether something else was going on. I couldn't afford any distractions at this critical juncture. Locating him would need to wait. I left the hotel via the service entry that led into a side lane. Making sure the coast was clear, I flagged a taxi and headed to the Moto residence. I needed to synch up with Hiro and Kayoko to check on their progress. If they have completed their bit, then the only thing left to do is a quick equipment test. Assuming all is well, tomorrow will be operation 'Go Live.'

When I arrived at the gates, the small inlaid entrance door was locked. I looked around and noticed the little bell recessed into the stone wall. I picked it up and gave it a shake. Aki immediately responded by frantically barking. I heard footsteps and then a latch release that revealed a small sliding window with bars on it.

"Hello. I never knew that was there. Why is the door locked?"

"Harper yes. One momento kudasai."

Kimiko slid the viewing window closed and opened the door. As I entered, she locked it behind me.

"Did something happen? Why are you locking the door?"

"Eto, better safe?"

"To keep safe."

"Hai. Safe."

"Hiro in kitchen. I dinner make."

"Have you heard from Roman? Has he stopped by?"

"Hai. He brings wife yesterday. We lunch. Now go on holiday."

I was relieved. "Great."

We entered the house and headed for the kitchen.

"Dōmo Hirosan," I said, smiling as I approached.

"Dōmo."

"How did you go? Are all the cameras up?"

"Hai. Camera in many tree. Children help. Berry secreto."

"Good. Did you have them overlook the whole area? Facing inward and outward so we can capture anything approaching? Like I drew in the picture?"

"Hai." Hiro pulled out the piece of paper I had scribbled on. "Red you. Blue camera."

"These blue marks are where the cameras are in place. Is that what you are saying?"

"Hai."

"Are these the exact geo-coordinates of the location?"

"Hai so desu."

"How sure are you that it is the right place?"

He pulled out the digital camera and switched it on. "Berry sure. Forest no grow same. Big circle."

I flipped through the images and could see that there was a disturbance in that area. It was sunken as though the soil had settled. "Okay. Did you show the boys how to use everything?"

"Hai."

"The night vision goggles. The camouflage suits. Everything."

"Hai. Everything. Children hide in mountains."

"Okay. Perfect. I need to go and organize a few things."

"Please stay dinner ready soon."

"Thank you, Kimiko. I really need to make my way back. It will take me hours to return to my hotel."

"Stay, I make bed for you. No problem," she said.

"It is safer for you if I am not here. If anything goes wrong, I don't want there to be any connection to you. The rest of the plan I can do on my own. It is important that you continue to do everything the same. Hiro you go to work. Normal. Okay."

"Hai. We understand."

"If the tests I organize on the cameras work tonight, then tomorrow morning the information will be released. Then we just sit back and watch. I won't return again until it is safe to do so."

"Plan work?"

"I'm not sure Hiro. This is the only thing I could think of that will help to expose what has happened and hopefully allow the children to return home safely. We can only try."

"Hai."

I stood up. "Please say goodbye to Kayoko and the children for me. Tell no-one about your involvement, not even Roman. Stay quiet and safe."

"Hai. Secreto," replied Kimiko.

"Thank you." I bowed "I am grateful for everything."

Hiro stood up and bowed, "Grateful to Harpersan."

There was a feeling of hesitation about leaving them to face this portion of the plan without me being present. Pausing for a moment to look at them both, I took in the scent of the incense that was burning near our feet and exhaled, releasing a sigh. "Until we meet again." I placed my hand on my heart, tapped it, then turned and walked out of their home.

* * * * *

The sun was rising on a beautiful still morning. I purchased my ticket and just boarded an express bus taking off from Kanazawa station headed for the smallest city in Japan called Suzu. It is set by the seaside in the Noto Peninsula of Ishikawa Prefecture. I knew from the remote locale that it would be an unlikely tourist hot spot. Positioned far enough away from Toyama prefecture but close enough for me to return if the circumstances warranted.

I'd spent most of my night on the move using burner phones to send and retrieve encrypted messages from my offshore team. They were busy testing the connectivity by remotely accessing the cameras in the field. Each unit had its settings optimized for day and night surveillance. The aspect ratio was checked to validate that there weren't any significant blind spots. The cameras had their unique sim card that transmits the strings of footage in real-time to an encrypted server. The team set up the primary server to be backed up incrementally every eight minutes through five other encrypted servers, all located in different underground data centers worldwide.

The transfer is routered via multiple virtual private networks, configured never to utilize the same branch of IP addresses more than once. At worst, the most prominent risk was the connectivity being blocked or the link between the cameras to the primary server getting discovered. The team is manually deleting any trace of data that is older than an hour to mediate this. They first confirm the transfer to the backup servers are successful and then proceed with removing the old data on the primary server. Our entrapment plan was underway.

It would take approx. two hours before I arrived in Suzu. Instead of paying for a room, I organized a short-term rent of a small house situated along the fishing village's shoreline. I was looking forward to getting there. It had been a few weeks of hectic planning, sourcing, preparing. As nerve-wracking as it was, I felt relieved that we had arrived at the execution phase.

When I had reached out to the team at Sanctorum Avow, they were excited to hear from me and keen to participate in the mission. The last time I had significant involvement with them was when orchestrated to leak the details about the governing body GHOP wanting to expedite the release of a synthesized chemical called eXileanon straight into human trials. It was pitched as the apparent cure for a new disease termed Euphoric Death. Marketing campaigns promoted fear with suggestions that Euphoric Death could become a pandemic. It was the first time the public was aware that a chemical I aptly called Anathema had been leeched into human biology for decades using vaccines as the conduit. Anyone who had been vaccinated as a child for anything had a masked dose of Anathema in their system. I was principally applying the same strategy here as I had done so before. Expose the situation in the hope that it reveals a trail that leads directly to the enemy. Perhaps this time we will have better luck.

Less than thirty minutes was remaining before the crew at Sanctorum Avow pressed the button. The team was poised to flood every media outlet, reporter, and social media platform with the hashtag Lost Boys. Compelling snippets conveying the story of how hundreds of children had been taken by force through a massive covert operation by unknown assailants two years prior. Children disappearing without a trace. A two-minute short of the incident in the form of a re-enactment had been created for added effect. There would be a call to action to hunt the perpetrators and find the children. Using old KGB techniques, subliminal messages were seeded into the communications broadcasts to implant the suggestion of government involvement.

The key is to make people aware and outraged. Millions will now know this previously unremarkable village called Tatszuki within the Toyama prefectures. In a matter of hours, the roads will be jammed with a flux of incoming traffic. The streets inundated with reporters, volunteers, and such. I had no way to predict how the villagers would respond to the exposure of a painful secret that is steeped in shame and tragedy. Insensitive questions, not to mention loads of judgmental bias, will be hurled at the community for not speaking out when the incident happened. It was an unavoidable cost of the process.

The fact that I was continually making decisions that impacted many was an ever-present burden. My thoughts drifted to my college friends Peppy and Sam, their female companions, and Liam too. The consequences for being associated with me had a potentially high cost. In their case, it was the ultimate price, their lives.

# Mirage

Roman and his wife were still nowhere to be found. I had thought he would be easier to locate than this. My team of hackers had tracers on his wife's cell phone before it was switched off. They seemed to be somewhere in Osaka. It was too risky to send a text. I hoped he had the common sense to understand it would be madness for him to enter the hot zone. Any foreigners wandering around Tatszuki village would be a beacon for the media to approach. I had gone to great lengths to put everything in place to ensure nothing could be easily traced back to him. All the local hotel reservations were executed under a false identity. I'd organized to pay for his plane ticket and other expenses via a shelf company that would lead nowhere. Then used another shelf company to pay for the costs incurred by his false identity. He entered Japan via Tokyo and made his way to the Toyama prefecture utilizing bus routes. The paper trail for Roman Air showed he was in Tokyo staying at the Mirankoto Hotel. I had even arranged a person who roughly fit his appearance to utilize the room. Security footage would show him entering and leaving the suite during the time Roman was with me. Roman had inadvertently created a gaping hole by not letting me know before bringing his wife over and checking out of the hotel in Toyama. I still had his pseudo doppelganger checked in at Tokyo Mirankoto. If circumstances arose where he required an alibi and became closely scrutinized, there would be a mismatch around where he first used his bank card in Japan vs. the Tokyo check-out.

Someone started creating strings of paper cranes, leaving them strewn around lamp posts, shopfront windows, and so on, with the message, '*For the children.*' When a story was aired featuring the origami cranes, others participated. Within a matter of days, the village was littered with them. Many of the locals locked themselves indoors, trying to avoid any media coverage. One by one, husbands and wives were called into the local authorities to lodge a missing person's report and make a statement on what occurred on the night in question. Everyone feared reprisal and did not want to be falsely associated with the instigation of this onslaught of global interest. A rare few were willing to seek the reporters' attention to tell their version of the story. The rest of the villagers shunned those that did speak.

No one had visited the unmarked gravesite bar a few wild animals. The most action recorded was a spider busily making a web that crossed back and forth over the lens of one of the cameras. There seemed to be no discernible change in the various government bodies' behavior for all the social media noise and physical search parties that were underway. We had hackers accessing feeds into every department with extra monitoring of research and military facilities. There was either something we were missing, or we had planted sniffers in the wrong divisions. I would have expected someone to raise some flags, start deleting large volumes of files. We detected nothing.

I had received word that the lost boys were safely tucked deep in the Hida Mountains, where only Hiro, Kimiko Kayoko, and I knew their location. They had enough supplies to last them four months. Up until now, they successfully managed to avoid detection. If luck were on our side, they wouldn't have to be hidden for much longer.

I sent the signal to trigger the commencement of the next phase of the strategy.

* * * * *

The fire was now roaring in the woodstove. While waiting for the pot of water to heat to make myself a cup of tea, I turned on the little antique black and white television to surf the news channels. Every station was covering the situation. We had recently released the longitude and latitude of the burial site using a broadcast switcher to redirect random signals to a singular feed. Poster Images that had been released of the missing children were repurposed to be the wallpaper backdrop. This, together with the geolocation of the gravesite overlaid on a white cross, was on air for two minutes. It was enough time to have people capture the information and cause another tidal wave of reactions.

I switched to a burner phone to access the latest news from an English station.

*'Coming to you live from Tatszuki in the Toyama prefecture, Japan, I have received confirmation that the search party was reconvened and are about to accompany local police to the site where leaks have rumored a mass grave exists*

*containing the missing children. If this is true, it will bring a black stain to this day for all the families who have held hope across the years that their children would one day be returned.*

*As you can see behind me, there is heavy machinery being loaded on the trucks. Convoys of search and rescue people and volunteers are queued in their vehicle, ready to follow closely behind the law enforcement squads to the location. We will be monitoring their every move. Our next update is expected to be coming live from the site in an hour.'*

I switched off the phone, took out the battery, destroyed the sim, and tossed it in the used pile. Placing the lid on the box, I shoved it under the sofa. The kettle was boiling, the water spilling over was making a hissing sound against the cast iron cooktop. I went and removed it from the heat. Leaning forward on the bench, I stared into my empty teacup. My jaw was clenched, foot-tapping, I had to get out of here. Time would feel like it is passing quicker if I distracted myself. With this thought, I grabbed my wallet, jacket, and beanie to help shield me from the crisp winds. I looked around for the house key, placed it in my pocket, and walked out the door.

The little cottage I'm renting is situated on the shoreline only meters from the main pier, where all the medium-sized marine trawlers are docked. At the start of daybreak, I can hear the seabirds calling as they circle the returning ships' hulls. This morning was no exception. I walked across the road, gazing up at them hovering above, patiently awaiting the moment a rebellious fish manages to leap from the netting to frantically flip flop on the wooden slats of the dilapidated pier. All that energy expended on a chance for freedom, only to have half a dozen birds swoop down in fierce competition to capture it.

The fisherman didn't seem to notice me approaching. They were all in their respective positions doing what needed to be done to get the haul safely loaded into the truck's opening that was parked below the crane. Just in the short time I was observing, I could appreciate how physically demanding their job was. The cold winds were blowing a gale so hard I could taste saltwater on my lips. It made the seas choppy, and along with it, the boats were bobbing to the command of the water. Just watching all the erratic motion made me feel a little queasy. I had been indecisive about whether I would at some point organize to go on a boat tour. I had seen a few locally advertised. The itineraries were very similar in offering an all-day adventure to the various islands seeded around the area. Standing on the dock, feeling my stomach churn, I realized it probably wasn't for me.

Walking along the boardwalk with the open seas to my left and the village to my right, I casually looked at the window displays. In the select few that were targeted at the tourist market, it seemed popular to follow a maritime theme. Some of the old parts of ships were for sale, like the buoy and rusted anchors. What continually caught my eye was the detailed craftsmanship in the model boats. It was truly outstanding. I didn't linger at the windows for too long as it created false anticipation with the shopkeepers who watched in the hope that I might enter and buy something.

I finally succumbed to crossing the threshold into a store that attracted me with their eclectic mix of old and new items. There were so many interesting pieces intentionally displayed in ways that suggested alternative domestic uses. A large field rice sifter had been overfilled with plastic fruit. Three-pronged pitch forks fashioned into hat stands. It was quirky and kind of fun.

The shop was oddly larger than it looked from the outside. I weaved my way around the shelves that were crammed with items and was amused when I noted the distinction between stacking styles immerge. There were two very different people operating this store. One of them was neat, and the other might have tendencies of a hoarder in the making.

Thus far, my favorite section was a row of perfectly displayed pottery urns of varying shapes and sizes presented beautifully. In contrast, the shelf above had a doll's head with one eye missing glaring down from between a pile of vinyl records which were precariously resting on the edge of some wooden kitchen utensils. The display was a complete mish-mosh of elements stacked together, likely because they had been unpacked in that order. How positively delightful and odd. I continued to peruse with amusement.

Occasionally I could hear the sound of the chair creaking as the shop owner lent across to try and see where I was. I'd freeze in position to make it harder to detect my location. I don't know why this place brought out the child in me. I stared and touched everything and felt happy.

There was a particular section of the store where the secondhand goods were spread wide and staked high on an oversized singular table that piqued my interest. Nothing of note stood out. It was the way I felt standing there. It made my senses tingle. Carefully I moved layers of items to the side to expose everything in sections. I visually scanned from left to right and back again. I trawled through the things as though I was on a secret treasure hunt. I even went around and stood on the other side of the table to gain a different perspective. Something here was calling to be found. I just knew it.

I decided to continue to explore the remaining portion of the store. I honed in on the little details. A used candle wedged into a kerosene lamp where the wick would typically sit. The outside of the lamp has a light patina of rust forming around remnants of fingerprint stains. An empty packet of camel cigarettes lay crumpled next to a faded dried flower arrangement in a tattered weave basket. It was easy to write this stuff off as junk, yet each piece felt as though it had secrets ready to reveal to an unsuspecting observer.

Slowly I gravitated back to the table to recommence sifting through the items. I found myself sorting the objects into various piles. The hairs on my arms stood on end when the tips of my fingers brushed the tattered edges of a book. I shifted the large glass jar that was perched on top of it to get a closer look. A Hungarian magazine. What is an eastern European magazine doing in the smallest village in Japan? I flipped through the pages staring at the pictures and article layouts. There were stains on some, slight pen marks, and a sentence circled while others were underlined. Whoever this used to belong to had left me with the impression that they read every detail in this magazine. I came across a folded piece of paper that may have served as a bookmark lodged tightly just past the midway point. It released what felt like a light electric jolt when I first touched it. My hand recoiled as I smiled at the mystery paper. This is it.

Unfolding the white sheet of paper revealed something written in oversized Kanji using traditional black ink calligraphy. There were some light scuff marks from where the ink had been rubbing against the paper along the crease line. I checked the back; it was blank. I turned it over again. I honestly had no idea what it said. I decided to keep hold of it in my left hand while turning the rest of the magazine pages with my right. When I got to the end, I flipped it over to look at the front cover again. The picture featured was of two men in business attire shaking hands. The Hungarian flag was displayed in the backdrop. I quickly flipped through the magazine to see if I had overlooked something that would provide some insight. I then checked around the table to see if there were any other magazines and found nothing similar. All I knew was that I didn't want to let this piece of paper go.

Satisfied that there was nothing more to do, I walked over to the man sitting at the counter. I showed him the piece of paper and in and asked how much.

"Kon'nichiwa, koreha ikuradesu ka?"

"Kon'nichiwa," he said as he looked at the piece of paper in my hand, then tilted his head to look under the desk while using his left hand to fumble about for something. Moments later, he straightened up and revealed a tiny calculator. He typed in some numbers, then subtracted a few, looked at the paper again, then at me. I tried not to burst out laughing. He was making a legitimate attempt to appear as though he had some science to his application of the cost.

Finally, he pressed the equals sign and showed me the damage. ¥520

I gave him a thumbs-up, opened my wallet, and counted out the money, which was roughly equivalent to five USD. He watched intently as I placed the notes neatly on top of each other. Creases on his forehead appeared as his eyebrows raised when I intentionally put one of the notes down without aligning it as I had with the others. His eyes jutted up for a second to look at me and then returned to the pile. With both hands, he collected the money, tapped it down on the desk to get them all aligned before placing it in front of me to add the rest of the notes. This fellow was not the messy one, I mused.

The transaction was complete. He seemed delighted that I had purchased something. In turn, I was pleased to have found this mysterious little treasure. I carefully folded it using the same crease lines and stuck it in my pocket. I gave the shopkeeper an enthusiastic wave then left the store. I was famished.

I'd already walked past two restaurants that were overlooking the waterfront. I wanted to find an obscure place like that fantastic sushi bar I discovered in the Higashi Chaya district. My tummy was protesting as I made my way through the maze of streets, looking for a gem. I didn't stop to glance at the window displays of plastic food in case my mind sided with my stomach to convince me just to walk in. Persisting with the idea of finding a place to eat that offered an experience with my meal, I noticed I was gravitating further away from the coastline.

After an hour and a half, my resolve had started to wane. None of the establishments grabbed my attention, so I didn't feel the need to backtrack. There was a place I could see in the distance with a familiar wooden sign secured by chains out the front swinging with the breeze. I'll go in there.

The front of the building had large wooden doors with no windows. A small sign displaying an arrow indicating the direction to slide it open, some kanji characters, and the word in small letters underneath '*welcome.*' I wrapped my fingers around the handle and began to slide the door. A lady came rushing over to push it the rest of the way.

"Irasshaimase, dozo."

"Arigatōgozaimashita," I said, thanking her as I walked in.

"Eto no ingrishu gomen'nasai." She said, looking a little concerned.

I nodded my head and gave her a thumbs up that I understood she doesn't speak English. My tummy made a loud noise that made me pat it. I smiled and asked if I could please eat, "Watashi wa tabetaidesu onegaishimasu."

"Hai, hai," she replied with a smile and a series of little bows.

I followed her through another set of sliding doors down a rather dreary-looking hall that led to an open space where the dining tables were located. I took off my shoes and placed the traditional slippers on and sat on the tatami mat in front of the table. I wasn't sure how to ask for a cushion in Japanese. I couldn't see any around, so I decided I would have to tough it out. My stomach took precedence over my ass.

The host scurried off then quickly returned with a menu and a fresh jug of water filled to the brim with ice. She poured me a glass of water before placing the pitcher on the table. I accepted the menu and gave a tilt of my head, "Dōmo."

I could see her hesitate, wanting to say something as I opened the menu. It was all in kanji and hiragana with no pictures. I looked up and smiled. She accepted this and left to give me some time to peruse the menu.

For the second time today, I found myself feeling delighted. This quaint little establishment mainly catered to locals. It meant that whatever I ordered on this mystery menu would be more traditional than what I was likely being served at other places. I stared at the words and wondered what they might be. The only kanji character I recognized was the one for fish.

A solitary man tucked in the corner on the opposite side to my right. He was tucking into what looked to be a bowl of udon filled with thick noodles. There was a family of five dining to my left. They had a banquet of food in the center of the table they were sharing. My tummy grumbled.

I politely waved to the host.

She glanced over as I pointed to a few things on the list. I figured if I ordered enough, I would get some of it right. I closed the menu and placed it on the table. With this queue, the lady scurried off down the hall.

Sipping on my water, I took a better look at the room. The walls were made from wooden slats that were dark brown. There wasn't any artwork on the walls. The abundance of light came streaming into this space from a series of rectangular windows situated close to the roofline. It didn't seem in keeping with other architecture I had seen. The décor was rather plain.

The sound of a page flicker caught my attention. The elderly gentleman held a book in his left hand while mindlessly using his right to stir the contents of his bowl of udon with his chopsticks. The title 'Inner Decree' was diagonally displayed with bold orange font on a black background on the front and back page. I wondered if it was in English or Japanese. Conscious not to get caught staring, I waited until I heard the page-turning then glanced across. Right to left. It must be in English.

The host and a helper arrived with two trays containing my order. The aromas wafting up my nostrils smelt tantalizing. I picked up my chopsticks before they had placed the last bowl down.

"Dōzo omeshiagarikudasai," she said with a smile.

"Dōmo arigatōgozaimashita," I replied, thanking her while making the assumption she was telling me to enjoy my food or some such sentiment.

I was salivating in anticipation of the first bite. Using my chopsticks, I focused on selecting a portion of the foods I recognized, steamed salmon, along with some wilted greens that were covered in a light brown sauce with a sprinkling of sesame seeds. I placed it in my mouth, closing my eyes while I chewed. It was incredible. The flavors were surely enhanced by hunger and my untainted palate. Joyfully I swallowed my first morsel of food for the day and wasted no time loading my mouth up with another.

Stacking the empty plates then pushing them to one side, I slid the bowl of ramen over. The dish was presented so beautifully it was almost a shame to eat it. Two halves of a perfectly cooked egg floated on the surface of the light soup. Loads of vegetables were splayed in the center of the bowl. Bamboo shoots, some tofu, grated cabbage, shallots, and seaweed were the only items I could recognize. First, I sampled the soup. It had a very delicate flavor. Collecting an array of the veggies, I took a bite, then another to fit it in my mouth without liquid dribbling down my chin. They still had a crunch to them. Everything was delicious.

In terms of selection, I managed to choose an excellent range of food. The only item that looked a little odd was this clump of tubular white sacs of something foreign. It reminded me of intestines, except it was blistering white. The way it was piled high on one side of the plate, I envisaged they could be chubby maggots the thickness of my pinky finger. I poked it to see if it would wriggle. Thankfully it didn't. I'm not sure if it suddenly came alive how I would react. Eating the refreshing cucumber salad that accompanied the dish, I tried to determine whether I should be adventurous and taste it. The more I stared at it, the weirder it looked. Shifting it to one side, I went back to the safety of the ramen.

Nearing my limit for consumption, I was impressed with the amount of food I had managed to eat. I'd ordered a large quantity that could have easily satisfied three people and polished off enough for two. I picked up my glass of water and took a few hearty gulps. Looking across, I noticed the family of five were still in the throes of feasting. However, the elderly gentleman had left.

There were two things I was presently consumed by now that I had more than satisfied my stomach's demands. I was starting to feel uncomfortably full, and my ass was killing me. Shifting my position on the floor to relieve my numb butt cheeks, I simultaneously raised my hand to flag the host over.

As she came across, I waved my hand over the banquet and said, "Totemo oishī arigatō," to let her know the food was delicious. I then pulled out my wallet to show her I would like to pay. I learned how to say the words to enquire how much is something but wasn't familiar with requesting a bill. Not to offend, I decided showing her my wallet was a solid signal for her to let me know the amount due.

The host walked to where the elderly gentleman had been sitting, retrieved a box, and returned with it in hand. She placed it down on the table, bowed, and then waited. It was a wooden box painted in the same glossy, traditional red lacquer seen everywhere in Japan. There was a slit at the top where people can, I assume, place money inside. I'd heard about these places. Establishments that let you pay what you can afford. It prevented the need for less fortunate patrons to beg. The community in a more favorable position overpay, which affords someone struggling to come and have a meal for very little. It was an eloquent solution that helped those who needed it while maintaining a modicum of dignity. Pulling out money from my wallet, I happily began feeding a note at a time into the box. The host bent down and placed her hand over it when I had reached ¥5000.

"Totemo oishī," I said, gently moving her hand away to continue adding more money. This got the attention of the other group who were now watching. In the end, I had put in just shy of ¥20,000, which was around $200 USD, give or take a few dollars. I flipped my wallet upside down and shook it for effect while letting her know how delicious the meal was, "Totemo, totemo oishī." The expression of surprise on her face was priceless.

"Dōmo arigatōgozaimashita," she said, bowing several times.

I stood up and bowed in response, then took a step toward the hallway. The host placed her left hand up to suggest I stop, and her right hand pointed behind me.

"Dōzo," She said as she began to walk in that direction. I followed.

As we walked by the other patrons, I gave them a smile in response to their nod of acknowledgment. It felt lovely to know such places exist.

The host used both her hands to open the door, then stepped aside for me to walk past. "Kitekurete arigatō, sayōnara," she said, thanking me for coming as she began closing the door.

I replied in kind, "Arigatō, gochisosama deshita," while in awe of the most enchanting garden I had ever laid my eyes upon. The understated room I had dined in was a stark contrast to the glory of its external surroundings. How impossibly beautiful it seemed. The vibrant green wide-spanning fronds of a somewhat rather spindly plant shaded another plant which showcased an abundance of star-shaped yellow flowers. The water trickling down moss-covered stones fell directly into a vast winding pond bubbling with movement from the Koi. I felt as though I had ventured into a fairy tale. I slowly began to walk the path, not wishing to miss a thing. The details were so well thought out I knew moving too quickly might hinder my ability to appreciate this living masterpiece. Air ferns draped from the arms of maples. Japanese lanterns were dotted about. I imagine seeing them lit at night would be heavenly. I stopped at the midpoint of crossing the bridge to look into the pond at the Koi.

"You possess the expression of a child experiencing wonderment."

I turned to my left to see who had spoken. A puff of smoke was release from the long thing pipe. He grasped the end with his teeth and smiled.

"Hello, I guess I am; this place is rather extraordinary. I saw you inside. You were reading a book. I think if I recall correctly, it is called, 'Inner Decree.'"

He lifted it from where it laid on his lap. "You are correct," he said, waving it. "I am glad you are enjoying the fruits of my labor. Many of the plants you see here were cultivated by seed, giving birth to this garden. It is a long and rewarding process."

"Did you create this?" I asked, looking around in amazement.

"Indeed. I am still creating it, and, in many ways, it creates itself. What you see around you is forty years in the making."

"Forty years? I'm sorry, how is it that you have no discernible Japanese accent? You sound like you are from the US, right? New York?" I wouldn't think he was any older than early to mid-fifty.

He balanced his pipe on the edge of a stone and began waving his hands in the air, "New York, New York. That's right."

"I'm trying to do the math. If you have been building this garden for forty years, how is it possible that you don't seem to have a hint of a Japanese influence to your speech?"

"I was born and raised here until I was old enough to go to school. My uncle had migrated years prior with his family. He was located in Michigan. For a long time, he campaigned to have my father let my brother and I live with him. When my mother fell ill and then passed away soon after, he agreed to send us to live with our uncle. My father was a fifth-generation fisherman. Maintaining tradition was important, and as the eldest son, he had a responsibility to support his father and continue the legacy. Every summer, we would come home to spend the holidays with the family. When I graduated from college, I moved to New York to do an internship with a stockbroker and eventually met the woman I was to marry. Celia."

"Did you forge a career as a stockbroker?"

"Eventually."

I smiled, "What I'd like to know is which of these glorious plants was the first seed you established for this garden?"

His eyes twinkled. Picking up his pipe, he rushed off. "Come, I will show you."

I followed him down a pebble stone path to an open space where the area was transformed into a Zen garden. Large stones nestled into the earth, raked sand, and amongst it all was a glorious tree with long curved branches casting ominous shadows across the landscape.

The man stood upright and proud as he looked at it. "This is the first seed I planted. It is the Mizunara Oaktree. My father was a fisherman by trade but a gardener by heart. Before my brother and I left to go to America, we planted a seed with our father. He nurtured them as a symbol of his love."

"How incredible. Without the insight, this was a spectacular tree. Now knowing its origin has transformed the way I feel. This magnificent oak represents the significance of a father's love for his children."

"Yes. He was a splendid father."

"Thank you for sharing such a special memory with me. I feel so profoundly honored to be here right now."

The man turned to look at me. "What brings you to this place?"

"I was hungry."

"Ah yes, but to Japan. To Suzu."

Pursing my lips as I thought about my father, my mother, the insanity of it all.

"I guess I came here to get lost in an attempt to be found. A lot has happened that has left me questioning everything. It's complicated. In essence, I wanted to find a space where I could hear myself. I'm not sure if that makes any sense. I've been walking the streets of Japan for some time now."

"What you run from comes with you. Nothing is ever left behind."

"Yes, the sentiment is very true. I'm not running. I just needed some space to breathe, away from everything. I felt depleted, defeated; foreboding darkness was looming. I had to find a way to re-establish balance."

"And have you?"

I looked into his eyes and pondered the question. A sudden rise of a smile beamed on my face as I felt the answer come deep from within, "Yes."

He returned his gaze at the tree. "I got so caught up in my life in New York that I found little time to return to Japan to see my father. He never complained and was grateful for when I brought the family over to visit. At one point in the peak of my career, I received word that he had fallen ill and could no longer manage the ships. Instead of returning, I sent him money. I thought as a dutiful son; I was providing him with what he needed. My brother had lost himself in the indulgent Las Vegas lifestyle that took him to the brink of death. Overconsumption of all the party treats, gambling debts, mixing with the wrong crowds, He was the opposite of me. To save his life, I placed Mako in a rehabilitation center and then returned him home to live with our father. At first, my brother was very angry with me for leaving him behind. Eventually, he apprenticed with the seamen out on the trawlers to learn the trade and later took over the family business. He runs it still to this very day."

He paused for a moment to take in a deep breath, then released a sigh. "I worked hard to make my father proud only to realize as I sat beside him during his last hours of life, all he ever truly wanted was my time. He told me it was now up to me to take care of the tree and ensure it always maintains good health. After the funeral, my brother thanked me for saving his life. Returning home helped him to find his way back to living again. He treasured the remaining years he got to spend with our father and discovered a love for the open ocean. He told me stories of how father had him withdraw large sums of the money I had been sending. They would sneak out to people's homes planting it in places that could be easily found, allowing them to think it was good fortune rather than offending them with charity. Across the years, father had helped many struggling villagers. I was very moved to hear of this and also sad. I was learning more about him after he was gone. I should have spent the time when he was alive."

"Is this the driving force for the restaurant's business model? No set price. Patrons pay what they can afford."

"Yes. It is in honor of my parents. The restaurants maintain their legacy of imparting generosity and support to those who are struggling. We have fifty-two operating across many prefectures. All the residents of the village contribute as they can. If a farmer has an abundantly large crop, he will send a bushel to contribute. Many people across Japan now see the restaurant as an opportunity to support in ways that don't rely on donations. Every day people will arrive to assist and work for free, cleaning dishes, chopping vegetables. Notable Chefs from five-star restaurants will travel to different regions to teach the local cook's new techniques and recipes. It has evolved."

"The food was delicious. The only thing I wasn't sure about and decided not to try was this dish that had something white stuffed in what looked like intestines. I almost convinced myself to try it then chickened out."

He chuckled, "You ordered Shirako. This is a dish for an acquired taste. Even for the locals."

"The menu had no pictures for me to reference against, so I pointed out a few items on the list with the hope that one or two would be something I would eat. Everything else was fantastic. You're still laughing. What is Shirako?"

"It is the sperm of the codfish served raw. Shirako translated means, white children."

"Yuck, talk about trusting my instincts. I have never been so happy with a decision I've made in my life." I said, thoroughly disgusted.

The man released a hearty laugh.

Reaching around in my back pocket, I pulled out the paper I had purchased earlier and carefully unfolded it. "Can you tell me what this means?"

He looked at the paper quizzically. "This is oshichiya. On the seventh night after the birth of a newborn child, the father writes the given name on a piece of paper. This is presented to the extended family at a dinner celebration. Usually, it would have the birth date at the top and then the name. On this one, there is literally the kanji for the year, and the rest is the boy's name."

"Oh, what is the name?"

"Peter Jacobs."

"That doesn't sound Japanese," I said, a little surprised.

"Do you know who this boy is?"

"No. I found it in a store. I liked the aesthetic of the lettering and decided to buy it." I said, not wanting to divulge anything more.

Placing his hands behind his back, he let out a little, "Hmm."

I began folding the paper, then returned it to my pocket. "It's nothing. I was just curious about what it said. I thought you were going to tell me it had some deep zen message."

"There are no accidents. It is strange to have such a treasured item being discarded or even sold in a shop. Usually, all the names of the children are displayed within the home, mounted on the wall in the meals area. It takes pride of place."

"That makes sense for a Japanese family, but a child called Peter is likely connected to a foreign family. Perhaps they wanted to experience some of the local traditions, and this was a practice attempt before creating the one that hangs on their wall. Or maybe it was someone using their name to learn the calligraphy technique. At least now, I won't be staring at it and wondering whether I am holding the answer to the secrets of the universe." I said, laughing.

"How long are you planning to stay in Suzu?"

"I'm not sure. A few more days, I guess. I've rented a small cottage on the shoreline not too far from the pier where all the trawlers dock their boats."

"If you would permit me to be your guide, we can meet tomorrow morning near the pier. I would take great pleasure in showing you around."

"That is very generous of you. I'd like that. Thank you."

"My name is Naruto; most people call me Naru."

"I'm Harper. Pleased to meet you, Naruto."

"Likewise, Harper. Is nine am too early?"

"Not at all. I guess I will head off now and see you at nine tomorrow."

"See you then."

"One final question. How do I get out of here?"

"Straight back to where we were, except you will need to stay on this side, walk past the bridge toward the fence line. There is a gate that will place you on the corner of the same street frontage where you had entered the restaurant."

"Got it. Thanks again," feeling content, I turned and walked down the path toward the bridge.

* * * * *

Tears welled up in my eyes as I watched the news footage. I felt partly relieved and despondent. How could people be so fucking cruel?

"They appeared from nowhere, linked hand in hand, walking toward us. Covered in dirt, tattered clothes, it was very surreal. Everyone was momentarily stunned until mourning parents' wailing was replaced by screams of recognition of some of their children. It was overwhelming. Names were being called, parents trying to cross the cordoned barrier line, while the local police force stepped into formation to prevent them. That's when we intervened to help. Reporters united to begin crossing the barrier to distract them. Parents broke through, searching, hugging the children. Tensions increased with a riot about to ensue when the police received orders to step aside. Floods of parents scrambled to find their children, a cacophony of names being called and sounds of grieve-stricken whaling. As miraculous as this has been for the few families who get to have their children return home, the outcome for many others is not so fortunate. The manual excavation of the site continues. The tally is believed to have crossed two hundred with an expectation that hundreds more will be uncovered in the days to come. More forensic experts are en-route to help with the analysis and identification of the remains. The police have since tried to shut down the area, citing it was to reduce further contamination of the crime scene. This has not deterred the families who are standing their ground. More and more people are arriving from neighboring villagers in support. As the sun begins to set, candles can be seen flickering around the area's circumference, where a vigil is commencing. The forty-six survivors I've been told are united with their families. We are still trying to receive permission to be granted access to interview them. Until then, the mystery remains. Who is responsible for this horrendous atrocity and why?"

I switched off the phone, dismantled the battery, and snapped the sim card in two. There wasn't any more that I could do, at least for now. The surveillance footage at the burial site would remain in place. All the sniffers planted into the computer networks would also continue to be monitored. It was alarming not to find a single lead available so far. For the perpetrators, laying low and perhaps even blending in was a clever strategy. I was sure the survivors emerging would make them react. Yet, we identified nothing.

It was a haunting image to see the footage of the boys walking hand in hand silently. Futoshi had been planted in amongst them to ensure he too was identified as part of the survivors and could thereby openly return to his family. All of those boys were now our allies. They knew not to say anything about the assistance the Moto family had provided. The boys, I hoped, would be safe now that the world was watching. I was banking on everyone in the village being so enraged that they band together to be on alert and protect one another at any cost. There was way too much attention brought to bear for any type of threat, intimidation, or forced silence. The villagers were thrust into a harsh reality, some stripped of hope, but all received the freedom of no longer being enslaved to fear. With the Moto family's influence, they will be instigating the largest active civilian coordinated hunt to identify and find the people responsible. No stone would be left unturned. It made me feel confident that a day of reckoning was looming.

I tapped my finger on the window ledge, causing fragments of dust particles to stir. I watched them rise upward in a swirl then shifted my gaze to look outside at the birds circling above the noisy trawler coming in. My mind drifted to the conversation I had with Naruto. He asked if I had found my balance, and I had responded yes. I know what drove me to come to Japan, but I wondered whether there was any further need for me to stay.

# Revelation

Naruto held out his hand to clasp as I took the last few steps over the unstable wooden plank and onto the trawler. His brother Mako was busy shifting things and calling out orders to the crew. I noticed the tiny fish scales trapped between the creases of the bundled netting. The way they reflected the light to glisten held improbable beauty given the reason for their presence was linked to the fate that was bestowed to its owner.

"I thought it would smell fishy," I said, scrunching up my nose.

"Fish don't start to have a smell until they are decomposing. It's the way we can easily prove what we are selling is fresh from the ocean. No smell commands a much higher price. Once Mako took over the business, he made a few changes to ensure his haul's longevity provided even higher quality to the purchasers. He modified the fleet to have open bays that draw in a constant stream of seawater. This keeps the catch alive and breathing. A similar modification was installed in all the carriages of the transport vehicles. Mako invested in bigger trucks that could handle the additional heavier loads. This way, shipments traveling across the country are well maintained. He has tripled the business just with local demands alone."

"Why is it heavier? Don't the transport trucks already carry tonnes of dry ice to keep it fresh?"

"Salt water is denser than water or ice, so there is a difference in the weight. Also, carrying liquid causes more sway. To counter the impact of the movement, there needed to be some adjustments to the container to ensure the loads were secure."

"It seems Mako was born to be the sixth-generation fisherman."

"Yes. I'm afraid it might stop here. My three children are established back home. Mako's two children live in Tokyo. His daughter works in a lady's salon, and his son is in the throes of completing his culinary apprenticeship. He wants to be a chef in his own restaurant."

"At least that's food-related. He may not become a fisherman, but that doesn't mean he won't look at running the business someday. Your brother fell into it. Never say never."

Naruto laughed. "He is a devout vegan who wears T-shirts that have slogan messages such as 'Meat is murder.' I don't imagine he is the right person to be heading up this business. Mako Jnr has aspirations of establishing a high-end vegan restaurant."

I felt the deep rumbles run up through my legs as the throttle was shifted into a higher gear. I turned to my right to confirm that the ship had started to move away from the pier. "Oh my, I think this was a bad idea."

"Nonsense. Once you acclimate, everything will be fine. Here chew on the end of this. Don't swallow. Chew slowly to release the flavor.'

He handed me what looked like a weathered old piece of leather. "What is it?"

"Sundried ginger. It may have a little heat to it. Ginger settles the stomach. Look at the crew. Any of them that appear to be chewing something is guaranteed to have this in their mouths."

I smelt it to confirm it was ginger, then popped the piece into my mouth and started to chew. "Wow, this has some serious kick to it."

"It does. If you chew on it now, it will prevent you from getting seasick later."

"I honestly didn't think when you said you would be showing me around that it would entail a cruise on a shipping trawler."

"The best parts of Suzu have to be seen from an ocean vantage point. I've also arranged with Mako to take us on the route near the islands so you can see the wildlife."

"It sounds incredible. Thank you."

Mako approached, sporting a big smile, "Is there anything you need?"

"No thanks. Your brother just gave me some ginger to chew on."

"Ah yes. The ocean gets rather choppy. It's best to prepare yourself now so that you don't feel seasick for too long when we are way out there. Spending the next couple of days at sea with us will give you your sea legs."

My expression changed as I looked at Naruto with confusion, "Day's? No." I switched back to address Mako, "You're joking, right?" I looked at the distance between the ship and the pier. "It's not too far. I can still swim to the shore."

"What in these shark-infested waters? I wouldn't like your chances." With this, Mako roared with laughter.

"OMG, you had me for a moment. Seriously tell me we aren't going to be out here for days. Are we?"

"A few days, perhaps a week at most. I promise no longer," he said, slapping my back as he turned to re-join with his crew, all the while still laughing heartily.

I looked at Naruto, who was also clearly amused.

"My brother is joking. We will be out for the day and back before dark."

I released a sigh. "Okay."

"Come. I'll give you a tour of the place."

I followed Naruto down a narrow flight of metal steps. "Behind this door is the toilet. The kitchen and eating area is through there. Over here are the sleeping quarters."

There was a light scent of diesel. The air felt humid and thick to breathe in. I looked at the four bunk beds while feeling the sway of the boat. "There are more crew than there are beds."

"Yes, on long hauls, the ship is always crewed in rotation, four on and four off plus the cook who is a seasoned fisherman. Most of the men who work for the company are linked generationally. Their fathers worked with our forefathers. They are not just employees; they are family."

"Incredible. Loyalty must run deep with such connection to historical lineage." The ship moved with a motion that made my stomach flip.

"Best we get you back on deck for some fresh air. You look a little pale."

I immediately turned to head down the hall and up the stairs. "I'm not sure the ginger is working." At the top of the steps, my sweaty brow was cooled by the sea breeze. I tried to shut my eyes for a moment to stabilize, but this exacerbated the tension I felt in my stomach.

I looked around in a slight panic as I rushed to the edge knowing there was nothing more I could do. With my hands firmly grasping the border, I opened my mouth while positioning my head over the side, releasing a healthy stream of vomit into the waters below.

Ten minutes into an onslaught of cramps and vomit had me wishing for solid land and my bed. I couldn't establish a comfortable position that allowed me to lay my face against the side of the ship's cold steel. The icy sting seemed to be the only thing that made me feel better.

"Here, rinse your mouth out with this."

I slowly shifted my position to see what Naruto was handing to me.

"It's just water. Swill it in your mouth and spit it out. Do that a couple of times, then sip a little at a time to get some fluids back into you. That was a lot of vomit."

I mustered a slight smile as I accepted the glass, "Thanks for noticing." Propping myself up, I did as he suggested, then passed the glass back. "I'm sorry. I don't think this is going to pass anytime soon. I feel awful."

"We have all been through it. Your body will adjust to the way of the seas. We have set up a hammock. The seafarers cure to motion sickness."

"A hammock?"

"Yes, sleeping it off. The hammock rocks to the sway of the oceans. This will settle the imbalance caused by all the movement. Trust me, it will help."

Naruto placed his hand under my left arm to support me as we walked over to the hammock.

"Are you sure about this?"

"Absolutely. Get in, sleep it off for an hour or so, and when you wake, your system will have adjusted."

I climbed in, repositioned the pillow, and closed my eyes to see how it felt. Naruto loosely tucked a blanket around me. My body was limp.

"Sleep. You will feel better soon."

I closed my eyes and surrendered to the motion.

* * * * *

"Harper."

I felt Naruto's hand ever so gently nudging my shoulder.

"Harper."

I smiled as my arms lifted, toes pointed, allowing my body to indulge in a stretch.

"Do you feel better?"

My eye still closed, I replied, "Much, much better."

"Great, do you need help to get up? There is something you must see."

I turned my face into the sun's rays and squinted my eyes open. "I'll be right," I said as I began shuffling, then almost lost my balance as the hammock swayed on one side. When my first leg touched down, I placed a hand on my knee to brace before the rest of my body followed. It wasn't graceful by any means.

"Come over here."

I felt the shift in the boat as it went up and over the waves. The hammock seemed to mask the movement. It took a few moments to reset my balance as I walked over to where Naruto, Mako, and the rest of the crew stood.

"Look," said Naruto pointing out at a rocky shelf on the side of an Island.

"How incredible," I replied while feasting my eyes on countless sun baking seals barking at each other. There were thousands of squawking seabirds hovering over nested babies. Landslides of white streaks marked downward into piles of shit. The waves rhythmically rolling in were crashing hard against sharp stony crops tossing misty sea spray into the air.

"This is my favorite part about being a fisherman," said Mako.

"Do any people live on this Island?"

Mako smiled, "No. The three others are neighboring. You can see one of them in the distance."

"Ah, yes, I see it."

"They are owned by our family. We have held the titles for the last three generations. Land developers, pressure from the government, many people have tried to force the sale. No matter the cost, we have never relented. Our family's creed is," Mako looked at his brother.

Together they said, "Take from the sea and give back what she needs."

"Baransu," I whispered.

"Hai, Baransu," replied Mako. His crew members all acknowledged with a slight bow.

"We do not see this as our land. We are the custodians, the protectors. Our ancestors knew there was a price to pay if we only spent energy on the flow of taking. We were taught where there is take; there must also be an equal amount of giving. There are stories of fishermen who would slaughter the seals and kill the birds to reduce the competition for the fish. This caused mother nature to be angry with them. She retaliated with a tsunami that wiped out the entire village. When the fishing boats returned from their trip, they found little remained. Very few people had survived. Fishermen are superstitious and believed the tsunami was their fault. This was instrumental in shifting the way things were approached.

Each of the owners of the fishing trawlers agreed to make amends with mother nature. Our forefathers purchased the four islands to protect them from poachers and gave them back as an offering to the sea."

I was smiling, "This place renders me speechless."

Mako leaned in, "Notice how the seals don't care that we are here? That is because they know there is nothing to fear. We are just something they see passing by from time to time."

"Hmm, that might not be a good thing. I think a little bit of fear is a healthy response."

"The rocky crops surrounding these islands are too treacherous to bypass. This is the closest you can safely get. Even with a small boat, the currents would toss them about and have them capsized before getting close enough to do anything. You see, we protect the land from being commercialized, and mother nature does the rest."

"I know I was off to a rough start when we left this morning, and as horrible as it was to be so seasick. I'm thrilled to be here right now."

Naruto passed me another piece of ginger.

I looked at him puzzled, "I feel so much better. I don't think I need it."

Mako once again laughed, "We are yet to arrive in the deep seas. Chew on this and hold on for your life." He turned and headed off with the crew to prepare the ship to move.

"Seriously?"

Naruto scrunched up his face, "Actually, he's not too far off. It can and often does get rather choppy out there. It is rarely calm waters."

I popped the ginger in my mouth and chewed.

* * * * *

Glad to see the pier in view, I felt myself relaxing for the first time in hours. Indulging in a deep breath, I looked up to enjoy watching the seabirds circling the boat. Up high, they effortlessly swirled while making a ruckus. Only a few minutes lay between me and the feel of the solid ground I was longing for. Although the experience was incredible, I had reached my tolerance for endless nausea and the taste of vomit that remained in the back of my mouth despite chewing copious amounts of ginger. The seas had been wild, more so than they had anticipated. The turbulence on the surface did not deter them from retrieving a bumper yield. There were a couple of times when big waves had lifted the ship and slammed it down so hard; I was sure something would have broken. When I saw the crew scattered about and Naruto handed me a life jacket, I would be lying if I said I wasn't frightened. The sheer power of the lift in the swell was incredibly intimidating. I couldn't imagine being caught out there in a storm.

I felt a tap on my shoulder and turned to look. Naruto and Mako were at the helm of the boat chatting. I felt another tap on my back. I swiveled around, but no one was there. How odd. Walking across to join them, I felt something hit my leg. I looked down to see a big streak of white. Mako mid-conversation registered what had happened and burst out into uncontrollable laughter.

"I must be the luckiest person alive. I've been shat on three times." I said as I pointed to my shoulder and turned to show them my back. Mako was lost in his amusement. Tears filled his eyes as he said, "Oh, I can't breathe, too funny, I can't breathe."

Naruto, on the other hand, was smiling but sympathetic as he offered me a tissue.

"Thanks."

"Sorry, I should have warned you. The closer we get to the pier, the more they seem to unload. You were standing in the drop zone. Here, do you want me to help you wipe them off?"

"I'll just do my leg. We are almost there. When I get back, I'll soak this in the basin. No biggie."

Mako came over, "Sorry, Harper. I didn't mean to laugh. It's just three, you know, not one but three." Off again, he succumbed to fits of laughter, this time bending over while holding his stomach. "So hard to breathe," he squealed joyfully.

Naruto and I looked at each other and smiled.

Voices from behind were calling out to each other as they secured the boat to the pier and set up the plank for us to be able to disembark. The truck was waiting at the dock for the signal to come and pick up the load.

"I guess this is it," I said, trying not to contain my glee.

Mako did his best to compose himself as he offered me a hug, "You are welcome anytime."

"Thank you. It was lovely to meet you."

He stepped across and embraced his brother. "See you tomorrow for dinner?"

"Perhaps. I will let you know."

"Okay, brother. Come, anytime."

I made my way onto the pier with Naruto following close behind.

"I'm so excited to be back on solid ground. I'd kiss it, but I don't want your brother to strain his heart from laughter." I said, looking up to wave vigorously at him and the crew.

"Yes, Mako has a hearty penchant for laughing, especially at other people's expense."

"I noticed."

"You must be hungry. Would you care to join me for dinner? I can meet you at the restaurant in an hour or so."

"I'm starved but also exhausted. Honestly, as much as I would love to eat, I feel I need to have a hot bath and go to sleep."

"Of course, yes. I'm sorry it wasn't as enjoyable for you as I hoped it would be."

"Oh no, I wouldn't trade that experience for the world. It was amazing to be out on a big trawler in wild open seas. The motion sickness was awful, but the rest of it was incredible. I'm delighted you took me. It was humbling to feel so small and helpless; the human ego dissipates. You know? Being surrounded by the energy of this vast expanse of turbulent water was terrifying. That first time when the boat lifted with the wave and the ocean below seemed to disappear beneath us. My heart was in my mouth. I've never felt anything quite like it."

"That wave came out of nowhere. When we smashed down, the crew was running around yelling to check for cracks. Mako signaled for me to get you secured. I tried to look casual as I gave you a life jacket. Even I was unnerved and was doing my best not to show it. When that second one took us up and slammed us down, I was starting to feel queasy too."

"It certainly became surreal pretty fast and then stopped just as quickly. I don't know how they do it."

"Mako says it's a calling. He explained it once as an extension of who he is. Out there, he feels alive and has a purpose."

We reached the end of the pier. I turned to look back at the trawler. "Yeah, I get that."

"Are you sure you won't consider joining me for some dinner? I think you will sleep better if you have something in your stomach."

"I know you're right. I honestly can't muster up the enthusiasm to dine out. I'd rather skip dinner."

"Then I'll make you a counteroffer. Go have your bath and get some rest, sleep. I'll organize some food and bring it over in a couple of hours. That way, I'll feel less guilty about the number of times you were sick on the trawler."

I shook my head, smiling, "I don't want you going to all that trouble. The guilt is not necessary either."

"Please say yes."

I looked at Naruto, "Sure. Okay, yes. I am staying at that little house, third from the end."

"Great. I'll drop off some food in a few hours."

"Thank you. Are you sure?"

"Yes, absolutely. I will see you later." Naruto had a pep in his step as he left.

"Okay, bye." I turned to look at the trawler one last time before crossing the road and heading back to the cottage.

* * * * *

It felt like the moment my head had hit the pillow; there was a knock at the door. I stumbled out of bed, placing my light on to find a tie for my hair. I swooped it up into a messy bun then went and answered the door.

"Hello."

Naruto was neatly groomed with his long grey hair flowing. "Did you have a good rest? I waited an extra half an hour to ensure you had plenty of time."

"I was so tired it felt like minutes. Please, come in."

"Oh no, I don't want to impose; here is your meal."

"Naruto, come inside and eat. You're not imposing. It's the exact opposite. You have been very generous."

He stepped over the threshold and placed the food on the coffee table.

"I used to play with the little boy who lived here when we were very young."

"Do you still keep in touch?"

"Yes, we did, on occasion, see one another. He died a few years ago now."

"It's never pleasant losing someone," not knowing what else to say. "I'll grab some plates. I don't have anything other than water to drink. I hope that's okay."

"Water is my drink of choice."

I returned with everything bundled in my hands.

"Here, let me grab some of that."

"Thanks. Do you have a preference of where you would like to sit?"

Naruto dropped down to a crouch, "Just here is fine."

Walking to the opposite side, I sat on the floor. "This smells delicious."

He pulled out the containers and popped the lids off. "I prepared it myself especially for you. Are you happy for me to serve?"

"Sure, thanks." Picking up my chopsticks in preparation.

"This is wok-tossed native greens seasoned with sesame oil and a sticky soy balsamic glaze, steamed salmon on a bed of cauliflower and creamed rice. Squid legs marinated in chili paste and fried that is finished off in dried garlic, salt, and pepper seasoning. Oh, and some potato salad."

I gladly accepted the plate of food, "You made all of this?"

"Everything except the potato salad. I took that from the restaurant fridge."

"Well, it smells divine and looks outstanding. Let us see if this feast passes the taste test. It looks so good I don't know where to start. Itadakimasu."

"Itadakimasu. Try the vegetables first, then the salmon and squid last. The flavor will build if you eat it in that order."

I followed his suggestion and ate in a circular motion around my plate. "My lordy lord, this is delicious. Your wife must miss your cooking when you are here."

Naruto smiled, "She does say that a lot. I am glad you are enjoying it. The chili paste on the squid too hot for you?"

"No, not at all. It gives off the perfect amount of heat. This is all so yum." I took another mouthful. "How often do you come to Japan?"

"Usually once per season. Four times a year. My wife Misako travels with me usually once or twice, depending on her schedule. We have our first grandchild now, so she tends to want to stay close to our children."

"Do you ever travel anywhere else?"

"No, not really. Our honeymoon was in Bora Bora. We have spent time camping in the summertime in different national parks around the USA. That's about it."

"When are you returning home?"

"My ticket is set for Monday week. I have a few more people to see, some business matters to tend to, and then I'll be off. And you? When are you returning?"

I gulped water to wash down the niggly bit of squid that was lodged in my throat. "I honestly don't know. I feel as though it is time, but I am not convinced that returning is the best way to go. I've discovered a real love for travel. I might country hop and just keep going."

"Do you have any place in mind?"

"Hmmm, not really. I want to go where the wind takes me. Maybe I'll head to the airport one day, look at what is scheduled that day and arrange to go. I'll see. I don't have any plans at the moment."

"It sounds wonderful. An unplanned adventure."

"Look at how we met. I had decided to explore the streets, venturing further and further until I came across your restaurant. Chatting with you in your glorious garden led to spending a day on a fishing trawler, and now we are sharing this delicious fare. I couldn't have planned a better experience."

"I must say it was out of character for me to divulge so much. It's just that you seem so easy to talk to, and I liked how I felt when I was around you. I am hoping that we can stay in touch. I'd love to have you meet my wife and the rest of the family."

"I'd like that too."

I looked at my empty plate, "My compliments to the chef. This was so good. It hit the spot." I released a yawn.

Naruto used his hands to push himself up. "That's my queue. I'll use the bathroom and then help clear this up before I go."

"It's just down the hall,"

"I know where it is." He called out already on his way.

I put the lids on all the containers, placed them in the bag, and stacked the plates on top, carrying them to the kitchen. When I returned for the glasses, Naruto was standing at the hall entrance holding my kimono in his hands.

"Harper, I saw this hanging on the back of your bathroom door. Where did you get this?"

"From an obscure little shop when I was traveling around the Toyama prefecture. Why?"

"You bought this in a shop?"

"Yes. I believe it was a Kimono shop. Elegant kimonos were showcased in the window. When I entered the store, there were dummies with kimonos on display scattered everywhere. The one you are holding is the only one she would sell to me. She was very insistent. No matter what I looked at and asked how much, the shopkeeper would indicate it wasn't for sale. I thought it was strange at the time. In the end, she presented me with the one you are holding. It was very plain in comparison to the others she had on display. At the time, I wondered if foreigners were restricted to what they could purchase. I decided to get this one and didn't think much more about it. You're staring like you have seen a ghost."

"Have you worn this in public?"

"Sure, once. What is this about?"

"Did anything strange happen when you wore it? Anything at all?"

"Nothing comes to mind. What's so significant about this kimono?"

"This is going to sound a little fantastical. You will need to keep an open mind."

"I've led a rather inexplicable life. Try me. I'm rarely surprised."

Naruto draped the kimono over his left arm with an expression of excitement on his face before sitting down in the recliner. I shifted a cushion and made myself comfortable on the sofa.

"Have you heard the fable about the koi and the golden dragon?"

"Maybe. Isn't that where one koi persisted above all others to travel against the current traveling upstream and then fought hard to swim up a treacherous waterfall.

Eventually, the koi reached the top and was rewarded by the Gods for demonstrated bravery and perseverance. They transformed the koi into a golden dragon."

"Yes, precisely. The legend has been reduced to this version and connected to the famous yellow river in China. Our ancestors have a version that is about our lineage."

"I'm assuming you are one of the believers."

"I am."

"Okay. You've piqued my interest."

"There was a little boy called Daisuke who lived in a local village situated near the river of rainbows located in the Ibaraki prefecture. Villagers referred to it as the rainbow river because in the afternoon, the suns shimmering light reflected off the backs of the many koi that would swim in its waters. Daisuke would spend hours every day at the river with his great grandfather, who would tell him stories about the koi's legend and their plight to reach the top of the ominous cascading waterfall. It had big expansive shelves with rock pools and was a whopping one hundred and twenty meters high. He filled Daisuke's mind with so many different stories about the individual koi he named and observed across the years, all attempting and failing to make the journey. He would hike with Daisuke up the mountain to the top of the fall to show him the two bowed trees that reached across both sides of the river to touch one another. A strangler vine was binding them into an arch to form the legendary Dragons Gate. The legend foretold the first koi ever to cross over would be granted anything they desired."

"What does that have to do with the kimono?"

"There's more. Daisuke was told a secret by his Great Grandfather that had not been shared with any other grandchildren. They were evolutionary descendants of the koi. That is why some of the family, including him, had the extra skin between their toes. The webbed feet stood as a reminder of where they originated from.

Daisuke was teased when he braggingly retold the story to his friends, being called the fish boy and such. One night he overheard his father telling his Great Grandfather to stop filling his child's mind with nonsense. Great Grandfather insisted it wasn't nonsense and said he was blind because he didn't believe it. He was no longer connected to his ancestry. The last Daisuke heard was his Great Grandfather saying he would prove it.

The next day Daisuke went to the river to be with his Great Grandfather. He walked up and around the riverbed; he was nowhere to be found. Eventually, he sat at their rock under the shade of a sprawling tree, splashing his feet in the water and waiting. That's when it happened. A big koi swam right up to the gap between his feet and playfully splashed some water onto Daisuke. As he laughed, the fish turned about to show off all his lovely markings. Big black, silver and brilliant orange splotches of color covered his body. Daisuke put his hand in the water and rubbed the koi's belly. It was turning to its side to look up at him, swimming around his feet. Then it picked up a pebble and placed it on his big toe. Then another and another. Daisuke wished his Great Grandfather was with him to see this as he knew no one else would believe."

"Shape shifting? The koi is the Great Grandfather, right? He was able to transform into a fish?"

"Well, yes. It is the Great Grandfather, but it is not shape-shifting, not exactly. Let me finish, and then we can talk about it afterward."

I made a motion to zip my lips shut.

"Okay, so when the fish left, Daisuke went home soon after. The next day he returned to the river and saw his Great Grandfather was there waiting for him. Daisuke was so excited he wanted to tell him everything. The Great Grandfather stopped him before he could say a word and instead told him what had happened. Daisuke was amazed and wondered how he could know all this if he wasn't there. That's when he explained he was a fish, and all born with the web between their toes can revert to their traditional form as the koi. He warned the transition was not without danger. He pointed out the predators that lurked; birds of prey, foxes, and bears would all like to make a tasty meal of him if he was not on guard. By right of birth, he was able to will himself to transition to a koi and then return to human form three times and no more. If he did it a fourth time, he would remain a koi thereafter. His Great Grandfather had used his own third time to reveal the truth to the boy to ensure he believed as there was a favor he was set to ask. The boy knew in his heart that all he was being told represented the truth. The Great Grandfather said that when his body shows signs of decline, just before he becomes too feeble, he, like all his ancestors before him, will transition to live the remainder of his existence as a koi. The ordinary koi possesses a lifespan of twenty-five to thirty-five years. An ancestorial koi lives for a few hundred years. This is why the koi are kept in elaborate ponds at home. Most of them are people's relatives.

Daisuke had so many questions. He wanted to know why his Great Grandfather had transitioned the previous two times. Like so many others, the response was simple; he wanted to be the first to swim up the waterfall and go through the dragon's gate. It was this piece of information, above all else, that changed the course of Daisuke's life. He agreed to be the caretaker of his Great Grandfather when the time came for him to become a koi and set to work to start training for his own attempt to be the first.

Daisuke was running and swimming to increase his endurance, rock hopping to build strength, walking in the riverbed against the current, using the rocks on the side of the waterfall to attempt time and time again to climb to the top. His Great Grandfather gave him pointers and insight into his own experiences. Daisuke was determined to be the one.

The first time he transitioned, as hard as he tried, he could not muster the strength required to achieve his goal. After countless attempts across weeks, he succumbed to accept defeat and returned to human form. Understanding how it felt to be in his koi body, he adjusted his training to involve compulsion, leaps, and thrusts. He needed to condition himself to get stronger and make traction without using his legs and arms. Knowing he only had two remaining chances and a human life to lead, he took his Great Grandfather's advice to pace himself.

Daisuke was the last of his lineage at the time to be born with the webbed feet. He held a responsibility to nurture the next generation, so this meant he would likely need to forfeit one of his transitions just as his Great Grandfather had done for him.

Years had passed by. Maintaining his training became tiresome. He grew impatient, that is until he found a new distraction. He fell in love with an apprentice seamstress whose garments were known for their high quality and hand craftsmanship. They soon married and had many children. None of which had webbed feet.

A magnificent koi pond was constructed just before the Great Grandfather transitioned for his final time. He reminded Daisuke of the importance of keeping the ancestral secret and waiting until the next child with webbed feet is born. It was now left up to him to be there to guide the child. Although he agreed, he was disheartened, knowing that decades would pass before his children gave him grandchildren. His wife was not interested in having a sixth child. She was already struggling to maintain her shop and the upkeep of a house with five children.

One evening his frustration surfaced in such a manner that his wife insisted he explain the underlying cause of his increasing outbursts. When he said, he couldn't tell her she was devastated. Up until that moment, she believed they harbored no secrets. It didn't take long for him to relent and have his wife sworn to secrecy. Daisuke told her everything. It was with this new knowledge, along with her deep love for her husband, that she agreed to have a sixth child. When their son, whom they named Takato, arrived in the world with webbed feet, Daisuke was overjoyed. Finally, he could recommence his training with vigor and attempt the climb up the waterfall.

After many months of training, he was confident he felt ready. He bid his wife farewell and went down to the river. What Daisuke hadn't paid attention to was the weather. Soon after he changed into his koi form, he saw the edge of the waterfall insight when a roaring thunder came from the skies and along with it a torrential downpour. It didn't take long for the mouth of the fall to widen with so much water causing the river to swell with rapids. As hard as he fought to maintain a position, he could not get close enough to the falls to try to climb. Instead, he found himself caught in a swirl or turbulence that had him being tossed and dunked, hitting rocks along the way. Daisuke, much to his disappointment, woke naked and bleeding on the edge of the bank. His body had been bruised all over. Shivering out of control, he retrieved his clothes, placed them on, and headed home, wholly deflated that his last chance had been wasted.

His wife watched him embrace a deep depression. He had been obsessing over this his whole life and now felt he held no purpose in the absence of it. As scared as his wife had been losing him to his plight, she was more frightened now that her beloved husband may take his own life. The further he fell into despair, the harder it was for her to reach him. This was when she decided that he must use his third chance to make it up the waterfall. She assured him that if anything happened to him, she would impart the knowledge to their son. She felt it was more important for her husband to try than to watch him waste away wishing he had. The only request she demanded was for Daisuke not to return to his human form until he achieved what he set out to do. Without hesitation or thought to consequences, he eagerly agreed.

The day had come to bid his children farewell and kiss his wife goodbye. She knew in her heart that this might be the last time they would embrace, so she held him extra tight and told him how much she loved him. She promised Daisuke that she would visit him at the river's edge in the same place where he and his Great Grandfather met. And that she did. Each day they met, he would place pebbles on her toes and rub against her feet while she told him about the kids and her day. In some ways, she realized they were closer than they had ever been. He seemed happier now that he was on his quest.

Years passed, the seasons came and went. His devoted wife would attend the same spot every day, sometimes bringing their grandchildren to play with him in the shallow waters. There were times when Daisuke wanted to transition to human form so that he may hold his gracefully aging wife in his arms but knew she had sacrificed so much for him that he had to keep his promise and stay in koi form until the job was done.

Finally, after decades of attempts, an extra-long dry season reduced the water's flow, and then the winter presented so cold that most of the fall's water had frozen in place. This provided Daisuke with a real chance of making it up the waterfall and through the mountain gates. He gave it everything he had and then some. Leaping onto rock shelves, flip-flopping until he got to the rock pools, then up another rockface and onto the next ledge. It took him an entire day of exhausting effort to achieve the unthinkable. Daisuke couldn't believe it. He had reached the top and finally traveled through the legendary Dragon's gate. There was less than a moment to celebrate the joy's before he felt the waters beneath him bubbling. His body began to swirl into the center of a whirlpool. He felt himself stretch and grow; his mouth opened as sharp teeth pushed from his gums. His body felt heavy. His arms stretched out as he rose into the sky and then came plummeting down with a thud. When he woke, he realized he was no longer a koi, no longer a human but a magnificent Golden dragon. The legend was true. He was the first and had been rewarded by the gods. In his claw, there was a scroll. He tried to open it but struggled with his talons. He knew whatever was inside contained the actual reward and that he needed to use his hands to open it.

Daisuke spread his golden wings and lunged upward toward the sky. He soared high above, looking at all the regions and peaks to find the perfect place to secure his precious scroll. Deep in the rooftop of a remote cave, he hid it out of view. Later he could retrieve it, but first, he wanted his wife to see he achieved the quest. Only then would he return to human form. Satisfied it was safe, he flew straight down to see his wife, who was waiting for him by the river. She marveled at the Golden dragon who appeared before her. She stroked his head as he bowed down, so proud that he had achieved his quest. He used his talons to write her a message in the soft soil. Advising of the scroll and drew the map that would be needed to retrieve it.

Now that this was done and his wife had seen him in his glory, Daisuke stepped back to will himself to return to his human form. He felt this overwhelming emotional ache to hold her and thank her for her devotion and patience. He wanted to spend time with his children and play with his grandchildren, take them on adventures, and such. As he watched the expression on his beloved wife's face change, he felt himself reduce in size until he sunk into the waters. A koi fish once more. An impossibly beautiful iridescent golden gleam sparkled from his scales. Try as he might, he could not transform again.

His wife continued to meet with her husband at the river's edge every day. Daisuke would have messages he created out of pebbles for her to read. At first, they were about the scroll and his need to find a way to get to it, for he was sure it held the secret that would allow him to transition to human form. To hear this angered his wife. Daisuke spent his life wanting to be other than what he was. Now achieved, he wanted to spend the remainder of his life finding a way to return to his original form. She was furious and wanted to take no part in it. There were days when she would not visit. Too much of her life had passed away for her to continue with indulging his whims. The visits became so infrequent and then not at all.

Whispers emerged around the village about a spectacular golden koi that was seen in the river and the mysterious messages created with rocks. Things such as, I love you, I miss you, and I want to go home. Most laughed it off as children playing until talks about maps and mention of treasure had surfaced. Groups formed to begin a search to find this elusive golden koi. When the wife heard this, she feared her husband would be hunted and rushed to the river edge. When she called out his name, Daisuke swam over. His wife placed her hands in the water and scooped him up. Placing him safely in a bucket of water, she took him home to live in the koi pond he had made for his Great Grandfather. Each day she would spend time watching the two of them swim about and around one another.

Daisuke's wife had never intended to tell their son Takato about his ability to will himself into a koi. The gift of the Golden Dragon was achieved. She convinced herself there was no point in him knowing that he can convert. She had lost her husband to an obsession and didn't want her child to befall the same fate. Instead, she encouraged him to pursue his career as a fisherman, fall in love, marry and have children of his own.

One day she received news that Takato had been lost at sea in a storm so harrowing only two of the men had survived to tell of it. Guilt-ridden with the realization the knowledge of his ancestorial gift may have allowed her son to will into a fish to weather the storm and return safely to the shores had her grief-stricken. She understood the gravity of what she had done by denying him his birthright to knowledge. This was weighing her down. There were no other grandchildren with webbed feet, so her hope of correcting this error in judgment reduced as her own time for living was quickly waning.

In her desperation to make amends, she captured the details of everything that she knew from what her husband had told her, combined with what she had witnessed. She complimented the writing with elaborate drawings of the koi, the river, and the golden dragon. In her letter, she mentioned the dragon's scroll with no details about its specific location. The wife did not want the information to fall into outsiders' hands. Instead, she devised a plan to create four plain-looking kimonos with the most detailed embroidery. On their own, they would be lovely, understated kimono's but laid out together in the correct order; they reveal the precise location of her husband's dragon scroll. The only reference in her writings to them was a painting of four Geisha wearing kimono's climbing up the side of a snow-capped mountain.

Once her work was complete, she marked it in her will that this dowry of four kimono's and the letter must be inherited only by a direct descendant with webbed feet. She emphasized to her family the critical importance of never selling the home. To ensure her wish was obeyed, she created a tale that linked their lineage to the house, the sacred koi pond, and the resident koi who lived in it. She drummed into her children and grandchildren that it would dishonor the family should anything happen to it. Shortly after putting everything in order, her body was found lying beside the koi pond with her hand in the water. The koi were solemnly surrounding her hand in mourning.

Years had passed before their thought to be lost at sea, son, Takato, crossed the threshold of his home to greet his wife and children. He told the story of how he was caught in a storm and had somehow found sanctuary on a cargo ship that took him to foreign lands. Without any means to communicate and money to return home, he found shelter with a religious order which provided him food, protection, and tutelage in exchange for daily labor. Once he developed a proficiency in the native language, he sought to find work on ships headed for Japan. It was a tight nit community, and they were distrusting of foreigners. After many attempts, he was finally given a passage in exchange for labor, and this is how he managed to return home.

Takato didn't dare to tell his wife that after being tossed about violently in the stormy waters, he found himself to be a fish and that he swam and swam for days then blacked out with no memory of how he was to be naked on the shores of a foreign land. He was then found and arrested, left in jail for many weeks until rumors of a naked foreign man found onshore reached the monks. It was they who came and offered him sanctuary. This was too much madness.

His wife explained what happened and of his mother's death, the will, the house, and the fable of the koi pond. She gave him the unopened letter that evening to read, for Takato was the only living descendant with webbed feet. He sat alone and read the pages and pages his mother had written. Knowing that everything disclosed felt true in his heart, he rushed to his childhood home in the middle of the night and headed straight to the koi pond. He waved a single finger in a circular motion in the water, out from beneath a rock; an iridescent golden koi shone in the moonlight as soon as Takato spoke and said hello, father. Daisuke leaped out of the water, up into the air with a backflip. He then swam to his son, affectionately rubbing against his finger.

The following day Takato had asked to see the kimono's his mother had created. His wife produced three. When he inquired about the fourth, she confessed that she had worn it a few times and was approached by a lady who wanted to know who made it as she desired one as unique. Once the lady understood there could be no more made, she offered to buy her one. It was such an overly generous offer, and without Takato to provide, she thought it a blessing for her family. After all, there were three more; what would it matter if one was sold for such a good cause? Takato, after that, spent his life searching for the fourth kimono. It had simply disappeared."

Naruto patted the kimono that was still folded on his arm. "This Harper is the long-lost kimono of the Koisato clan."

"How can you be sure?"

Naruto turned the garment inside out. "See, the seams here and here are not as flat as the other areas."

"It looks like there is something trapped inside."

He smiled, "There is. Come outside into the moonlight."

We both headed out the front door where Naruto held the kimono up, so the inside seam was exposed to the moonlight. A golden flicker was shining through. It increased its glow to look as though a light source was trapped between the cloth.

"What is it?" I asked, smiling.

"Daisuke's fish scales. When charged with moonlight, they glow."

"This is extraordinary," I said, running my finger gently over the seam.

"There is more that I feel I need to tell you."

"More?"

"I know it's getting late, and you're tired, but I want to show you something. Will indulge me for a little while longer?"

"I'd love to."

"Great." Naruto opened the passenger side door. "Hop in."

We drove for ten or so minutes before parking his car under a carport. He jumped out, and I followed suit. He eagerly opened the front door of a quaint house, switched on the lights, walked down the hall, and then straight out a back door. He waited for me to get closer to him before he flipped a switch that lit the garden transforming it into an enchanted forest. I smiled when I realized where we were.

"This is the restaurant garden, right?"

"Yes. This is my house, and the restaurant is over there on the other side of the block."

Naruto turned and headed down the path with me in close pursuit. We passed the glorious Mizunara Oaktree, continuing until he stopped in front of the koi pond.

Naruto's face was filled with delight, "Call him by name."

I looked into the blackened pool of water, crouched down, and said, "Daisuke." I placed a finger in the cool water and swirled it gently. A sliver of light appeared out from under a big stone. The fish, as it revealed itself to the moonlight, glowed impossibly golden bright.

The koi looked at me with caution and then up at Naruto, standing behind me to the right.

"Ī nda yo; kanojo wa shinraidekiru yūjindeari, watashitachi no nagaiai ushinawareta kimono o mitsukemashita," he exclaimed.

The fish leaped in the air executed a perfect flip before returning to the water and swimming to my finger. He gracefully swam by, rubbing his scales and blowing bubbles that popped as they hit the surface.

"He seems excited. What did you say to him?"

"I assured him that it's okay; are a trusted friend who has found our long-lost kimono."

"Your long-lost kimono?"

"Yes," replied Naruto slipping off his shoes to expose his webbed feet. "This story I have told you is about my ancestorial family. I am Daisuke's great, great, great, grandson."

"Are you telling me you can change into a koi?"

"Yes, well, kind of. Something changed after Daisuke turned into the Golden Dragon. He was only able to transition to the last thing he had previously been. A koi. After that, he was trapped in that form."

I looked at the golden fish, then back at Naruto. "Daisuke's son was able to transform to a fish and then back again."

"Precisely. Yes, he was able to transform automatically while under extreme duress. You must remember that Daisuke was taught to will it to occur. Tako had no idea it was possible, so it was beyond any conscious request. Even after he was aware of what had happened and acquired the knowledge of his ancestry, he remained in human form, unable to transition. Only in the moment of death was he miraculously transformed again. He too lives in this pond with his father, Daisuke."

"What about Daisuke's Great Grandfather? Is he here as well?"

"Sadly no. I never had the pleasure to meet him. He passed away before I was born."

"Oh, of course, even as a Koi, he would have been ancient. So, you believe that the only way you can transform is if you are under extreme duress?"

"Exactly. I believe the gift of transformation has been reduced to occur through some form of primitive survival instinct."

"Have you ever tried to put yourself in that position to see if you can?"

"No. You see, I spent my life feeling very self-conscious and highly embarrassed about my feet. Being raised in the USA with their idealism of beauty and the pressures to conform when I already had an outsider's appearance was difficult. When I became financially successful, I had consultations with the best plastic surgeons and was seriously considering surgery."

"Why didn't you go ahead?"

"Something was stopping me. Whenever I was close to proceeding, I would feel this looming dread as though the act of removing it would leave me feeling trapped into not being accepting of myself. Eventually, I ceased, knowing that I was already married, and my beloved wife didn't care that I had webbed feet. She loved me just as I am and therefore so should I."

"In the absence of having actual proof, how did become convinced it was real?"

"You don't believe me?"

"Quite the opposite, I do. I have experienced enough to know nothing is ever as it seems. It's just that you, on the other hand, would likely have no such exposure and therefore be less accepting of the truth. Your webbed feet are just that until you transition into a koi to prove to yourself that it is real. A golden fish can be fed bioluminescence to make it glow and be trained to do tricks. There are so many alternative explanations to cover all of this. Yet you are in no doubt that it is all true. I'm trying to establish what events took place to make you believe."

Naruto looked down at Daisuke as his voice spoke quietly, "My father tried to tell me. Whenever I brought the family to visit, he would discuss our lineage and history, always pushing me to accept my destiny. The older he got, the more he spoke about it with urgency. I am ashamed to say that it was just the ramblings of an old fisherman who lived his life telling tales. On his deathbed, he insisted, I read to him Daisuke's wife's letter. He then had me hold up the three kimonos to explain his thoughts on how to read the map. Indulging a dying man's wish, we spoke about it all. During those last few days, I felt a shift. I started to believe there may be some underlying truth. My father made me promise to look after the tree we had planted together and implored me to take special care of the koi in his pond. Mako inherited the business. Everything my father owned was now his. I was the beneficiary of the letter, three kimonos, and the koi in his pond. I also received a note that said, believe."

"Did you begrudge Mako inheriting the business?"

"Not at all. The moment he took over for father, it was rightfully his. He looked after him, managed the fleet, and raised a family here. It already belonged to him."

"So, receiving the letter, kimono's, and the koi was enough to convert you?"

"Not quite. There was a part of me that wanted to believe in it all, and of course, I had a raging internal skeptic that seeded doubts. I mean, the whole thing sounds crazy. The days between my father's passing and the funeral, I began to visit my father's koi pond to reflect. Daisuke would be distant; he'd swim about out of reach. He watched me intently. It was a reasonably hot day giving me the thought to put my feet just under the surface of the water. Things changed after this moment. Daisuke came rushing over, eagerly inspecting my feet. He then swam off to gather pebbles in his mouth that he carefully placed onto my webbing. Puzzled and feeling a little foolish, I said his name. That's when he soared into the air to do his first of many backflips. Surely it couldn't be true, I thought. Still, there was something very intriguing about this fish's behavior, and the pebbles gave me an idea. I had been using mini plastic kanji symbols and flashcards to teach my children Japanese. The next day, I returned with a bunch of mini kanji and a flat white marble piece. No sooner had I put them in the water, Daisuke was hovering over studying the kanji. Using his mouth, he would scoop them in and begin creating messages. The first of which was a message of condolence for the loss of my father. I never doubted again."

"Do you communicate with his son Takato and the Great Grandfather as well?"

"No. It seems that when they leave their human bodies for the final transition, they fully commit to becoming fish. Daisuke is the only one who remembers his human form. When his wife first placed him into the pond, he tried to communicate with his Great Grandfather only to realize after many failed attempts that he was indeed a fish."

"That seems like a lonely existence."

"Yes. When I return home, Mako visits and plays Go and other board games with him."

"Mako knows?"

"Yes. It seems that father had an easier time convincing him and made Mako swear he would continue the plight of trying to get me to see the truth. He was never to stop trying to get me to believe."

"The only other thing that I'm wondering is why you are sharing all of this with me? You could have stolen the kimono or offered to buy it from me. I would have been none the wiser. Why do you include me into your inner sanctum?"

"I have to believe there is a reason you possess the one item my family has been searching for across generations. When you first entered the restaurant, I watched you and felt something rather special about your energy. That is why I had arranged for you to be escorted out through my private garden. I wanted to observe who you are when you think no one is watching. Then we spoke, and I found myself wanting to tell you everything, to spend more time with you as though we were kindred spirits reclaiming a long-misplaced connection. This evening when I saw the kimono, it confirmed to me that you are more than what you seem. I felt compelled to tell you the truth and somehow knew that against all odds, you would believe."

My eyes were feeling heavy. "Aside from getting some well-earned sleep. What happens next?" I asked.

"Oh yes." He bent down to put his slippers back on. "I'll drop you off and then return to get some rest myself. If it's alright by you, I'd like to borrow your kimono so I can study it alongside the others."

"Borrow it? No, it was never mine. Consider it returned."

Naruto paused to look at me as I gave Daisuke a gentle rub on his underbelly then stood up. He stared into my eyes with a serious expression.

"No one would give up such a treasure without demanding something in return. This is the missing link to finding the dragon's scroll. It is priceless."

I shrugged my shoulders, "I guess I'm the exception to the rule. Your family spent generations on this quest. Everything that Daisuke and his wife sacrificed shouldn't be without reward. It is yours; the kimono is back where it belongs. No strings attached. I promise."

Gratefully Naruto clasped his hands and bowed. "I will find a way to repay this kindness."

"Naruto look at me. There is nothing to repay. It is gifted willingly. Believe."

"I do." He bowed again. "Thank you, Harper."

"You're welcome." I turned and waved at the koi. "Bye, Daisuke. Time for all of us to get some sleep."

With this, we left the garden, got into his car, and headed back to my place.

# Serendipity

There was a restlessness that began to grow inside me. Naruto was devoting all his time to interpreting the map, while I braved a couple more day trips out on the open seas with Mako and the crew. There was an allure to the raw energy out there that somehow made me feel rejuvenated. No longer a complete victim to seasickness, the sway and endless rocking of the ship became, for the most part, soothing. When we came across our first pod of whales, I was in awe of their majesty. Contrary to their mass, they seemed gentle. My heart was palpitating when one inquisitive fellow came closer. He was longer than the trawler and almost as wide. Feeling anxious about his proximity soon subsided and was replaced by a wide smile. I now appreciated why these men stuck to their vocation and endured the risks of the sea's unpredictable temperament. As intimidating as the open waters are, they also presented indescribable beauty and provided sanctuary from the mayhem that existed on land.

It was now the morning of my final day in Suzu. I didn't want to offer to help or be seen to be interfering. Naruto was emersed with trying to identify the route according to the map. He hadn't asked for assistance which made me assume he preferred to work on it alone. I had replayed the sequence of events that led me to the store where I purchased the kimono. The curiosity for me stemmed from the shop keepers desire to sell me that particular item. How could she have known to sell it to me? Was she trying to offload an item sitting in her store for decades, or did she know of its significance? No clues were readily identifiable to me. Yet, I was somehow connected to a thread of subconscious energy that tapped into the direction needed to unite the gowns in the absence of even knowing they existed. It was fascinating. More and more, it seemed that we are vessels of energy misdirected by ego and conditions of the mind. The closer I became in tune to this surplus of energy that surrounded everything, the more I seemed to feel in balance.

*Tap, tap*

I jumped a little, then saw a shadow cast near the window. I opened the front door.

"Hello, I was just about to come past your place to say goodbye."

"Mako told me you were leaving. Is there a reason you need to go? If not, I would like you to stay. I'm sorry if I'm being selfish, but I don't think I can do this without you."

I touched Naruto's arm, "Is everything okay. You seem a little frazzled."

"I've been awake for days trying to figure out where the map begins. I can't seem to find the origin. Each time I drift off into a short burst of sleepless delirium, I find myself walking beside you in search of the Dragon scroll. I believe there is an ancestral calling for you to be a part of this."

"Come inside, take a seat. I'll make us some tea."

Naruto entered and followed me into the kitchen. "I can't understand why the kimono was given to you, and after learning all of this stuff about my family, you find it so easy to walk away. It's as though none of this craziness has unhinged even the slightest part of your reality. Seriously, who are you?"

I topped up the water in the kettle, placed it on the stove, and then used a match to light the kindling. "This is going to take a little while to build some heat." I blew on it to increase the flame's spread, then left the hatch slightly ajar to keep it burning.

As I headed back into the sitting area, I propped myself on the sofa and pointed to the armchair. Naruto sat down and waited.

"Have you asked Daisuke for help?"

"He doesn't remember. I've shown him the kimono's, and nothing seems familiar. We think it might be because he is no longer in dragon form."

"Does he remember anything about the time when he was a dragon?"

"He knows he was a dragon. He recalls the sensation of soaring through the air. He remembers not being able to open the scroll and deciding to hide it."

"Well, let's focus on what we do know."

"Don't you want to see the kimono's first?"

"I think if I see them, my mind will try and make things fit. In the absence of them, I can look at what we do know, determine what the information may mean, and then look at how it integrates with the details depicted in the kimono. You have to consider that what Daisuke's wife created may not be completely accurate. She was operating from memory too. So, what do we know?"

Naruto placed his hand on his chin as he thought about it.

"Let me start," I said, feeling it would be easier to kick things off. "When you were reciting the story, you mentioned the dragon hid it in a snow-capped mountain. How many mountains are capped with snow in Japan?"

"I don't know."

"Well, that's one thing we need to find out. Assuming that the telling of the tale is accurate, that will help to eliminate everything else."

Naruto's face lit up, "The mountain on the kimono is snow-capped."

"Great. It sounds like we are on the right track. We can't eliminate all the snow-capped mountains, but it does make sense to narrow our focus to any of those near the rainbow river. I think you mentioned the Ibaraki Prefecture, right?"

"Right. What did you say you do for a living?"

I jumped up and made my way into the kitchen as the kettle began to whistle. "I think you should look up records if you can find them of fables about a Golden Dragon to see if it leads anywhere. I can't imagine a dragon would be inconspicuous. It may have been translated into folklore and could even name the mountain with a stroke of luck. It might be a long shot but worth looking into."

Returning with a fresh pot of green tea, I poured Naruto a cup, and then he poured mine. I grabbed it and sat back on the couch.

"I have something I'd like to know. When you realized I had the kimono, one of the questions you asked was if anything strange happened when I wore it. Why? What were you expecting to hear?"

"I wanted to see if anyone had approached you. This kimono is sought after by many who seek to obtain the scroll for themselves."

"How do they even know about the kimonos? I thought it was a secret."

"They were until they weren't. Much like Daisuke's wife, Takato's wife experienced the same fate of losing her husband to an obsession. He spent his entire life looking for the kimono that she had mistakenly sold. When his time had come to die and transitioned into a koi, she was misguided in thinking he was still Takato. Each day she would visit him at the pond expecting him to be happy to see her, yet he would ignore her. The more time passed, she developed a bitterness in her heart. She knew Daisuke and his wife created a closeness and felt entitled to receive the same. She had no way to know that in the final transition, Takato was now just a fish.

Consumed by her husband's rejection, she had become spiteful for all the years lost. This was when she got the idea to seek buyers for the remaining three kimonos. She revealed what she understood of the ancestorial secrets and all that it entailed. Word spread, and expressions of interest grew. It didn't take long for counterfeit copies of the design to emerge on kimonos, wall hangings, and such. Soon, the villages were saturated with noise about a secret dragon scroll hidden in a cave in the mountains.

The kimono's would have been completely lost had their children not intervened. They understood the shame their mother had brought to the family with her betrayal. Knowing there was no reasoning with her, they cleverly made arrangements to have three replicas made in the authentic materials with some components of the embroidery details subtly changed. Thankfully, no one had seen the insides of the garments, which were also adorned with more crucial information about the map. This, at least for the time being, remained a secret. The children switched out the originals for the substitutes and also took possession of the letter. Thankfully they had the foresight to anticipate the worst and had relocated the koi in their ponds for wild ones caught in the river. A week later, their mother joined the families for a lavish dinner where she was distracted with entertainment provided by her grandchildren. While she was with them, her two eldest children returned to her home and orchestrated a robbery taking the counterfeit garments and all the koi with them. When she returned home to discover everything was stolen, she was immediately remorseful and pleaded with them to find their father. Even on her death bed, her children never told her the truth."

"Why make faux copies and then steal them?"

"They wanted to ensure they passed as the real thing. They couldn't risk getting caught while executing the robbery. It was a precaution in case a neighbor saw something suspicious and alerted the authorities. If they were caught in the act, they would have the fake ones."

"I'm missing the connection between what happened back then and the current day. After all this time, people outside of your lineage are still looking for the kimono's and dragon scroll?"

"Absolutely. The robbery somehow heightened the profile of the story. It began to have a life of its own. Some say the dragon scroll reveals the location of the holy grail. Others rumored it to reveal the secret to life. It goes on and on. Teams of people were tearing through the local mountains, trying to find it. The faux garments were worn by trusted friends in different regions to steer attention away from the region. Sightings were being reported all over Japan. Once again, a phenomenon was born whereby commoners in villagers all over started making their version and wearing it as a sign of prosperity and hope. Japanese authorities paid attention when hundreds of sightings turned into thousands. They concluded that without intervention, there might be an impending uprising. This resulted in a country-wide notice that this style of kimono was outlawed."

"Yep, people thinking for themselves is always a scary prospect for authoritarians who like to suppress and control. That's one thing that never seems to change."

"Exactly. Then you can appreciate that outlawing made the movement grow, and it soon became the Japanese underground symbol for freedom. Just like when opium became illegal, it also triggered the same response. It shifted to the black market and flourished. This style of kimono, to some, now symbolizes the fight against oppression. In those times, Christian missionaries were trying to convert people, and they said the kimono was the work of the devil and would try to encourage their followers to shun people they saw wearing them. You were lucky nothing happened when you wore it. If a police officer had crossed your path, you would have been under arrest and likely interrogated."

"How positively odd. This means the shopkeeper who sold it to me knew that she was going to get me into trouble."

"Yes, I'm certain of it."

"Do you think she knew it was the original?"

"Honestly, I don't think so. Why would she have given something of such value to a stranger?"

I shook my head. "It's got me stumped. I'm not sure either."

"Also, it is well known that there is a big reward offered for the fourth kimono issued out by the Japanese museum of historical art in Tokyo. They have three fake kimonos on display with a spot reserved for the fourth detailing the notice of a reward."

"Really? Do they know they are fake?"

"I'm not sure. There have been reports of a few attempts made to steal them, so I assume some people believe they are the originals."

I took a sip of my tea, "Hmm, I wonder how they acquired them."

"I know you have been avoiding my personal questions, and I appreciate you may prefer to maintain your privacy, but I'm wondering if you are a trained detective."

"I'm not a detective. I am a behavioral scientist who specialized in the assessment of cognitive reasoning in the field of criminology. That was a whole other lifetime ago. I'm retired from the profession now."

"That sounds intense."

"It sure was. The other consideration is that the cave would need to be wide enough to fit a dragon inside. Daisuke hid the scroll in the roof of the cave. I know we have no measure of what the size of the dragon might be, but that at least rules out any caves with a small opening."

"Yes. That's good. I'm going to note all of this down."

"Do you know when Daisuke's wife would visit him at the river?"

"Not exactly. It would be in the afternoon for sure. She had the shop and the children to look after."

"No, the children had grandchildren by the time he was successful, so let's say it was late afternoon between four and five pm. Daisuke took all day to make his way up. Assuming he started at first light and made it past the Dragons Gate by four at the latest. That gives him an hour to fly there and return to meet his wife in their usual spot by the river."

"Thirty minutes each way?" Asked Naruto.

"No. I think it would be less. Daisuke was searching for a place to hide it. That would take time, which further supports the idea that the mountain he was circling was likely close by. All things considering that seems plausible. Although we don't know the speed at which a dragon can fly. Hmm, close by might not be close at all."

"It sounds like you are talking yourself out of your theory."

"I am, and I'm not." I sat up and placed my empty teacup on the table.

"Would you like me to pour you another one?" He asked.

"I'm good for now, thanks." Rubbing my hands together. "Let's think like Daisuke. He believed he needed hands to open the scroll, so he hid it until he could transfer back into human form. That means his hiding spot was only intended to be temporary. We know he placed it up in the ceiling, but it must be accessible for him to retrieve it. This is what is key. Daisuke needs to access the cave and get the scroll in human form, supporting the theory that the location is close. Do you have internet?"

"Yes, of course."

"Look up the list of all the mountains in the region."

"There are three, Mount Kaba, Mount Tsukuba, and Mount Yamizo."

"Do they all have snow-caps?"

"In winter only, but yes."

"Okay, we know that it took place in winter because the waterfall was partially frozen over. All three would be snow-capped. Hmm. Let me think for a minute." I tapped my index finger on my lip as I ran through the story as it had been told to me. "Which of them is the tallest?"

"Mount Yamizo."

"Which one of the three is the closest?"

Naruto readjusted his position, "Mount Yamizo is the closest. By car, it is less than an hour.

Mount Kaba and Mount Tsukuba are both over two hours."

"Can I borrow your phone for a minute, please?"

"Sure." Naruto stretched his arm out to pass me his phone.

I searched for information about Mount Yamizo and began looking at the pictures. I scrolled down, then to the next page, and the next. There it was.

"You're smiling. What have you found?"

"I have reason to believe that it is Mount Yamizo."

Naruto walked over. "What makes you certain?"

"It's just a hunch. You said the kimono has a snow-capped mountain on it, which is of itself not that distinctive. They are all snow-capped in winter. What makes Yamizo so interesting is that it seems to have a white flower covering the peak in springtime and throughout summer. At a distance that could give it the illusion of being snow-capped. Daisuke in dragon form had traveled high up in the sky. This is the tallest of the three and the closest. It is another possible clue. I mean, I am making this stuff up as I go along. What do you think?"

"Amazing. I think you're amazing."

I laughed as I passed him his phone, "Your family are descendants of koi, and you think I'm amazing. Too funny. Okay, I'm ready to go look at the kimonos." I stood up and headed for the door. Naruto was still fixated on the images. "Are you coming?"

"Oh, yes, of course."

* * * * *

The four kimonos laid out on the floor formed a spectacular embroidered landscape.

"This must have taken her years to create. It is so detailed. She was very talented."

"They are beautiful."

"You said you and your father discussed how to sequence the kimonos. Is this the formation?"

"Yes, we thought this was the order."

I crouched down to take a closer look at the detailing in the first kimono. "Okay, talk me through it."

"This first one depicts the river's edge where they met. That is her sitting in wait. Daisuke, as a koi, is shown trying to get up the waterfall. The next one shows the dragon's gate at the top of the waterfall, with him transformed into the golden dragon. The third is the dragon soaring over a snow-capped mountain. The fourth, which is the one you found, has a cherry blossom in full bloom with a snow-capped mountain in the background."

I shifted over to be closer to the last kimono, "This doesn't look like a map to me. It seems to be the sequence of the story. The cherry blossoms depicted in this one means Spring. The snow-capped mountain in the third kimono is designed differently from this one. Look, you can see she has overlaid loads of tiny white starlike shapes. I believe that increases the possibility that she is trying to differentiate the snow-capped white from the springtime bloom of white."

"Are you saying that there isn't a map?"

"I'm saying the way you have sequenced it is aligned to the story and not the map. Can I pick these up?"

"Of course."

I flipped the first one around to see what imagery was pictured inside. Then did the same with the three remaining kimonos. I alternated between them being face forward and back to see if there was anything that stuck out. I stood up, walked around them. I was wracking my brain to understand how these four items could become a map.

"Do you have the letter she had written? I'd like to see the drawings."

"I'll get it." Naruto disappeared down the hall.

"Can you also give me a big piece of paper and a pen so I can scribble out some thoughts, please?"

"On it. One sec."

"What am I not seeing?" I said to myself as I continued to scan each of the kimonos.

Naruto returned with the letter in hand, "Here you go."

"Thanks," I replied as I collected the pages with both hands.

"Where do you want these?"

I looked at the pen and paper he was holding. "Would you happy to scribe as I put out some thoughts?"

"Sure." He shifted some items from his coffee table and dragged them across to where he had sat. "I'm ready."

"While I'm looking at this, can you jot down all the things we discussed when we were at my place? It would be good to have it there as a refresher."

"Okay. Did you want me to translate it for you?"

"Not at the moment. I'm interested in the pictures for now. I'm following a hunch. Are these pages in the right order?"

"Yes, they are. Can I ask what your hunch is?"

"I think you can't decipher the kimonos without the letter. I am guessing that the words telling the story are a distraction from the pictures she drew. My hunch is that they reveal something. See, straight away on this first page, there is the golden dragon with the scroll in his hand. There is only one kimono where the dragon is depicted with the scroll. The inside of number three." I shifted it across to the first position. I flipped to the next page. "Cherry blossoms."

Naruto walked across and shifted the kimono with the cherry blossoms into the second position. "What's next?"

"The dragon's gate with the Golden Dragon."

"Yep." He moved it to the third position.

"Okay, so that leaves her sitting by the river's edge."

"This one has Daisuke in it as well as a koi."

I smiled, "Flip it over. On the inside, it is just her at the river's edge without him."

Naruto flipped it over, putting it in the last position. "You are right."

I looked at the order of the kimonos, then at the fifth page. "Four geishas." I released a sigh. "Four geishas."

"What does the number four in Japanese represent?"

"It is traditionally seen as an unlucky number because it is associated with death."

"If it is considered bad luck, you would think she would avoid it. I'm not sure if there is a significance to it other than her grief and guilt over the death of Takato."

"I've never thought of it before. Four is a number to avoid. They don't have fourth floors in a lot of buildings for that reason."

"Does anything about Geishas stand out as significant to you?"

"They are a recognized symbol of Japan, idolized. Every little girl over here grows up wishing she could become one."

"Maybe it is just because she was a seamstress and made kimonos for all the Geishas. Can you write the word feminine down."

"Absolutely." Naruto walked over to where he left the pen and paper and wrote the word in cursive.

I put the letter back in order and placed it down on the coffee table.

Naruto looked up at me with a smile, "What's next?"

"We eat. I'm starved, and, in all honesty, I am beginning to hit a mental roadblock. I'm confident that we have them in the right order. I need a break so that I can look at it with fresh eyes. Are you okay if we stop to eat?"

"Are you kidding? Yes, yes, thousand times yes. Let's go. I'll get the restaurant to make up a feast."

"Do you want to put all this away first?"

"No, it's fine. The doors are locked, and no one knows it's here."

We walked over to the restaurant and went across to the same corner that I had seen Naruto seated the first time I had eaten here.

"I gather this is your spot?"

"It is. Take a seat. I'll be back in a minute."

I grabbed a couple of cushions, piled them on top of one another, and sat down squarely in the center. I could hear some people behind me muttering something. I assumed it was related to me walking in with Naruto. It was strange to think about him as a man who can transform into a koi. I'm not sure if I was in the same position whether I would ever switch. It seemed curious to have the ability to do it just before death. I wonder what the purpose is.

"The food will be here soon. I hope you are hungry. I ordered a lot." He said, placing two glasses filled with water on the table.

"You just made my stomach grumble. I'm starved. I just realized I didn't bring my wallet with me."

Naruto scoffed, "Please, you can't possibly think after all of this you are going to pay for your food. No way. I have you coved." He took a sip of the water, "What I saw today amazed me. You have an incredible gift. This ability to see things, brcak them down into their components. I've never seen anything like it."

"It's handy for sure. I find it can be exhausting too. Sometimes I don't want to see and understand as much as I do. It would be nice to get to wear rose-colored glasses, Switch them on and off. Allowing me to become more oblivious to the horror of the world."

"There is certainly a lot of that. I'm not sure if you have heard, in Toyama prefecture, they found a mass grave of children that had been kidnapped and used in experiments for biowarfare. It's all over the news."

"I did hear snippets. Some things are all too hard to comprehend. It's the stuff of nightmares."

"They are on the hunt for the people who did this. Some child survivors have come forward. What they need is you to assess the information they have gathered to find a lead."

"Nah, I do not doubt if there are leads, they will find them. The whole thing is truly horrific. I feel for the kids that survived and have to endure the knowledge of what they were subjected to. Knowing they got used, discarded, and buried in a hole. As I said, it's the stuff of nightmares."

Naruto nodded his head, took another sip of water, and then pursed his lips. "I have to confess. I felt a little bit dumb today."

"Dumb? Why?"

"You deduced more in three hours than anyone has in decades. When you talked me through it, I could sense you were on the right track, yet I couldn't leverage your lead to make new connections. I could only follow."

"You were exhausted when you arrived at my place this morning. It's just a loop you were stuck in. When you get caught up in the details rather than establishing the facts and then making educated assumptions."

"You're being kind."

"I'm not. There are experiments out there that prove that the mind takes over in an autopilot mode. You think you are paying attention when in actuality, you aren't. You must have come across some of those mind game experiments. You know when they tell you to read a sentence, and you do. Then they say read it word for word aloud. That's when you notice particles such as and, the, etc. are missing. Words are misspelled, and some are back to front."

"Sure, I'm familiar with them."

"Now consider that you have had this story told to you over and over by your father. A story which, for the longest time, you fought against believing. Then add reading the letter and staring at those kimonos, trying to make them fit the story your mind is conditioned to. It's only natural that you see what you think you know rather than what is there. That's why it was easy for me to spot that the two snow-caps differed. When I bought the kimono, I saw the cherry blossoms denoting spring and recall marveling at the detail in the snow-capped mountain, all those intricate little white stars on a white backdrop. See, I had made an assumption. This morning I was revalidating what I believe I knew from the story and then exploring the possibilities. When I asked to look at your phone, I wasn't quite sure what I was looking for but knew I needed to see images of that mountain in different seasons. That's when I found the magnificent display of white flowers. It gave me a new perspective on why she might have spent all that time adding tiny white stars all over the snow-capped mountain. At your house, the first thing I wanted to validate was my new assumption. Were the snow-caps depicted in the same way? If they had been, I would challenge my theory and start again."

"Fascinating. It all makes sense. How do I become more like you?"

The host arrived with a platter supporting a fantastic display of all kinds of sashimi, nigiri, and sushi.

"Oh, my, this looks insane. How spectacular. Great choice." I placed some soy in a small dish and dolloped a colossal clump of fresh wasabi in the mix. I took a piece of nigiri, smeared some more wasabi on top, and finished it with a bit of ginger.

"Are you sure you want to do that?"

"I love wasabi. Here it's the real deal. Fresh and packed with a solid punch." I dipped the piece into the soy wasabi mix, then popped it in my mouth and chewed.

"Wow, I think you might be more Japanese than me. I can't stand it. The way it burns my nose and throat."

I took a sip of the cold water, "That's the best part. I like the after taste as well. I'm a fan." Taking another couple of pieces on my plate to dress.

"So, going back to my question. How do I become more analytical in my thinking? Did you do some special training? Is there a course?"

"I'm sure there are some courses that teach the fundamentals of critical thinking that might help. I didn't get trained. It's the natural flow of my thought process. It's a type of discipline that you would have to work at."

"How?"

"Well, for a start, you would begin to question everything you know to bring it back to what is real vs. what is assumed. Maybe look at exercising your mind by extending its queues to push beyond the norm. Um, let's see." I scanned the items on the table. "Here, this glass. Tell me what it is."

He looked at it and raised an eyebrow, "Is this a trick? I don't know what you mean. It's a cup. It holds water."

"Are you sure that's all it is?" I said with a smile. "Think about it." I continued to eat while Naruto rested his head on his hands and stared at the cup.

"I don't know what I am meant to see. It's a cup, nothing more."

"Great. Hold that thought and the way you are feeling inside." I reached over and picked up my glass. "If a spider crawls by, I can flip this upside down, and it becomes a bug catcher. I can place it close to objects and use it as a magnifying glass." I placed it back down on the table, wet the tip of my finger over the edge, "And now it is a musical instrument."

Naruto smiled, "I get it. Wow. I was feeling tight like a coil. Then the frustration dissipated into a sense of wonderment. It's hard to describe. You made me feel like a kid again and a bit dumb too. I'm so ridged in the way I see things. God, my whole life, I've been blind."

"It is freeing to allow yourself to imagine, create, extend beyond what is obvious. The world presents differently when you start to see things for what they are. The function of a glass is limitless. You may feel dumb, but you are far from it. The way we are raised promotes rigidity. Society is built on the foundation of encouraging conformity, not free thinkers. Lookup anyone in history that was challenging the status quo, and you will uncover a tragic story. People who are celebrated now for their contribution to advancement weren't embraced for their forward-thinking. It was common to be subjected to ridicule, ostracized, even jailed, or worse placed in mental institutions."

"It's like those conspiracy theorists that get shut down, are humiliated, and then decades later, documents are revealed that confirm what they were saying is true. MK Ultra."

"Exactly. You're spot on. Think about the recent events around those children. How is it possible that all those kids can be taken through a large-scale coordinated effort and disappear with no links to who is involved? This group then experimented on the kids. People willingly participated in this, and not a single person has leaked any information or been identified as connected to the crime. That is some seriously intense human conditioning. MK Ultra on steroids."

"Yeah, you're right. I can see that now."

"Mark my words, there is going to be some scapegoat in the next couple of weeks presented. The pressures of global calls for intervention and the negative media providing a black stain on the country increase political interest in getting it resolved to save face. Emotions are high, and people demand answers. These perpetrators cannot escape from having something sacrificed. It will only be the pawns in the game that are thrown on the altar, with a feeble story that provides enough to satisfy the well-conditioned masses to see a cup, just as a cup."

"My heart aches for those children and their parents. I can't imagine what they been through and are going through right now."

"And theirs your cup again. You have compassion and recognize the parents and children's plight but haven't considered the other victims. The people who were subjected to extreme conditioning led them to participate in executing this heinous crime. It's too easy to want to blame them and judge their actions as willing participants, but are they? Sure, some are willing. Most will be conditioned to follow orders, not question authority, not think for themselves. Martyrdom is not an easy path, and the consequences are often fatal. Self-preservation places a shield over the act, and fear can make people do almost anything to stay alive."

"I can't feel sorry for them. They hurt innocent children. It's not right for them to go unpunished, no way."

I took a slice of sashimi, dipped it in the sauce, and placed it in my mouth.

"You really believe they are victims?"

"I know they are. Like I said, not all but most. Narcissists and psychopaths lead the charge for sure. The rest are, to varying degrees, victims of circumstance. Everything you just said, they hurt innocent children. It's not right for them to go unpunished. That plays directly into the hands of the sadistic people who instigated the crimes against these children. They know that you will judge, blame and prosecute anyone involved, and so do the conditioned minions that have participated. It reinforces the silence. Making it less likely to establish the truth and easier to orchestrate some fiction that will be fed to the angry mobs. You might consider them weak and without morals. The reality is that unless you were there, how do you know what you would have done under the same conditions?"

"I'd like to think I would be brave enough not to conform, to find a way to fight."

"Sure. Then to find a way to fight, you need to live. To live and remain so, you must conform. That is how you convince yourself to begin to do things that compromise your morals, believing that you are biding your time to find a way to help eventually. I'm the same as you. I want to think that I wouldn't conform. What if this act of being a martyr resulted in an immediate death sentence? Would you rather die in a fruitless act of rebellion or comply and live to try and fight another day? Look up Nazi stories told by actual Nazis. Some said they felt they had no choice. They watched comrades speak out, question authority, and were shot and discarded. Even the display of the slightest hesitation in executing a commanding officer's order could result in a bullet to the head. The price was high, and the message very clear. You are either with us or die. There was immense pressure to conform, with fanatics amassed everywhere watching. Some soldiers who participated in doing the most atrocious act to other humans did so because they would have the same fate if they didn't. It's not so easy to judge a person when you stop to consider the circumstances."

Naruto released a big sigh, "You're right. It is far more complex, and we are quick to judge, especially when it comes to crimes involving children."

"I'm not suggesting that they are not to be held responsible. I just don't believe that the same weighting can easily be applied to all those who were involved." I looked at the remaining food on the platter. "It is curious that some children survived, and others didn't. It seems so random on the surface. But…"

"What are you thinking?"

I looked at Naruto and considered whether it was wise to say anything. "Look at this platter of food. It followed a pattern in the way it was grouped and displayed. Sashimi in one section, sushi in another, you get the idea. The way we selected from the platter was to follow what we like to eat. I went for the salmon nigiri first, then the California rolls, while you preferred to start with the tuna sashimi, then the salmon nigiri. There was an order in the way we chose to eat. It's only natural to select what we like or what is familiar. How we selected what we ate seems random, but."

"But it's not."

I smiled. "No, it's not. I'd hedge my bets those children that survived weren't random either. Someone did something to help them, give them a chance to survive. I'm not sure what they needed to do. I just know it would have involved some medical skills for sure. That mass grave was an inhumane act. I believe the people in charge thought all the children were discarded. It's likely the children saved are all somehow connected to the person or people who helped them. That's the thread."

"The thread?"

"It's my analogy. When I was interviewing criminals, I related it to the hunt for a thread. Similar to a needle in a haystack, except mine is a messy, ugly, impossibly entangled ball of twine. My search begins with identifying a single thread. Then I follow where it leads while unwinding the ball in the process."

"What if there is no thread?"

"Impossible. There are always threads. You just have to know where to look to find them. If there was an ability to establish what the link is to these children, it could lead to sympathizers who could then be convinced to blow the whole thing wide open."

"We should tell someone about this. I can speak to the police and give them the information."

I shook my head, "No, you can't tell just anyone. You would be executing a death warrant. This was a large operation that was kept secret for years. That means it runs deep with many people involved. There's no telling whether the person you are speaking to is clean. Even if they happen to be one of the good guys, they don't, and you don't know which of their colleagues is corrupt. The minute information like this is divulged, the likelihood of those sympathizers, if they do exist surviving, is low. They would be hunted and killed."

"Seems impossible to know what to do. If we can't trust anyone, then what can we do?"

"I didn't say there isn't anyone who can be trusted. I said, you can't just trust anyone. There's a difference. And Naruto, there is no we here. These are dangerous people. You are limited by the constraints of seeing a cup as just a cup. I've still got some connections with the right kind of people who can take a quiet look at this. We can leave it with them to identify and follow the thread. Okay?"

"I understand. I won't do or say anything."

"Cool. Now back to the task at hand." I paused and looked at him with a big smile.

He squinted his eyes as he smiled back, "What are you thinking?"

"I'm pretty sure I know how to read the kimonos as a map."

"Seriously?"

"Seriously. Can we take this with us? I want to finish it later. I don't want it to go to waste."

"Of course. I'll get them to pack it up for you." He jumped to his feet and headed down the hall with the platter in hand.

The conversation had been so stimulating I completely forgot how uncomfortable it was to sit on the floor. However, the extra pillow did make a huge difference. With the grace of an elephant trying to stand and turn around in a confined space, I got to my feet, only to realize as I faced toward the center of the room the restaurant was almost at maximum capacity.

Naruto waved at some of the patrons as he walked toward me. "They will pack it and store it in the fridge. We can grab it before I drop you off at your place."

"Awesome, thanks. I had no idea how many people came in. I was so engrossed in our conversation I didn't pay any attention. It's really unlike me. I'm usually hyper-aware of my surroundings."

"It gets hectic. This is a popular time to eat."

"For sure. Okay, time to unravel this mystery. Lead the way."

Naruto opened the sliding door to enter his garden and closed it with a latch to secure it shut once I was through.

"You know I realized the other day when I was saying goodbye to Daisuke that I was speaking English. I guess the wave of my hand is universal, and the fact that we walked away was a clear sign too."

"I did notice. Yes."

"You should have said something to me."

"It's okay. He got the gist."

Naruto unlocked the back door and allowed me to enter first. I went straight to the coffee table, picked up the letter, and flipped to the back page to have another look at the four geishas. I glanced over at Naruto with a cheeky smile, "How're your skills at origami?"

"It's been a while. I could figure it out, I guess."

"We have the sequence; the only thing now is to reveal the map. These embroideries are just a diversion. Look, here." I pointed to the kimonos. "See the pictures on their backs are origami folds. I think each one of these kimono's needs to be folded to match these. Grab your phone and google the instructions to fold an origami dragon."

Naruto pulled out his phone and searched.

"Holy cow. Look," he said, holding up his phone. "The shapes match."

"Ta daaaa! Mystery solved."

"I'm deliriously tired and hyped at the same time. So, we need to use all four kimonos to make the one big origami dragon or fold each of them into an origami dragon?"

"Neither. You need to fold this first kimono into the same shape as displayed on the first geisha. Then match number two with the shape of displayed the second geisha and so on. Look at how the geisha are positioned, each slightly higher than the other. The map on the kimonos will probably flow in the same way."

Naruto was walking around the kimonos. "Okay, okay. I think I've got it."

"Remember the way each of them is facing up aligns with the pictures she drew in this letter, so I am assuming the maps are revealed when you do the folds and keep them facing up."

"Right."

"You look confused."

Naruto glanced up, "No. I get what you're saying. I'm just can't quite see how it will become a map."

"I think that's the genius of her design. If we are on the right track, then these folds will transform what we see now into a map. I'm going to leave you to it. I can be back later tonight or tomorrow morning if that suits you. I think that after all of this, you are going to sleep well."

"You're leaving? Don't you want to stay and help me work this out?"

"I have some things that I need to attend to. How about you catch up on some sleep while I run errands. We can synch up later tonight to work on this together?"

"Sure. I'll get you your food. One sec."

"No, don't bother. If we are regrouping tonight, I'll eat it here. No sense in taking home and bringing it back."

"Okay. Well, let's go. I'll give you a ride home."

"Thanks."

As we got into his car, a big gust of wind rocked it and made his door slam.

"Shit, that was close. It almost closed on my foot."

"Look at those grey clouds. They seem to be moving fast. Is your brother out today?"

"Mako and the crew are out every day. Rain, hail, or shine, they face the open waters."

Naruto started the car and began to drive.

"Those seas were rough the first time we went out. I can't even imagine voluntarily facing an actual storm. It seems like madness to me. Why wouldn't they take the day off and wait for the weather to settle?"

"Some of their biggest hauls come from hectic days out there. Fishermen have long believed that bravery is rewarded."

"Seems like complete insanity to me."

"I agree," said Naruto with a laugh.

I stared out the window looking at the deep grey clouds. I was set on leaving today. The only plans in place were making my way across to Tokyo. I'd stay a couple of days and then figuring out where to from there. I felt like the time had come to leave Japan. Eight hours later, I'm still in Suzu, I've managed to manifest a possible positive lead to help find the sycophant's who hurt those children and am helping Naruto with his quest.

"Harper, we're here."

"Ah," I opened the door and got out.

Naruto leaned his upper body across to the passenger side, "Hey, thanks for all your help today. I know you had plans to leave. I appreciate everything you've done for me."

"No problems. Do you know what time you might be coming back to pick me up?"

"Is eight pm too late?"

"Perfect. That will give me enough time. I might even squeeze in a nanna nap myself."

"Great I'll see you then."

"Okay bye." I shut the car door, and he promptly drove off.

It was time to contact my team to compile a complete dossier built around every person in every family who had a child returned. There had to be a link.

# Quest

The noises from the trawlers horn and rumbling engine was calling out to me in my dreams. The birds circling in a frenzy around the hull, squawking, was grating on my nerves. It caused the dull ache on the left side of my neck to spasm. I twisted my body around to the side, quickly opening my eyes as I felt myself plummet to the ground. It took me a minute to realize where I was. I climbed back onto the sofa and squinted my eyes to reduce the glare from the early morning sun. Mako and the crew were heading out for the day. I turned around and sat upright on the sofa, stretching my neck to one side; I gave it a little rub to release the tension. Naruto didn't return to pick me up last night. By eleven pm, I gave up waiting and decided to get some sleep. Crashing on the sofa in case he swung by, I managed to get in an awkward position and gave myself a stiff neck. Naruto not turning up seemed really out of character.

It would take a considerable amount of time to have the team collate all the information we needed on the children and their families. A data-mining program is being fed the raw data in real-time to search and list all the threads. It could take months before we get enough information to identify something that might be a helpful lead. Out the window, I could only see a speck in the distance. The trawler was well on its way to the open seas. I glanced around to look at my half-packed clothes. The urge for me to leave Japan was quietly bubbling to the surface. Perhaps I'll go tomorrow after I've made sure that Naruto has revealed the map. With this thought, I got up and headed for the shower.

* * * * *

*Knock, Knock*
"Naruto, are you there?"
*Knock, Knock*
"Hey Naruto, it's me, Harper."
I heard some shuffling, then footsteps coming toward the door. As it opened, Naruto stood there looking somewhat disheveled.

"Someone had a rough night," I said as I walked in. "What happened last night? I thought you were going to come to pick me up?"

"Yeah, I know. I'm sorry. When I got back from dropping you off, I decided to try to piece it all together. It was harder than I thought. I got frustrated, then overtired. I ended up falling asleep. By the time I woke up, it was already too late. There was no way I was coming over to get you. I went back to sleep and woke up just now."

Standing over the quasi-folded kimonos trying to assess the progress he had made, I could immediately see there was something wrong with the origami theory.

"I was worried about you. It seemed out of character, that's all. Did you at least sleep well?"

"Kind of. I kept dreaming about these dam kimonos."

I walked over to the coffee table and picked up the letter. I was flipping from page to page to cross-check them with the kimonos.

"Do you want to get some breakfast before we start?" He said as he stretched out his arms and released a big yawn.

"Nah, I'm good. Why don't you have a shower, get dressed, and I'll look over this? We can get started when you're ready."

"Okay, I'll be back soon." He turned and left the room.

"Take your time," I hollered.

I crouched down to take a closer look at the kimonos, then back at the four geishas. He did follow the shapes. It wasn't perfect but close enough to expect to reveal something of the map. Instead, it was a mish-mash of bits of the embroidery, a jumbled mess with no discerning message and no map. It was clear what laid before me was not right. I stared quietly at all of them, waiting for something to stand out.

"Hmm." I picked up the first kimono and laid it on my lap. Lifting the left sleeve, I inspected it closely, then the other. Previously we had spent so much time devoted to the actual embroidery I wanted to see if there was anything hidden in plain sight that we had missed. I turned the kimono inside out and began the same process. I felt a hot flush as my eyes detected an anomaly. Instantly I sprang into action.

Down on my knees, I began to fold the kimono into shape. Then slid across to the next one to find the marker and folded it accordingly. By the time Naruto had surfaced from getting dressed, I was standing over the kimonos, looking down at a map.

He looked at me and down at the map, "Oh, come on. How the fuck did you figure that out? Those aren't the origami shapes on the picture she drew?"

"I know. I was wrong about that but right that she was hinting that it was origami, aka folding. I was thinking of it in a literal sense last night. When I saw how it turned out this morning, I knew it was wrong. Even though you didn't have the folds completely perfect, it was close enough and should have revealed something, but it didn't. So, I went back to looking at the kimonos themselves to figure out what I missed." I bent down and ran my finger along the edging. "It is the seam. This one is in a completely different style and color to the rest of the gown's seams. I used the seam as a guide to fold the garment to expose the edging on all sides. A new perspective is revealed. Combined all together, and we have a map."

"I know I should be happy right now, but I'm so jealous of your brain."

I laughed, "Well, I've changed my mind about breakfast. I'm hungry."

"Me too. Hey, there are two snow-capped mountains on the map."

"Yes. While I was waiting for you to arrive last night, I decided to do a little more research on the three mountains. I had strong reason to believe it was Mount Yamizo, but the two peaks we see here indicate that it is Mount Tsukuba. That rules out Mount Kaba and Mount Yamizo."

"Okay, this mountain's covered in spring flowers, and this is snow-capped, right? How does that fit into being Mount Tsukuba? They are two different seasons. Do they get covered white flowers in Spring-like Yamizo?"

"No. See how you are holding onto the theories we had yesterday and now trying to make them fit. Toss that thought of springtime and flowers looking like snow-caps out. Instead, you need to look at it with fresh eyes because you are presented with new information. Lookup a picture of Mount Tsukuba. Tell me when you have it."

Naruto pulled out his phone and searched.

"I've got a picture."

"Come over here and look at the mountains. Do you agree that they follow a similar line to the way Mount Tsukuba is shaped at the peaks?"

"Without a doubt."

"Great, now if you look at the cherry blossoms and the peak with the star-shaped flowers on them, what could that represent?"

"Spring?"

"No, you are still using yesterday's theories. What it represents is female. If you look up the details around this mountain, the peaks are referred to as male and female. This confirms that the map is indicating Mount Tsukuba. This peak is referred to as the feminine, and this is the masculine side. My hunch is the Geisha symbolize femininity, and therefore the dragon scroll is likely in a cave on that peak."

"Amazing."

"It sure is. Honestly, to know that this was all conceived and done by hand so long ago is next-level mastery. Very clever work."

Naruto let out a little laugh, "I'm talking about you, and you're talking about the kimonos."

"Come on; you have to be impressed with it. She went out of her way to make sure that it wasn't easy to ascertain the information."

"It had me stumped, that's for sure. I would never have been able to figure this out."

"I'm sure if you kept at it, you would have solved it. Think about how many times I've been wrong on the path to getting to the right solution? I kept creating a hypothesis and following that line of thinking until it started to display aspects that stopped supporting it. The trick is to be able to let it go when it is not making as much sense. A good example is that I am aware that I might still be reading too much into the geisha painting by connecting it to the mountain's feminine peak. Either way, you need to start the search somewhere. If you don't find anything on the feminine peak, you know you've narrowed it down to the other peak. Based on what we see on this map, you know it's hidden on Mount Tsukuba. Now it's just a matter of time before you find it."

"You're coming with me, aren't you?"

"Oh, I was planning to leave tomorrow for Tokyo."

"Is there any chance you could delay for a little longer? You are somehow connected to all of this. I'm not sure I can retrieve it without your help. I certainly wouldn't have gotten as far as we have, and if I'm candid, I don't want to do this without you. As selfish as it may be, it's nice being able to talk to someone about all this. I mean, I am a descendent of koi. This is seriously next-level insanity."

I looked at the kimonos and then at Naruto.

"You have Mako. He knows about this."

"Yes, but he has a business to run, and it's out of his wheelhouse."

I chuckled, "The stuff we've been doing is out of everyone's wheelhouse."

"Yeah. I guess."

I released a big sigh, "Alright. Let's do this."

Naruto clapped his hands together. "Deal."

"I have some conditions. We must prepare to do some research upfront to narrow down the focal point to known entrances to caves with large-sized openings. I'm not interested in wandering out there for weeks, hoping to stumble across it and likely miss it."

Naruto was nodding his head so hard it reminded me of a bobblehead toy. "Absolutely. It makes perfect sense to approach it that way."

"We need to get some proper hiking gear, climbing gear and pull together a quality survival kit in case we get lost or hurt out there."

Naruto began typing into his phone. "I'll find a supply place we can go to on the way. There's nothing like that locally that I'm aware of."

"Well, I guess I'm in. Have you ever used climbing ropes and pulley systems before?"

He looked up for a moment. "No."

"Hmm, I did some abseiling when I was younger while camping with my folks. We'll have to watch a few instructional videos. If the dragon scroll is up high, we may have to climb the wall and then across the roofline. That takes some skills, serious upper body strength, and stamina which neither of us has. From what I learned yesterday; Mount Tsukuba has a lot of hard granite rock. That means we might need to take some extra equipment to secure any pegs in place. If we locate it and it seems too dangerous to attempt, we need to find another way that's safer. Okay? No taking unnecessary risks."

"Great. Agreed. I want to hug you right now."

"I'll settle for breakfast. Someone didn't pick me up last night, so I went to bed without any supper." I said with a pout.

"My bad. Yes. Let's get some food. Are you happy to try a traditional meal?"

"Sure, so long as the tradition part doesn't include white children."

Naruto burst out laughing, "There's no shirako served for breakfast."

"Trust me when I say there's never a time to serve cod sperm. Ewe."

He continued laughing as he led me out the back door of his home and down the path toward the restaurant.

* * * * *

Our base preparation time for the journey had taken a little over a week with an awareness that we were nowhere near ready for what may lay ahead. I had considered the options and decided that it was best to locate the dragon scroll and then determine what we require to get it down. The alternative was to carry everything with us just in case we needed it. That meant close to sixty pounds of extra weight on our backs as opposed to the twenty-two-pound ones we settled for.

The first stop was a slight detour to the rainbow river to get a sense of the place. A lot had changed. The trees were overgrown. Some of the banks were no longer accessible due to the mass of reeds in residence. Even a tourist platform had been built for people to view the stunning cascading waterfall easily. The water volume coming down and its impossible height made me wonder why any koi thought it was a good idea to try and scale up it. The river itself seemed empty. There wasn't any birdlife, certainly no koi or fish of any kind for that matter. It made me a little sad to think that it no longer lived up to its namesake.

As we arrived at the foothills of Mount Tsukuba, we entered the Shinto shrine. I looked around the outside while Naruto went off to pay his respects to his ancestors. I approached a display of wooden plaques hanging out on display. I'd seen them at other shrines too, pictures on one side and messages on the other. I watched them ever slightly sway with the breeze.

"If you would like to create one, you can purchase an ema over there."

I turned to see a young Japanese man standing beside me with his hands behind his back. He had a slender build, was wearing an off-white tunic, loose pants to match, and brown open-toe sandals. I glanced at his handwritten name badge, Lee Kim – Tour Guide.

"I can get one for you if you like."

"Your English is remarkable," I said.

His chest inflated with pride, "I know six languages and can speak them fluently. Japanese, English, Mandarin, Hindi, German, and my mother tongue Korean."

"Truly impressive. You must really like learning languages."

"No, it was just part of the job. A tour guide has a more competitive advantage if they can speak in the native tongue of the tourists."

"You work here?"

He scuffed some dirt away with his feet. "Um, no, not really. I travel to places, learn about them and then stick around to volunteer myself as a tour guide to get tips for my service. When I collect enough money, I move on to the next place on my list I'd like to visit."

"That's quite clever."

"Thank you, my desire to travel has always been the reason I study and work so hard. I don't have a place to call home or money in the bank, but my mind is enriched with experience, and I feel alive."

I appreciated his gumption. "Okay, you're hired."

"Really?" He said with a squeal. "Oh, you won't regret this. I'll be right back."

I smiled as I watched him run off to the vendor and then return with equal pace.

"Here this is ema. The blank side is where you place your wishes and desires. You hang it up here for the gods to see and fulfill."

I looked at the blank space on the wood. "What have people written. Can you read some to me?"

"It is for the Gods to read and fulfill. We cannot read them."

I let out a little laugh. "You can't read it, can you?"

With a crimson flush upon his cheeks, he scrunched up his face and shook it left to right. "No."

"It was a good sell, though. I almost believed you, but your body language gave you away."

"Damn, I do get fidgety when I tell a lie."

"It's fine. I'm not sure what I would write."

He did a little bounce with a clap of his hands, "The shrine is said to grant divine favor to people who are fated to be together. A lot of single people come here to write on ema wishing to have revealed to them the location of their mate."

I tapped my finger on the blank board, then looked at the countless others hanging. "I wonder how many people have had their wishes fulfilled?"

"Well, I believe a lot. This location hosts so many weddings. On Weekdays, weekends, there are always celebrations taking place in Spring, Summer, and Autumn. Not so much in the wintertime."

I put my ema in my back pocket. "I'll think about what to write. What else do you have to show me?"

"Outside first?"

"Sure. Outside first."

Lee was measured in his steps, making sure to maintain alignment with mine. He must have studied something around mimicry, helping to build rapport. I tried not to laugh as he attempted to follow my lead subtly. If I folded my arms, within seconds, he copied. It honestly amused me to see him in action. We wandered around the circumference of the shrine in a clockwise motion. The shrine looked to be in fantastic condition. The beautiful thick timbers held up a glorious roof that in itself appeared to be a work of art.

"It is said that a deity descended from the heavens over a thousand years ago in search of a place to spend the evening. The deity arrived at the peak of the magnificent Mt. Fuji. When requesting safety and shelter in exchange for blessings, the mountain refused. It was already the largest and most beloved mountain in Japan. It didn't see any value in the offering of blessings, for it was already clearly blessed. The deity went on to offer the same deal to Mt. Tsukuba. The mountain graciously welcomed the chance to provide warmth and shelter for the guest. The deity was given safety in its largest cave, together with nourishment so a full belly may support the deity to help sleep soundly. Legend states that the next morning Mt. Tsukuba was covered in foliage that emulated a sunset's glory. Flowers sprung overnight in full bloom, adorning the mountain in sweet perfume. The deity acknowledged the kindness of the mountain with two peaks by holding a ceremony to marry them. As a symbol of their union during the new moon phase, two blessed seeds were planted. One was a South Giant Cedar, and the other a North Giant Cedar. By the time the cycle of the full moon reached its peak, the tree roots were intertwined, and the trunks grew side by side high toward the heavens with their branches wrapping around one another."

We arrived at the foundation of a spectacular tree.

With a wave of his hand, Lee said, "This is called the wedded cedar or Meoto Sugi."

"It's beautiful. What a lovely story."

"The legend is true. Look at how the trees hold one another. They are so close now you cannot see where one begins and the other ends. It is my favorite place to sit and eat my lunch."

I was smiling as I looked up to the spread of its foliage. "It is a rather special tree. It makes me wonder how old it is."

"I thought it was hundreds, but the tourist brochure states it's thousands of years old. I checked to see if it was a mistake. The tourism group assured me it was thousands."

"Thousands of years old," I repeated as I spread my arms out and twirled. "It certainly feels lovely to be around. Imagine the secrets this tree could impart."

"Many," replied Lee nodding his head. "Many, many."

I stood as close as I could to the tree without getting my feet trapped between the gaps in the oversized roots. I placed a single hand on the trunk and closed my eyes for a moment to feel its essence.

"Would you like to continue to the inside of the Shrine?"

I shook my head slowly. "No. This will do just fine." I opened my eyes and followed the line of the trunk up into the canopy. "Trees truly are majestic." I released a deep sigh, patted the bark's rough surface on the tree, and then turned to Lee. "My friend was inside; he's probably finished praying and will be looking for me. Let's head back to the entrance."

"Okay, are you sure? I will be quick. It is a great shrine. I would hate for you to miss out."

"I won't miss out. Maybe next time." I said, returning down the path we had just taken.

Lee paused for a moment and then scurried to catch up. As we turned the bend, I could see Naruto at the top of the stairs facing out toward the car park, trying to identify me.

"See, there's my friend." I lifted my hand and waved. "Naruto, over here."

He turned, saw me, and immediately smiled as he began jogging down the stairs on an angle toward us.

"I thought I had lost you," he exclaimed.

"No. I made an acquaintance who has been kind enough to give me some history on this place. Lee Kim, this my friend Naruto."

"Pleased to meet you, Naruto."

"Likewise, Lee." Naruto looked at me, "Um, are you ready to go?"

"Yes. One sec." I turned to Lee as I pulled out my wallet, "Here's some money for your time today. I admire your entrepreneurial skills. Keep doing what you love." His eyes widened as I placed ¥10,000 in his hand. "I hope this covers the cost of the ema and your time."

"Of course, yes. Thank you for the kind words and generosity."

"Okay, I'm ready. Bye Lee."

"Thank you. Thank you. Bye."

We began walking to the car. "Hey, do you happen to have the map on you?"

"Yes, here." Naruto pulled it out of the side pocket on his vest.

"I just had a thought." I turned and called out to get Lee's attention. "Lee, have you got a second, please. I want to ask you a question."

He looked up from counting his money. "Yes. Yes." He jogged over.

"Can you please show me on this map where the big cave is that you mentioned? The one where the deity slept for the night."

He shifted his position to look at the map. "It is around here. The cave had a big opening, so large you could not miss it. Rock quarries are being mined in the area that used explosives to do some blasting which is now illegal. I believe large rocks have since fallen that make the entrance very narrow, and vegetation has grown, so it is tough to find."

"Have you ever been there?"

He shook his head, "No. I am scared of dark, enclosed places; they creep me out, spiders too. I don't like spiders."

I looked at the map. "What makes you think it is in this area if you've never been there before?"

He pulled out the tourist guide and showed me the pseudo map on the back cover. "The spot is marked on here."

"Great. Thanks again. Take care, Lee." I said as I exchanged a glance with Naruto. We both headed toward the car again.

"Bye," said Lee.

I gave him a single wave from my hand without glancing back.

"That area he pointed out didn't have any recorded caves near it. The only three we found are on the opposite side of the peak. What do you think? Should we go on a hunt for this unmarked cave or head to the other three first?"

Naruto released a sigh, "I'm not sure."

"Yeah, me neither."

We jumped into the car.

"We can either get the cable car and leave the vehicle here, or we drive up to the summit and then walk down the mountain."

I thought about it for a moment. "Let's use the cable car to reach the summit; then we can walk down to look for the caves. Then head for the shrine to grab the car. At least that will make the journey a little less taxing."

"Okay, well, let me move the car, so it is out of sight." Naruto started up the car, reversed out of the very tight spot, and drove down to the car park's furthest point.

"This should do," he said, turning off the engine. "I'll grab our stuff from the boot and go get our tickets." He reached down, latched his finger under the lever, and pulled upward to release the boot.

I hopped out of the car walked to the back, pulling out his backpack to pass to him.

"Thanks," he said as he placed his arm through the strap and swung it on his back. "I can carry yours on my front if you like."

"No. I'm good. It's super light."

"Okay. Here are the keys, lock up when you are done and meet me at the ticket booth."

"Sure, see you in a minute." I accepted the keys.

My backpack was partially open, with a few of the items scattered. I stuffed them into the bag, then double-checked to see if I had everything. Satisfied, I was about to zip up the bag when I noticed a large roll of thick plastic in the corner. Reaching across the boot, I grabbed it and began unraveling. They were transparent medium-sized garbage bags. I took two, deciding that if the weather turned and started to rain, we could protect our packs from getting soaked. They were already weather-resistant but only to a point. The zips, front and side pockets would only stay dry if it was a sun shower, anything heavier, and our maps could be drenched.

"Harper."

I turned to see Naruto waving and pointing at the cable cart that was on its way. He walked over and lined up.

I crammed the plastic bags into the only free pocket I had, then promptly swung the pack onto my shoulders and slammed the boot shut. I clicked the security button on the keys and heard the car respond with a beep, then lightly jogged to where Naruto stood.

"Here," I said, passing the keys to him.

"You took your time," he said with a cheeky grin as we stepped forward in the line.

"Yeah, some of my stuff had fallen out of my bag. I was just checking to make sure I didn't leave anything behind."

Naruto passed the tickets to the fellow collecting them. We hopped into the cart and heard the doors promptly close behind us. I nodded at the other people already seated and then sat myself down.

"The mountain doesn't look that tall. We probably should have legged it."

Naruto laughed, "Yes, let's see at the end of today whether we are thankful for conserving our energy at the start."

Staring out the window at the passing view, I nodded my head, "I'm sure we will be."

The scenery was divine. The trees below displayed various shades of green, with some foliage sporadically providing a pop of yellow. The vibrant lime green leaves were my favorite. I would have loved to be able to stretch my arm out the window so my hand could glide over the tops of the trees. I was so emersed in my thoughts the noise of the other passengers talking and the occasional waft of flatulence didn't ruin the forty-five-minute ride.

When we arrived, I was a little surprised to see the row of shops and a circular building with a viewing platform. It wasn't developed in the same traditional keeping of the stylized Japanese architecture that I've seen everywhere else. These commercial buildings seemed to be more of a blight on the mountain.

"I know people need to make a living, but this all looks out of place up here."

"It's ugly for sure," said Naruto.

"Let's go over to that track, set our things down, and look at the map so that we can get our bearings."

"Okay," replied Naruto.

We walked around the circumference of the round building to get to the path I had seen. Simultaneously we placed our packs on the ground. Naruto squatted in front of his as he searched through the front pocket to look for the compass. He then laid the pack flat, using it as a surface to spread out the map. I hovered over his shoulder to look at it.

"We are here. The three caves we know are marked here, here, and here. This alleged cave that Lee mentioned is roughly in this region. It looks like we would have to walk past the area to get to the other caves. It might be worth spending some time looking?"

"I'm in two minds. We know Lee mentioned that there is granite build-up narrowing the entrance. Maybe we look at heading toward the first of the three caves. We can keep an eye out for it. If we see anything at all that looks promising, we'll detour to check it out."

"Yeah, that works. Are you ready to go?"

I lent down and grabbed my pack. "Lead the way."

Naruto took one last look at the map before folding it up and placing it into his jacket pocket. He stood up, swung the pack over his shoulder, and began to walk. I followed slightly behind on the narrow dirt path.

It was nice to have the tourist noise fade off into a distant murmur. The day was warming up. I could feel the strikes of heat from the sun's rays as it occasionally managed to penetrate through the canopy of trees. Sweat was beading across my brow.

"I'm going to stop for a second to grab a drink. Do you want to cross-check where we are on the map with the GPS?"

"Sure. I am confident, I know, but I'm happy to check."

Naruto got to work setting up the map while I rummaged around my pack to find the water bottle that had made its way down to the bottom. I pulled it out, popped the lid and took a big gulp, then swilled some water in my mouth before swallowing that too.

"Are we good?"

"Hmm, no. According to the GPS, we are gradually making our way down rather than going across. I've taken us too far on this track."

"So, we need to go cross country and head up?"

"Yes. We will have to make our own track. Can you give me a few minutes to set up the GPS with our route?"

"Of course," I said as I dampened a light towel to wipe down my face before placing it around my neck. "I'll take this opportunity to go relieve myself."

"Sure, watch out for fire ants."

"Will do."

I wandered off into the bush, far enough away that I couldn't see Naruto. I did a quick scan for creepy crawlies before dropping my pants and squatting to pee. Careful to produce a steady stream to minimize the side splash onto my legs, I watched the steam rise with a swirl. I smiled the smile that comes with the sweet relief of emptying your bladder. Rising from the squat, I gave myself a quick wipe and pulled my pants up. Before heading back to Naruto, I looked down at the puddle that was quickly disappearing into the thirsty earth. That was a lot of pee.

Naruto greeted me with a smile. "We're set."

"Great." I fastened my pack and followed his lead.

"Sorry for this. We need to head cross country and up for a while before we get in alignment with the first cave."

"Are you using the GPS this time?"

"Yes."

"Cool. One second." I pulled my back to the front, unzipped the side, and retrieved a canister of bug spray. "Let me spray your shoes and legs. Then you can do mine. It will help to keep any unwelcome guests from trying to hitch a ride."

"Good idea," Naruto stuck his left leg out.

I sprayed his footwear and lower legs thoroughly and then gave a general spray across the rest of his body front and back while he shut his eyes and held his breath. When I was done, I passed him the canister to do the same.

"You can open your eyes, Harper. I'm done."

"Thanks." I grabbed the canister and placed it back in the pack.

Naruto began walking. "We need to keep an eye out for snakes. That and fire ants are the worst of it out here. Oh, and wild boars and bears."

"So, nothing to worry about then?" I said with amusement.

I could see Naruto shrug his shoulders, "I'm not too worried. I've never seen any of those things in the wild."

"You obviously must hike a lot when you're in Japan."

"Ha. Um, actually no. Hardly ever. Yeah, yeah, I get it. You don't have to say it."

I laughed.

* * * * *

It had been a few hours coupled with detours to check piles of granite later before we managed to locate our first of three known caves. When we walked through the entrance, it was not a particularly remarkable cave, although it seemed to get cold relatively quickly as we ventured deeper into the cavern. Both Naruto and I automatically slowed at what appeared to be the mid-point to the cave. We both looked up.

"What do you think?" Asked Naruto.

"I'm not sure that I can see anything that could hide a scroll." I placed my pack on the ground, strapped my headlamp to my scalp, and switched the light on. I was rummaging through my bag, looking for the monoscope.

"Do you have the scope in your pack? I can't seem to find it."

"No. I'm pretty sure it was in yours."

I crouched down and began pulling out all the gear. "Yep. Got it."

Standing up, I switched it on and held it up to my left eye, staring up at the ceiling. Carefully I scanned left to right. When I was finished, I shifted position and did it again. This continued until I was satisfied that I had completed an assessment of the whole ceiling. Meanwhile, Naruto was using his headlamp to look at the sides of the cave.

"I can't detect anything that might be a potential hiding spot for a scroll. Granted, we have no idea what it looks like or the size of it."

"A scroll suggests it's cylindrical, rolled up, maybe between A5 and A4 size? I don't know. I can't see anything of interest on these walls either."

"If we head out now, we can find a place to stop and eat, then go to the next cave. It's about an hour away, right?"

"Yeah, as the crow flies, it suggests an hour. Maybe slightly over."

"Well, my instinct say's it's not this one," I said while bending over to return all my gear into the pack.

"Yeah, I think you're right."

I stopped what I was doing and looked at Naruto. "You seem flat, what's up?"

"I keep wondering whether we should be even trying to find the scroll."

"Okay. Where's this going?"

"Well, I've been so consumed by the chase that I have never stopped to consider the consequences. What if the scroll reveals harmful knowledge that I shouldn't have read?"

"Hmm, I just realized that we are both operating from two very different mindsets. For some reason, I assumed that the retrieval of the scroll was for Daisuke. It is, after all, his to read. I have no desire or intention of opening it."

"Aren't you even the slightest bit curious about it? I mean, sure, it's Daisuke's scroll, but I'm his last living relative with webbed feet."

I turned to look at Naruto, "Yes, you are, but Daisuke is not dead. He is alive and well swimming in your pond. The energy of the Golden Dragon still lives within him, and the scroll was earned by right of passage. It's not for anyone else to see. At least that's what I believe."

"So, you don't think I should open it then?"

"Naruto, honestly, you need to do whatever you feel is right. It's not my place to try and stop or convince you. Dealers choice, this is your family, your ancestry. Do what you feel is right." I shrugged my shoulders as I placed the pack on my back and headed for the cave opening.

Naruto followed, "You are annoyed with me."

"Not at all. Which direction do we need to head?"

He stopped, pulled out the GPS, and pressed a few buttons. "We need to go right and slightly down."

I stepped aside, "It's best if you lead."

"Sure," he kept the GPS in his hand and walked forward. "Harper, I feel like I need to see what's in it."

"Then look. I'm not going to judge you. I was just trying to convey that we had completely different ideas of what would happen if we retrieved the scroll. I'm good either way." Internally there was a twinge in me that still felt very adamant that the rightful and entitled person was Daisuke. I was being honest about not judging Naruto for succumbing to temptation. That was his prerogative. I held absolutely no desire in me to read the contents.

"Look over there to your left." Naruto said, pointing.

I slowed down my pace and turned my head. "What are they?" I asked as I stared at these two adorable brown animals that looked like a cross between a raccoon and a brown bear.

"They are called Tanuki. The locals believe that they can shape-shift to take on human form or disguise themselves as ordinary objects."

I pulled out my monocular. "How adorable. Look at those little ears. Are they ferocious?"

"Not that I'm aware of. They are referred to as mischievous, similar to the raccoons we have in the US. I mean, they are wild, so I guess if they felt cornered or were protecting their babies, they would bite."

I returned my monocular to my jacket pocket. "Are they specific to this area?"

"I believe they can be found all around Japan. They are pretty common."

"Well, they are adorable. Did you want to stop for thirty minutes to grab a bite to eat? That fallen tree looks like a good place to set up."

"Perfect, yes," replied Naruto.

We both went over to the log. "Hold on." I said, picking up a branch from the ground. "Wait a moment," I said as I smashed the stick on the tree, making a whishing sound with the leaves.

"What are you doing?"

I bent over as I ran the stick under the tree and into tiny gaps. "I'm checking for snakes and giving warning so they can either present to attack or clear. They love living under rocks and trees."

"Oh. Good idea." Naruto looked around for a stick and began doing the same.

After a couple of minutes of swishing and banging, I stopped to wipe the beads of sweat forming on my brow. "That should do it."

Naruto gave it a few more bangs then tossed away his stick. "Phew, I've worked up an appetite," he said, clutching the areas where a belly might be if he had one.

He put down the pack and pulled out two sandwiches, passing me one.

"I'm not sure what the ladies in the kitchen made us, but I'm sure they are both the same. Do you want to check?"

"Nah, I'm not too fussed." I unwrapped it and took a big bite.

Naruto sat beside me on the trunk and followed suit. We ate in silence, looking up at the mountain. The sandwiches were tightly packed with layers of color. Each vegetable was thinly grated, purple cabbage, carrot, cucumber, onion. In the center was a generous portion of avocado and a perfectly cooked egg with the yolk partially still soft. There was lettuce on the outside and seaweed fused to the slices of white bread using Japanese mayonnaise. It was finished with a light sprinkle of rock salt and cracked pepper.

"Geez, you finished that fast. Would you like another one? I have more in my bag," said Naruto as I shoved the last piece into my mouth.

I shook my head as I stood up to wipe the crumbs off my lap. "No thanks. It was delicious. The food tastes so good here. I could never get a sandwich like that back home."

"Yeah, I think it's the way they thinly slice everything and layer it. The food is honored by celebrating the flavor instead of drowning it in condiments."

I turned and looked at him, "That might be it. Less fat, more whole foods. I mean, the bread isn't that healthy, but as far as sandwiches go, it was pretty nutrient-dense." I pulled out my monocular and started surveying the mountain peak.

"Are you heading back home after we have finished here?"

I shook my head, "I have no idea where I might go from here. At the moment, it's unlikely to be the US. I wouldn't mind visiting the pyramids or exploring the Island of Crete. I just need to roam for a while until I feel like I know my next move."

Naruto was rummaging around in his pack and then walked over to stand beside me. "Do you want to rest some more or head off?"

"Actually, I want to head toward that ridgeline. Here take a look." I said, passing the monocular to him.

"I don't see it. What am I looking at?"

"Follow the ridgeline toward the peak. If you don't see anything scan back down slowly and let me know if you see it."

While I was waiting for him, I took a couple of mouthfuls of water to wash down the bread particles that were tickling my throat.

"I can't see anything."

"Okay, look for those birds swirling around in what appears to be a zig-zag pattern."

"Yes. I see them."

"Focus on them, follow where they go."

Naruto dropped the monocular, smiling, "They disappear."

I nodded my head, "Exactly. It could be an optical illusion, or there might be a cave. Those erratic flying little fellows look like bats feeding on insects to me."

"They might be swallows; they move similarly," he suggested.

"True," I replied. "Either way, both of those animals tend to like to set up nests in caves."

Naruto glanced through the monocular again. "Do you want to go up and take a look?"

"I think it's worth checking out. I'm game if you are." I placed my fist out to him. He bumped it.

"Sounds like a plan."

"Before we go, let's give ourselves a bit of a bug spray top-up." I passed him the canister.

"Sure. Hold your breath and spin around slowly."

I did as he suggested, and when I was complete, I repeated the same for him.

"All set?"

I smiled, "Indeed."

We started the long haul diagonally up the mountain. The first forty-five minutes set the pace for an even slow muscle burn. It was mainly building in my quads and calves. Part of me wanted to stop for a rest; however, Naruto was pounding away without a murmur, so I didn't want to disrupt the rhythm. We were making new tracks through the shrub. Occasionally we could see a short path likely caused by local animals in residence. We gave up trying to use them as they frequently led to dug-out holes or nowhere. The forest canopy continued to help shield us from the scorching afternoon sun. Unfortunately, it didn't protect us from the humidity. Each step seemed to disrupt groups of micro-winged bugs that flew up in a circle and settled down as we passed.

"Okay, we need a time out for a few minutes," I said while reaching into my pocket to grab the monocular. I stared up toward the ridgeline.

"What do you see?"

"I'm fairly certain they are bats." I passed him the monocular.

Naruto placed it to his left eye and scanned the ridgeline. "Yep. They sure are."

"We're pretty close. If we cut over this brush and veer right slightly as we climb, I feel like we will be able to get into that open space. That will get us there a little quicker."

"Hmm, if we do that, the sun is going to be beaming down on us. It will zap our energy." Naruto pointed in a slight deviation to the left. "I know it might be more of a loop, but if we stick to this line, we have canopy almost to that point in the ridgeline. By the time we get there, the sting of the sun would have reduced dramatically."

I unexpectedly released a yawn.

Naruto passed back the monocular. "We can rest for a while if you like. We've been on the move all day."

"I'll be okay. How are your legs holding up?" I asked.

"Not too bad. I play a lot of golf at home, so I'm used to long walks and hills. This is harder, of course, relentless inclines, more miles without stopping. I'm a little sore." He patted the sides of his thighs. "I can keep going."

"Yep, me too. I want to try to get to the ridgeline asap. If there is a cave, we can take a good look and then find a place to set up camp. There's no point going down tonight."

"We can visit the remaining two caves tomorrow and then walk around the circumference of the cap to see if there are any unmarked caves."

I nodded. "I should have bought a drone. It would have been easier to survey the area."

"What a great idea. Too bad you didn't think of that earlier."

"Well, I did. My hesitation was related to drawing attention to us. I'm certain someone would spot it, and then questions would be asked. Doing the hard miles on foot is less conspicuous."

"You're right. A drone would have been nice, though."

I released a sigh. "Yep, it sure would have." I bent down and retied a loose shoelace. "Okay, enough rest. We need to get to that ridge."

Naruto laughed. "Come on then."

* * * * *

An hour and twenty-three minutes later, we arrived at the spot where we believed the bats had been flitting about. We both split up to cover more of the area. I went right, and Naruto left. Sections of the ground were a little hazardous to walk on. Large cavernous holes were filled with decades of forest litter. A couple of times, I had taken a step, and my foot disappeared as the sticks compacted. The first time it happened, my heart jumped to attention, with my body immediately filled with adrenaline from the surprise. In the second one I had happened across, the hole was shallow enough for me to see glimpses of the bottom. Large quantities of bright white bones from medium-sized animals were scattered everywhere. It made me wonder what caused the granite boulders to wear in such a monumental way. They were of significant size and would have taken hundreds of years to reshape.

"Harper, over here."

I turned to see Naruto waving in the distance before he disappeared. I smiled as I turned and headed back. He had found a cave.

There wasn't a clear path for me to get to where Naruto was positioned. I decided to climb up on a diagonal above where he was stationed and then carefully descend. By the time I reached him, he was already geared up for the exploration. The headlamp was on, utility belt with a pick, ropes, and shackles were dangling around his tiny waist.

"This is the place. I just know it," he said with a massive grin.

"You found it?"

"No. It's the way I feel when I'm in there. It's like the scroll is calling to me."

"Oh, okay. Great." I dropped my pack, unzipped the top, and pulled out my headlamp. I secured it to my scalp and zipped the bag up again.

"Ready?" Asked Naruto eagerly.

"Let's do this."

"Careful. The first few steps are slippery."

"Okay." I followed him in through the narrow crack. "This doesn't seem that wide."

"I know, just keep going. We're almost there."

It took approx. fifteen shuffling steps before the passage led to an open cavern. I walked over to Naruto. "This is certainly something." I flashed my light back onto the entrance and up. "That is one big ass boulder."

"I know, right? Once upon a time, there must have been an ultrawide entrance. Then this boulder fell, narrowing the doorway. Isn't this exciting?"

I smiled, "Yes, it kind of is. I can't get over the size of that thing." I turned my head to the right. "Shh. Can you hear that?" I whispered. "It sounds like running water."

"There is. I'm not sure where it is coming from. I saw it trickling down the side of the wall. Come, I'll show you."

Naruto's headlamp bounced to his step.

"See, it appears out of nowhere from here, glides down the walls face, and falls directly into this pool that runs off over there." I watched his torchlight shine on the different areas as he provided his observations. "Oh, look at this. One sec I'm just going to turn off your light."

He switched mine off, followed by his own. It took a moment for my eyes to adjust, and then I saw it, glowworms on the ceiling of the cave, as well as tiny little fish that also contained bioluminescence.

"Pretty cool," I said as I happily glanced around. "It almost feels like we've entered a magical wonderland filled with mystical creatures."

Naruto clicked on his light. "That's exactly how I felt when I first walked in. I have this tingling sensation all over. I think this is the place where the scroll is hidden."

"I shone the light up to the ceiling. Where are the bats?"

"I'm not exactly sure. I think that this tunnel leads to other open spaces."

I walked over to the medium-sized opening and shone my torch. "It's a strange shape, and it almost seems unnatural in the way it's formed. Perfectly round."

Naruto took a few steps inside. "It's almost like a machine with a drill came through and made this hole. Look at all these perfectly made grooves. Where did all the dirt go from when it was excavated? How Bizarre."

"Don't go too far in. Let's focus on searching the roof of this big cavern first, and then we can decide whether it's worth it."

"The tingling is getting stronger over here. I think we need to go this way," he said in a soft tone.

"Naruto, I'm feeling a little uneasy about this. I think we had best stop for a minute and consider our approach. Come outside, and we can clear our thoughts."

"No, no, we need to go this way, Harper. Everything will be fine. The scroll is calling me. I can feel it."

"Naruto, STOP."

He paused for a moment and turned to look at me.

"I don't feel any good energy from this tunnel. I believe whatever is calling to you is not necessarily friendly. Please don't go any further. I need you to come back over here."

Naruto looked at the passage and touched the wall. He closed his eyes and breathed in deep, then exhaled. "I think you are wrong."

"Maybe I am, but we agreed that we wouldn't take any unnecessary risks. I need you to respect that and come back."

Naruto reached up to his headlamp and switched it off. "I'm sorry, Harper," was all he said before running down the tunnel.

"Fuck, Fuck, Fuuuuuck."

I paced up and down, anger building at his reckless and incredibly selfish behavior. I wanted to walk away, leave him to his quest. What was I even doing here anyway? I had no business being here. Naruto wanted me to come, and now he chose to set off on his own. What the fuck am I supposed to do now? I could feel the fury within me rise. He betrayed my trust. I looked at the entrance to the tunnel and wanted to scream.

Ten minutes passed, then twenty, then thirty. After an excruciating two hours had passed, I heard my name called in the distance, then nothing.

"Shit." I knew I couldn't ignore him. I shook my head. At least that was a sign that he was alive. I secured my backpack and walked over to the opening. As I headed into the tunnel, I could feel this force of air pushing me backward. Then I saw it, quickly I dropped flat to the ground and covered my head as hundreds of bats came barreling out at lightning speed. My hands were getting randomly scratched, and the funk they carried with them insulted my nostrils with a dust-filled cloud of musky scent. I waited until it was all over before lifting my head to confirm my path was clear. The existence of bats confirmed there was something at the end of the tunnel. My heart was pounding with adrenaline as I jogged down the passage. It took a few minutes to get to a point where I could see a solitary stream of light that I assumed was coming from Naruto's flashlight. My jog transitioned to a run when I realized it was on the ground. Naruto was in trouble.

At the opening, my reflexes kicked in when I leaped over the flashlight so I wouldn't step on him.

"What the fuck. Oh my God, shit. Naruto. Naruto. Hang in there, buddy." I slammed my pack on the ground and threw everything out to look for the plastic bag I had taken from the car's boot. I grabbed it, placed my hand inside to open it before scooping up Naruto into the bag and running back through the tunnel. He was flipping back and forth with his body convulsing, his mouth open, gasping for air. I ran as fast as I could to the water hole, thrust the bag in with a swing, and filled it mid-way with some water.

I lifted it, "You alright, buddy?" Naruto was swimming lopsided. I fell to the ground, still holding the bag slightly off the cave floor. "It's going to be okay," I said, still out of breath and in shock with my hand trembling from the surge of adrenaline.

I stared at him, swimming in a circle. His markings were rather extraordinary. He was solid black at the front with a switch to a vibrant orange that fades to a lovely peach color on his fins and tail. The inside of his gills revealed a flash of orange inside as well.

His lopsided daze was slowly correcting. "You scared me. I thought I lost you." One-handed, I fumbled my way to a stance. "I need to get our stuff and head back to your place."

Slowly I walked back down the tunnel and out to the other side. All my things were still scattered about. I couldn't put Naruto down without the bag flattening, so I had to find a way to do everything with one hand. Once I was done with mine, I placed the pack on my back and then put Naruto's bag on my front. I did a quick survey of the roof of the cave before turning to head out. Naruto started manically flipping about. I lifted the plastic bag to my eye level to look at him. Instead of swimming in circles, he was pushing up against the plastic bag. I turned to look in the direction he was facing.

"What is it?" I said, using my torch to glance around. "I don't see anything?"

I took a few measured steps forward, then some more, searching the ground. A sudden hissing sound appeared to my left that I knew wasn't coming from anything friendly. I switched my attention to the sound's vicinity and just turned as the light captured a snake striking at Naruto's pack.

"Fuck," I said, jumping out of the way. My right hand was cramping from the tight grip I had on Naruto's plastic bag. I moved backward in a shuffle rather quickly as the snake gained confidence and decided to stand its ground. Just as I turned to make a run for it, my footing twisted with my right ankle giving way. I fell backward on the floor, quickly composing myself to glance at my foot and then across to the snake. It was gone.

"Shit." I scanned around to try to relocate the snake. It had either taken the opportunity to leave or was quietly slinking its way to have another crack at me. My ankle was flush with fluid. I reached down to check if I broke anything. As I raised the foot to feel it, I saw a glint of something shimmering. Slightly panicked that it was the reflection from the eyes of the snake, I shuffled back then checked again sporadically while fumbling in the pack for a weapon.

"What the?" I froze. It was hard to comprehend the beauty of it. I looked at Naruto, "Holy snapping duck shit, you found it." I carefully pushed myself up. My ankle was throbbing in protest. Slowly I placed some pressure on it to see how it would feel. The flush of pain caused my face to exude warmth. Using my left leg only, I swiveled slightly and then bent down, grabbing the scroll before losing my balance, then just managing to recover by hopping on one foot. Poor Naruto must have felt like he was in the spin cycle of a washing machine. Finally, I placed my right foot down and winced. Exhaling the pain, I shifted my focus to making some room for the scroll in Naruto's pack. Nestled safely between a couple of t-shirts, I zipped the pack shut and began the painful journey of hobbling back through the tunnel. There were some random sounds of a menacing hiss coming from all directions detected in-between steps and my heavy breathing. That amount of bats had to attract its fair share of predators. Not wanting to stick around to prove my theory right, I ignored the sear of pain and picked up the pace.

I held Naruto up and in front to ensure the bag was clear from any sharp rocks jutting out from the walls. The last thing I needed to happen now was his bag to tear. In the light, his scales were giving off a shimmer that reflected onto the walls. In any other circumstances I would have thought it was pretty. Right now, I was struggling to overcome the burn in my leg, and the flickering shadows seemed menacing. I needed to get out of there.

* * * * *

Welcoming the cool of the night air on my face as I exited the cave, I was grateful to see the luminous moon shining bright. I had been in two minds about setting up camp inside the first cavern. The microtrauma of seeing the snake lunge toward me with its mouth open and striking the bag was still too fresh. I knew laying down there; I wouldn't be able to sleep a wink. My other concern was the oxygen levels available in Naruto's sealed bag of water. I'd replenished the water from the pool and filled both our drinking containers to the brim to carry them in case I needed to top up his bag. There were so many things that could go wrong between here and the car. Everything had happened so fast that I still wasn't able to fully process that Naruto is a koi, and the golden scroll has been found. The whole thing seemed surreal.

I took a deep breath while I surveyed the area. Aware that my ankle would set my pace back, I looked around for a branch strong enough to use as a walking stick. The first couple I picked up were knotted and cracked the moment I placed pressure on them. I hobbled about for ten or so minutes looking for a suitable staff without success. It felt like I was stalling the descent. Whether I rested and waited until daybreak, either way, I needed to make my way down. There was an enormous sense of pressure. Naruto's life was literally in my hands. If I fell in one of those pits or just tripped, his bag could tear, and I would be left with a fish out of water.

"That's it," I said. I unzipped Naruto's bag and pulled out one of his t-shirts. Carefully I placed the plastic bag inside and wrapped it around to protect it. I grabbed another and did the same. Now at least the likelihood of any branch scratching the surface of the bag was reduced. "Sorry, Naruto," I whispered. "I need to protect the bag. I'll unwrap you as soon as I get to the car." A thought crossed my mind. I'd have to drive a stick shift on the opposite side of the road and find my way back to Suzu. I released a sigh. This was going to be one long, exhausting trip. I pulled out the scroll that was now shimmering in the moonlight, lay down Naruto's puffer vest, wrapped it in there for protection, then returned it to the bag. It was time to go.

Going down was all the direction I would need for now. I started walking the left diagonal on the descent in the hope that at some point, I would cross the path that led back down the mountain to the Shrine car park. This would be my best chance of getting there quickly. I began taking steps, cautious that there were divots covered in forest litter that could cause my ankle some grief. I wanted to do everything I could to reduce the probability of me losing my footing.

Wandering the forest at night had a completely different feel to it. The nocturnal creatures seemed to be in abundance. I had passed an owl roosting on her clutch of eggs in the hollow of a tree. There was a curious fox that slinked around for a while, circling me with a wide berth, sniffing the air, staring. When I was passed a certain point, it would track and investigate the areas where I had been. I welcomed the distraction of my surroundings. It felt as though my body had given up sending pain signals to my ankle. Instead, it was so swollen the laces on my shoe was starting to cut off circulation. I truly wanted to stop and take it off. I imagined the immediacy of the relief I would receive. I also knew there would be no way to get my shoe back on, and I certainly wasn't going to walk barefoot through this litter. So, I persisted, step by step down the mountain.

I felt so elated when I came across the path. It gave me a renewed determination to get to the car and make my way back to Naruto's house. I hobbled down at an almost average speed and got excited when I could see the cable car lines visible through the treetops. When I saw the Shrine to my left, I was ready to cry from joy. The muscles on my right arm had long since seized from holding out Naruto. The squishy tingling of my foot as I placed it down was an unpleasant sign that I was nearing the end of my body's tolerance for weight-bearing.

Reaching the car, I checked that all the tires were inflated and windows intact. Back home, a car would have been stripped down to nothing if it was left unattended in a car park like this. I rummaged around the pack's side pockets and then inside to try to locate Naruto's car keys. The searing pain had returned to my foot, and this time, it wasn't something I couldn't ignore. Finally, I located the keys in the side zip pocket of his puffer vest. I unlocked the car, placed both the packs on the passenger seat, secured them with the seatbelt, and carefully wedged Naruto between them to keep the bag from flattening out. I walked across to the driver's side and opened the door. I sat down, leaned over, and peeled my left shoe off my swollen foot. Just as I suspected, the intense pain was released like the steam from a kettle. If I allowed myself to rest, I knew I would, without a doubt, pass out from exhaustion. It was less about physicality and more the mental fatigue. There had been too many times I had slipped and felt my heart race at the thought of losing Naruto.

Tossing my shoe to the back seat, I started the car and fastened my seatbelt. It was going to be a very long drive home.

* * * * *

Gratitude was what I felt as I bent down and released Naruto into his pond. We made it. He was safe, and I was beyond exhausted.

"Daisuke," I called.

It took a moment before the golden koi peeped out from underneath a giant rock ledge.

"Naruto," I said, pointing to him.

Naruto seemed to be in a bit of a daze. The shift in water temperature and being couped up in that bag was probably not the best experience. I wasn't even sure if he understood what had happened or whether he had transitioned to an actual fish with no memory. Daisuke swam over to Naruto and began nudging him. I knew placing him here in the pond was the best that I could do under the circumstances. I unpacked the clothes Naruto had been wearing on the hike. I left them beside the pond on the off chance he transitioned back into human form. I slowly returned inside to try to get some rest. At the moment, I wasn't going to be of good use to anyone if I didn't stop and sleep.

I laid down on Naruto's couch, propped a couple of cushions under my legs to elevate them, then placed one under my head with the other over it to reduce the daylight glare. I had finally made it. Barely able to move, I closed my eyes and drifted off into a deep sleep.

*BAM*

My body jolted with the shock of the noise. I looked around, dazed.

"What the?" I wiped the sleep from my eyes. Sitting up, I winced when I shifted my sore foot to an upright position straight into a large puddle of water.

"Naruto, fuck!" I leaped from the couch and straight to Naruto, who was flapping around on the ground. I scooped him up and began to run. My adrenaline was firing up as I flew out the back door and down the path toward the pond. I stopped just before reaching the edge and launched him into the water.

I heaved over, panting as I held my waist, trying to catch my breath.

"What on earth happened?" I asked as I watched him flit about the pond haphazardly. He wouldn't look at me.

I turned and hobbled back to the room. There were his clothes, a massive puddle of water, and the scroll. I picked it up and placed it on the coffee table. Walking around to the sofa, I sat down and stared at the golden etchings. It was impossibly beautiful. Finely marked interlinking patterns with emerald green stones encrusted on the outer edge of the handles. There had been a lot of artistic time devoted to the creation of this masterpiece. It made me wonder if the intention was to lure people into wanting to possess it, a trap of sorts. Naruto had been turned into a koi twice. Both times I suspect had something to do with his desire to read the scroll. It almost cost him his life the first time, and yet it didn't deter him from seeking the same fate the very next chance he had. When I touched it, I felt nothing.

No longer willing to let the scroll out of my sight, I tucked it under my left arm and went to the back of the house into Naruto's bedroom. I flicked through his wardrobe, found a plain white singlet top, a light checkered shirt, and some loose pants. It would have to do, I thought as I placed it all near the washbasin with the scroll balanced on top. I stripped down and jumped into the shower. The cool of the water fell onto my skin. The hot water, for some reason, wasn't kicking in. I gave myself a quick rinse and then switched off the cold all the way to see if that would encourage the hot water to flow. It didn't. Goosebumps rose on my skin as the water somehow managed to become even colder. I dipped my head under and scrubbed back and forth to wash off the sweat and grime. Satisfied that I had done enough, I shut the tap and hopped out. I grabbed a fresh towel from the open shelf above the vanity unit and scrubbed myself dry.

Once dressed, I returned to the sofa and stared at the scroll that was now propped up between two empty cups on the coffee table. I had no idea what the time was or how much sleep I managed to get before I was jolted awake. Naruto was now in his second transition as a koi. He didn't have many chances left to gamble on this scroll. The colors on the tourist brochure caught my eye. It was covered in pictures of Rainbow Falls. An image flashed before me of Daisuke climbing up the waterfall. A hot flush rose within me. I suddenly stood up and walked to the kitchen, looking in draws and cupboards for something. I shifted pots and pans, emptied draws; I was looking for a largish durable container. I went out to the garden shed and looked around, then returned inside to check the linen closet and bathroom. The only thing I could find was a medium-sized bucket and an extra-large silicone bag with a leak-proof seal. This would have to do.

I emptied mine and Naruto's pack before carefully wrapping up the scroll in a couple of tea towels. I put it in one of the packs on top of a length of rope. My body was holding this nervous energy. Still sleep-deprived, I couldn't tell whether the feeling was a sign that I was on the right track or a warning that I'm not. Still, I felt I had to try. I grabbed the brochure, the bucket, and the silicone bag and carried it out to the pond. I scooped up some water in the bucket and silicone pouch then placed it down beside me. Daisuke and Naruto watched intently as I opened the brochure and pointed to the falls.

"Daisuke, go, kuru," I said, asking him to come. He swam closer as I bent down and placed my left hand in the water.

"Shinrai," I whispered.

Daisuke swam across and hovered over the palm of my hand. I nodded my head, lifted him gently out of the water, and placed him into the bucket. Naruto began swimming about in a fury; he tried to lurch forward. I put my hand up.

"No, Naruto. This is Daisuke's scroll. I have to do this with him alone. It's too dangerous for you. Focus on transitioning into your human form. I don't want to be the one to explain to Mako that you are a koi now."

I could see bubbles rising to the surface. He was trying to say something. Fighting my compulsion to seek to understand, I turned my head away from him. It didn't matter anymore. The certainty within me was growing.

I knew I was on the right path. Carefully I picked everything up and walked at a steady pace. I grabbed the two packs, my wallet, and Naruto's car keys on my way out to the car. We were headed to the falls.

* * * * *

It took an exhausting nine-hour drive to arrive at the falls. The sun was about to set, which made me realize I had forgotten to pack my headlamp. The waterfall was backlit with globes that changed colors. This would make it easier to see during the climb. However, I still needed to find a safe way to get down to the riverbed and into the water.

Carefully I climbed through the visitor's platform onto the outside, placing my feet on the frame below. I used my foot to tap left to right to find the next length of angled steel and then stepped down. The narrow metal frame bit into the soles of my shoes that transferred a sharp pain to my feet. The additional load of carrying Daisuke in water added to the pressure as I tried to keep myself and him balanced. My right arm started to sear in protest from the vice grip I held. It had not been given a chance to recover from the hours of strain incurred from carrying Naruto. My nerves felt a little fried. There was a part of me that wanted to stop this insanity. It wasn't my journey to complete. How was I always getting entangled in these bizarre circumstances?

Thankful when I reached the bottom, I took a moment to wipe my brow, take a swig of water and compose myself. The river's edge was lined with oblong-shaped pebbles that made a crunching sound under my feet. I held the bucket up and tilted it slightly so that Daisuke could see the river.

"This is it. I hope you are ready. We're going in."

The icy cold water in the dark looked black and uninviting. By the time I reached the middle of the river, I was up to my waist in water rushing around me with my legs weighted by the currents drag. I kept my mind focused on heading toward the waterfall. Daisuke looked excited, swimming in circles inside the bucket. After a few minutes, the sensation of cold reduced, making the bite of muscle stiffness disappear. No longer finding it hard to breathe from the shock of the chill, I settled into a nice rhythm stepping with my left leg, pausing for a few seconds before shifting my right leg, and then waiting again. Each movement was intentionally executed on a slight diagonal. I continued until I reached the left edge of the riverbank, which displayed the lightest section of downpour from the waterfall.

I placed Daisuke on the edge of the bank and propped myself up, leaving my legs in the water. The pull of the flow dragged at my feet with a relentless rumble of bubbles popping all around them. I glanced up at the backlit waterfall, feeling the cool of the mist spray on my face.

"We have to get up there, my little friend," I said, pointing at the top of the fall. I knew that he didn't understand what I was saying but judging by his mannerism, I assumed that he was aware of what we were about to embark on. Daisuke was positioned at the tip of the bucket, looking up at the fall too.

Ten minutes had passed. It was enough time to rest my legs and also to gain a chill. My body was starting to shiver, a solid signal that I needed to get animated. I knew the ascent was approximately 394 feet with five distinct ledges along the way. I figured the best approach was to carry Daisuke up the vertical rockface and then allow him to swim the length of the rock pools on each ledge so that he was making the trip with me rather than being carried for the entire journey. If I could get him up and under the Dragons Gate, then he would be in the same space that he was when the scroll had been presented. I planned to open the scroll and allow him to read it. Something I suspect he should have done all those years ago.

"Let's go do this," I said, looking into the bucket at him.

I wrapped a small towel around the handle then secured it in place with a knot at each end before placing my left arm through it. The extra padding would help to ease the pressure. If possible, I wanted to try to restrict the climb to the far left side, where there was only minor water cascading down.

Reaching with my right hand, I felt around and tested the grip on the groove I found in the rock. I put my left foot into a nice wedge, grimaced a little at the sting in my ankle. I secured my right foot and then quickly lifted my left hand to grip the other visible groove. Daisuke and the bucket rolled down the length of my arm and whacked my rib cage. This was not going to be easy. I dropped my right leg back onto the river bank and then my left, then stepped back to reassess the situation. The bucket was too awkward to carry in the manner that I had planned. I wanted Daisuke to watch the climb, but I hadn't thought through the logistics. I needed a new plan.

Inside the left pocket of the pack, I grabbed the bag that I used to carry Naruto. Bending down, I swooped some water from the river into it then placed Daisuke inside. I emptied the water from the bucket and positioned the silicon bag in the bottom. Once it settled,

I grabbed my water container and topped up Daisuke's temporary home to ensure the bag held a shape that allowed him to move about freely. I shifted the scroll from the main compartment in the pack to the side zipper. The scroll's new position meant some potential discomfort for my back, but I figured it was better than a water bucket slamming into my ribs.

Removing the towel from around the handle, this time, I wrapped it over the mouth of the bucket and secured it with some rope. I widened the pack just enough to place the bucket inside and then did up the side zippers as high as possible to ensure it was snug. At least this would leave both my hands free, and if I did fall, the bucket would hopefully help reduce the impact. There wasn't much else I could think of doing with the materials I had on hand. It was time to recommence the climb.

My strategy was simple, lead with my right arm and left leg and then alternate midway through the climb to lead with my left arm and right leg. The rocks were porous, which benefited a rookie know-nothing climber like me. The section I had selected to climb had the advantage of not being built up with moss. There were patches where a hanging vine displayed its large ivy-shaped leaves that bounced with the impact of the water trickling down. I imagine during the monsoon season; it would struggle to maintain its precarious position under the weight of a more relentless flow.

I readjusted the straps on my pack, tightened the waist and chest strap, took a few deep breaths to get myself ready, and began the ascent. Just as I had done before, I scanned and used the most obvious jugs to hold myself securely to the rock. It didn't take long for my heart to be pumping. The soft baby tips of my fingers were alive with heat. My mind was laser-focused on getting up to the top as quickly as I can manage. One move methodically achieved after the next, I made it to the first ledge and then went straight onto climbing toward the second. My hands were getting micro-cuts with wrinkles beginning to appear from the exposure to water. I was quickly starting to realize why climbers kept their nails short. The pressure I felt from my fingers was hard to fathom. They cramped in protest, forcing me to stop on the third ledge for a break.

Sitting on the edge with my legs dangling down, I shook my hands, then wrists and arms to release the tension. I was overthinking my moves, adding too much emphasis on my hand grips. Given the burn in my arms, I would need to look at trying to find heartier footings that transferred the weight more to my legs. This was not a straightforward climb. There were plenty of places to grip but the rock wall thus far presented as a sheer vertical, which required core strength that I didn't possess.

After executing some deep breathwork, I felt better and decided to tackle the remainder of the climb. There wasn't that much left to go. Three ledges down, two more to conquer, and then the final stretch to the top of the waterfall. My fingers and toes tingled as images began to flash like an old slide reel in a viewfinder. My mom, dad, and brother all appeared in the form of a hang man's death mask. I shook my head to discard what was presented and refocused on the climb. A sudden surge of untapped strength aided my ascent. Moving up felt like I was leaving the parts that no longer served me behind. The grinding ache I held onto so tightly was releasing its vice grip from my core. Unsure of what was happening, I trusted the sensation of release and surged upward.

Reaching the fourth ledge was more effortless than any of the others I had done thus far. There were enough footholds available for me to comfortably leverage my lower body strength. My ankle was still raw from injury, so I was thankful for the cool of the water. It helped to numb the sensitivity. I dreaded the final ascent to the fifth ledge. I knew it would take its toll. The rock face seemed to have a vast number of sharp offcuts on the surface that threatened to cut my legs and arms like a hot knife to butter. I didn't possess enough coordination and strength to hold myself off the rock. Each move entailed dragging my body against the face of this unforgiving section. By the time I managed to drag myself up and onto the final ledge, I was covered in fine slithers of open wounds. Little strings of blood beaded to the surface then ran down to pool at the end of the cut before dripping free.

Grateful to be standing on the final ledge, I looked down. Even if the water was frozen in place, I still can't imagine how Daisuke, with no arms or legs to aid him, was able to get to the top of this fall. It seemed impossible.

Exhausted, sore, and cold to the core, I felt myself begin to shiver uncontrollably. I waded through the shallow pool until I reached the final portion of the rock face. Once again, I took the time to inhale and exhale a series of deep breaths before reaching my right arm up to wedge my fingers into position. The water cascaded down my left leg as I raised it to the footing. My forearms were burning in protest. Knowing I was almost at the top didn't make the remaining climb any more manageable. I gritted my teeth, releasing grunts of displeasure with every new placement. In my mind, I was chanting over and over, 'I can do this, I can do this, I can do this.'

Attempting to climb over the top of a waterfall is not for the faint-hearted. Several times I lost my footing and could feel myself slipping. In a final thrust, I engaged my arms to carry the bulk of my weight as I swung my right foot over the fall. Pushing off my left leg against the wall, I lifted my upper body over and into the river. My face welcomed the flush of cold water splashing about. I took a mouthful in swirling it around, then spat it out. I had made it. Inside my backpack, I could feel Daisuke moving about. Doing my best to maintain my balance, I stood up in the waist-high water, then slid the pack to the front to remove him.

"This is it. We do the last section together." I said as I tried to catch my breath.

I untied the bag and placed the opening just beneath the surface facing the dragon's gate. The water rushed in to greet Daisuke, who responded by swimming with earnestness to maintain his position. Stepping forward slowly, I kept Daisuke in front of my body. He stayed in the bag and shifted with the momentum. Chills from the rapid frothing water around me caused my system to shiver. The closer we got to our destination, the deeper the water became. I clenched my teeth and pressed on. We were moments away from the goal.

Daisuke jutted out from the confines of the plastic bag and began to thrash as he fought against the increasing current. I tried to keep behind him at pace. His increasing speed made it difficult to contend. I watched as Daisuke made a determined dash on his own across the threshold of the dragon's gate. The water bubbled around to consume him in a way that looked to be forcing his unwilling descent. Then he was gone. All around me, the river stilled to a pace that made it feel as though it was frozen in time. The surface became like glass producing a mirror reflection of the blackened sky. I continued to move toward the gate with my mind blown by the water's mysterious change in state. It displayed no visible disturbance. Captivated like a child witnessing my first magic show, I continued toward the gate. Poking my finger in the water was like submerging into a freshly set jello shot without the wobble. It was surreal.

Just at the point of cross-over, I felt myself hesitate. Pausing for a second, I closed my eyes and breathed in deep before taking the final step that positioned me directly under the power center of the gate. Almost immediately, a dizzying sensation of energy began to exchange between myself and the surrounding elements. The air tasted sweet as I inhaled lifeforce and exhaled a fragrant tart residue of stagnancy. There was a euphoria to engaging in the interchange that was strengthening my body as I felt my wounds heal. The sound of bubbling water made me force my unwilling eyes to open. The vibrancy and saturation of the colors overwhelmed my senses as I glared at the impossible black night sky now lit up with a vivid range of deep blue hues. The leaves on the trees lining the riverbank twinkled with flicks of lime green light. Everything was different, more alive, breathtakingly beautiful.

My hands and arms were covered in droplets of black sticky ooze that emanated from my pores. I dipped my hands in the water, wiping it away with ease. I splashed my face, neck, and upper arms too. The blood coursing through my veins was flowing with an electrical charge that made my nerve endings tingle. For the first time in my life, I felt truly alive. Greedily I filled my lungs to capacity, held my breath while looking forward at the rising pool of bubbles ahead of me. There was a twist in the water as it swirled upward. It continued until I released my breath. Synchronized to the millisecond, the shield of bubbling water succumbed to gravity. It fell away to reveal a magnificent shimmering Golden Dragon that towered way above the peak of the golden gate.

"Daisuke," I said with a gasp.

The dragon looked down at me with its eyes glaring, then softened in recognition as he tilted his head in a respectful bow. Slowly, I unzipped the pack's side pocket, pulled out the plastic bag that contained the scroll, and tore it open. Daisuke readjusted his footing and bent his head lower. In turn, I positioned my left hand on the top of the scroll, held it up horizontally, and began to unfold it with my right hand. Placing it as high as I could manage, I stood perfectly still to allow him to fulfill his long-awaited destiny by reading the content of the scroll. His breath simulated the response the moon has on the ocean by creating an effect of ebb and flow with every inhale and exhale. The small waves passed around me, then returned, pulling my body in a way that felt like it was encouraging me to cross over the gate. Consciously I quietly acknowledged that a small part of me wanted to.

My body felt a jolt as the claws of the Golden Dragon appeared, then swiftly snatched the scroll from my grasp. Providing no resistance, I had opened my hands to release the scroll. I watched as he scrunched it with force. Crumpled it into the shape of a ball, the dragon opened his mouth, swallowing it whole. The ball emanated a light source that shone through his skin. Traveling down to the center of his body, I watched it stop at a midpoint in his chest. The light began to pulse and grow. For a moment, there was an eerie silence where everything once again became still. I witnessed in awe as the light grew larger and stronger with each beat. There was a vibrance that made the golden luminosity of his scales fade in comparison. A part of me wanted to reach out and touch the light. It was hypnotic.

Once again, I found myself caught off guard as the dragon released an almighty roar that shook everything around us. A continual stream of light was shooting out of his mouth, upwards into the sky for hundreds of feet far beyond my ability to comprehend its full measure. The light source seemed to rise until it hit an invisible barrier causing a shift in direction. The beam was moving upward and extending outward into a convex. The altered display felt similar to standing within the underside of an umbrella. The sky lit up brighter than any sunny day I had ever seen. There was a purity to the almost blinding luminosity. The movement could be detected everywhere I looked, a sway and pulse responding to the magnetic draw of this field of energy that had been released. Something extraordinary was happening. I imagined it being a shift in the axis between energy extremes finding new positions of balance. I could tell by the way I was inexplicably sensing a connection to the blades of grass, the trees, and the light itself that positive change was likely imminent. Spreading his magnificent wings, the dragon without a sound launched out of the water and upward toward the sky. He followed the path of the light and disappeared out of sight. An unexpected tear rolled down my cheek as I felt this extraordinary experience move me.

THUD

I gasped as the water splashed up into the air and fanned out wide into a fine mist as it gently returned to the water.

"Daisuke." I said, lunging forward to place my hands underneath his naked, limp body while raising him back toward the surface. Balancing my left hand to support his back as I used my right to lift his head so he could see me. "I will get you some help; hang in there. Please hold on." I said frantically, trying to readjust his visibly broken body in a better position. He slowly raised his wavering right arm to press his hand against the side of my face. At that moment, the familiarity of his touch stilled me as I looked into his partially opened eyes.

In a breathless whisper, he said, "Watashi was anata ni kansha shite imasu."

I leaned into his hand, nodding my head as tears streamed down my face. He told me he was grateful for my assistance. I wanted to thank him for everything he had sacrificed, for his bravery, but I couldn't find my voice or the words. Instead, I started to sob uncontrollably as I watched the life drain from his eyes. Feeling his hand go limp just before he broke contact made me transition to an inconsolable mess. I placed my head on Daisuke's chest and cried the ugly-faced cry of a heart that has yearned to love and aches from the pain of waiting.

The water around his body began to bubble as I felt a current whirling circle's around mine, trying to draw us apart. I fought to hold on, using all my strength to resist the pull. I wasn't ready to let go. We had only just found each other. This wasn't happening, not again, not to us. I howled with grief as a jolt of energy forced my grasp to weaken. Through tear-stained eyes, I watched Daisuke begin to sink, then hauntingly fade away. The light in the skies dimmed, returning to darkness, and once again, just like that, I was all alone again.

# Requiem

Standing alone at the foot of the wedded tree located behind the Monastery on Mount Tsukaba, I stared down at the blank eba in my hands. After my experience at the river, I found myself compelled to send out a long overdue message into the universe to the love of all my lifetimes, my ethereal twin flame. I instinctually knew it was time to redirect my attention to finding my one souls' compliment, to begin the task of reuniting our energies. The dragons gate unblocked my chi, to interconnect my vibration with everything. I could feel that now on the deepest of levels. The Interferons relied on creating an environment filled with distractions and disparity. My new interconnection with the infinite provided crystal clarity. An intangible knowing that I was in the right place for the right reason. All that I had done, experienced and chosen had led me to where I needed to be despite the crooked paths the Interferons created to dislodge my journey.

I retrieved the felt-tipped pen from my pocket, crouched down to place the wooden eba on my knee, and began to write.

*'Twin Flame see me as I now see you, my one. Our unity is binding, Our love everlasting. Seek me as I seek you, no matter the time, distance, or cost. We belong. Let us feel our path toward one another and unite ad infinitum. My love for you eternally flows soul deep. Always in all ways for Always.'*

I read the words repeatedly like a mantra, wishing the energy of the moment to travel across the planes. I imagined it reaching my twin flame, providing reassuring energetic vibrations that I am on the right path toward our union. Nothing else mattered. I knew with every cell within my being; this is my soul purpose.

Pushing with my right hand, I rose to stand. Slowly I walked around the tree, looking up and down until I spied a knot that looked big enough to stick the eba in. Placing the edge of the eba in my mouth, I used both my hands and feet to carefully climb up the trunk until I was a few feet off the ground and right in front of the opening. I turned my head to the side and put the eba three-quarters of the way into it. Reshuffling my footing to a stronger position, I gripped with my thighs for added security. Using my right hand, I pushed the eba as deep as the hole allowed, then tilted until I felt it was tightly wedged into place. Satisfied, I made my way down the trunk.

There was a stinging sensation that stemmed from my left ankle and ran up my leg. I realized a bushel of ants were manically running in different directions on top of my clothes and underneath attacking me. I quickly stomped my foot on the ground to encourage them to drop, then brushed the remainder off with my hands. The sting from the bites held a sharp pain from the toxin released under the surface of my skin. Backing away from the base of the tree, I took off my pants, turned them inside out, and vigorously shook them. There were still a couple on my leg that I promptly flicked off. Not wanting to be bitten again encouraged my attention to be laser-focused on ensuring there were no more stragglers left on my pants. After a thorough validation that they were all removed, I turned my pants the right way out and put them back on.

I looked up at the knotted hole in the wedded tree, clasped my hands in the prayer position touching my lips with the tips of my fingers. I closed my eyes, then bowed as I whispered, "Find me."

* * * * *

The front door to my accommodation was slightly ajar. I pushed it open and entered.

"What are you doing here?" I asked Mako, who was sitting on the sofa staring at the box of burner cell phones he found.

"Who are you, and what have you done with my brother? He has not returned my calls. I've been to his home. He is not there, and the family golden koi is missing."

I closed the door and sat in the recliner. "I can explain."

"I came here looking for you, looking for answers." He frowned, "All these phones. Only criminals use burners."

Calmly I responded, "I'm not a criminal. For personal reasons, I've been cautious of ensuring that I am not easily found. Your brother wanted me to help him locate the golden scroll that was hidden in a cave."

Mako glared at me, "It's impossible to find something that doesn't exist."

"What? I don't understand. You told Naruto that your father made you promise to convince him of his destiny. He said you believed in the legends. That his webbed feet were."

"His webbed feet are a throwback congenital disability that skips generations. The story was created to make the children who bore the deformity feel special rather than freaks, nothing more."

"What about Daisuke? Naruto told me you play games with him."

"I promised my father and brother that I would look after the koi pond in their absence. They embellish the involvement I have to satisfy their delusions. The golden koi is unique, and at times it almost felt like it had human qualities, but I know that isn't real. Where is Naruto?"

I shook my head, "There's nothing I can say that you will believe. It is all too impossible to describe without possessing faith that what I am telling you is the truth."

"Tell me where my brother is?"

"He transformed into a koi as a consequence of touching the dragon's scroll. I put him in the koi pond. The scroll seemed to trigger the transformation."

Footsteps approached. The front door was unlatched and swung open.

Mako jumped to his feet and ran forward with his arms open, "Brother, I feared the worst." He wrapped his arms around Naruto.

"Where have you been? I thought something horrible had happened to you," asked Mako as he stepped back to look at him.

"I'm okay, brother. Harper saved my life. Twice." He turned his head to look at me. "Are you okay?"

I nodded.

"Saved your life? How? I don't understand. When were you in danger?"

"If you sit down, Naruto and I can explain. This time you need to listen and trust that we have no reason to lie to you."

"Come, let's sit." Naruto guided Mako back to the sofa where they sat side by side.

I looked across at Naruto. "Are you okay?"

"Yes. Thanks to you. I'm fine now."

"What happened," asked Mako, who was impatiently waiting.

Naruto turned to Mako. "Father was right. The legend was true. With Harper's help, we uncovered the map and found the dragon scroll. I was converted to a koi twice. Both times I was a fish out of water, literally. Harper placed me in water and saved my life."

"Where is the scroll? Show it to me."

Naruto looked over at me. "Do you have it?"

I shook my head, "No. I knew the second time you transformed from human to koi that you weren't able to touch it without consequence. That's why I carried Daisuke up the river of rainbows and had him pass through the dragon's gate so that he may reclaim his rights to read the scroll."

"What happened?"

"The rivers rose, consumed Daisuke, and then returned him to dragon form. I unraveled the scroll; he read it, ate it, and released a significant amount of light that lit up the skies. It was so bright; night became day."

Mako adjusted his position to lean forward, "Wait, do you mean to tell me that you caused the global energy phenomenon recorded by the scientists?"

"No, not me. It was Daisuke and the dragon scroll. What did the scientists say happened?"

"They are claiming a light anomaly encompassed the full circumference of the earth's exosphere. A burst of powerful energy."

"Exosphere? I don't know what that is." I responded.

"I know what this is. It's bullshit. You are latching onto the event and making some elaborate story to hide the fact that you drugged my brother and stole the golden koi. I've no doubt it's worth a fortune on the black market and an easy sell for a criminal like you."

"Mako, no. Stop this. Harper isn't a criminal. She saved my life. I did transition into a koi twice and was rescued by her twice. I believe what she is saying is true. I was the one who asked for her help and insisted she stay."

Mako picked up a handful of phone parts. "Wake up; that's what she wants you to think. You're playing into her hand by believing that any of this was your idea. Her masterful manipulations blind you. I found all these burner phones hidden in a box under the sofa. She is clearly up to something."

I released a sigh. "I'm telling the truth. The dragon flew into the sky, following the stream of light, and what felt like milliseconds later, Daisuke, in human form, came crashing down to his death. He fell with such speed that the water became concrete. His body was broken. He died in my arms before the river claimed him."

"What a load of rubbish."

"ENOUGH," yelled Naruto. "The legend is true. I may not be able to convince you, but I will not tolerate another negative word spoken toward Harper." He grabbed his brother's hand and placed it on his heart. "I swear on my own life and that of my wife and children. Everything that has been said is true."

Mako looked into Naruto's eyes and nodded. "Okay. I'll listen."

Naruto acknowledged Mako's words and then shifted his attention back to me. "How did you know what to do?"

"I didn't. When I found you in the cave converted to a koi, my instincts to protect and survive took over. I suspected the scroll was able to read a person's intentions. Mine was to retrieve the scroll for Daisuke. You wanted to retrieve it for yourself to claim it through ancestorial entitlement. It was only when I found you the second time in your living room flapping about as a koi that I realized you had converted to human form and tried to touch the dragon scroll again. Am I right?"

"Yes. I became obsessed with a desire to read it. The minute my hand touched it, I lost control of my body and found myself panic-stricken flapping about gasping for air."

"The second time confirmed how important it was to have the right person read the contents. I somehow knew there was a need to return to the place of origin. I had no idea that Daisuke would transform into the dragon or that he would eat the scroll, for that matter. It was all so surreal, and yet..." I looked down at my hands as I clasped them together.

"What?"

Naruto and Mako both waited for my response.

"I recognized that it was meant to be, buying the kimono, coming here, unfolding the truth's hidden within the legend. I'd lost my way in this life, challenged by untenable circumstances that made it almost impossible to breathe. Yet, I have acquired the knowledge that provides me no hesitation of a doubt that I was the only one who could touch the dragon's scroll without consequences. When Daisuke returned to human form, I recognized he was the one I entered this life to find, to free. This part of my destiny is now fulfilled."

"Are you saying you and Daisuke are somehow connected?"

I nodded. "We are. For a long time, I thought I had been abandoned or lost to him, but he was here all along, waiting for me to be ready to find him. To feel him."

Naruto, "Interconnectedness? Like karma?"

"Interconnected, yes, not karma. What we have runs soul deep. I felt the scroll presented the golden dragon a choice, and he chose the selfless option. Instead of accepting what was on offer for himself, the dragon provided the gift to the world. An opportunity to restore balance, perhaps even heal. He bound his lifeforce with that of the scroll and released it into the atmosphere. It cost him his life."

Naruto leaned forward, "So you believe that Daisuke needed to do this to fulfill his destiny?"

I shook my head, "I'm not sure whether Daisuke would have made the same choice if he read the scroll when he first became the dragon. The time he spent in the koi pond, the centuries of waiting may have provided an influence that drove him to sacrifice himself for the greater good. None of us can ever know the answer. All that truly matters is that he received his chance to read the scroll and chose the selfless path. This one-act placed him in favor as he passed the test of three of the seven deadly sins."

"You've lost me. I've heard of the seven deadly sins, but what has that got to do with what happened? I've never heard it referenced before."

"There are a series of universal truths. One of them revolves around the purpose of life. We all are subject to the test of sins. Lifetimes reborn to run the subconscious gauntlet of the biblical seven until we complete them all. Only then can we traverse the pure path toward enlightenment. All souls are born to cycle repeatedly until we conquer the intended sin. I know through my energy exchanged with Daisuke that he released all binds to pride, greed, and wrath."

"What sin was I born to face?"

"I don't know Naruto. It's not for me to say."

"I have so many questions. How can you be certain that he conquered all these sins? What does it all mean?"

"He and I are connected. I know his binds were released. I felt them dissipate. Pride was linked to his obsession with crossing the golden gate. He was selfish in his desire to complete the quest. He wanted to be the one to achieve the goal and was not willing to relinquish his chance to make it happen. A life filled with the love of his wife and children was sacrificed for a chance at glory. Greed fueled his pursuit. He believed the rewards and riches he imagined came with the inevitable conquest would outweigh the toll his loved ones paid by his absence. Wrath became his state as he indulged his fury over being trapped in the form of a koi. Robbed of his imagined entitlements, he could not see past his anger to recognize he was in a life of his own making. The only way to break the cycle was through selfless sacrifice. I made mine by entering this life to find him. He, in turn, made his choice to give back to the world with gratitude in his heart instead of claiming his long-awaited fortune. Daisuke is now free."

Mako stood up and made his way to the door, "I don't know what to make of all of this. I mean, I want to believe you both, I do. It's just too much for me to process. Years of listening to what I thought was dad's nonsense, and now this. I'm not sure if you are both sharing the same delusion or whether it's all real. Either way, I am relieved that you are safe, brother. I need to get back to work. Will you come by for dinner tonight?"

Naruto gave Mako a reassuring smile, "Sure. Tonight."

"Harper, you are welcome to join us too if you like," said Mako.

"I appreciate the offer, but I have somewhere else I need to be. Thanks anyway."

"You're not leaving, are you?" Asked Naruto with an air of concern in his voice.

"Yeah. I am."

Mako placed his hand on my left shoulder, "Please don't go because of me. You are welcome to stay. I may not understand everything that's happening, but I do know you are a good person. It was wrong of me to suggest otherwise."

I placed my right hand on top of Mako's and squeezed it. "I'm overdue to be somewhere and feel a sense of urgency about it. I had already planned to leave before I realized that you were here waiting to ambush me. We're good. I promise."

"The invitation is there if you change your mind, I'd love to have you join us."

"Thanks."

"See you tonight, brother," Mako left, closing the door behind him.

"Why do you have to leave?"

"Why do you need me to stay?" I replied.

"I don't know. We've been through so much together. To have you leave now feels like a loss. You saved my life."

"Twice." I said with a smile.

Naruto released a little laugh, "Yes, twice. Don't go, Harper. Stay a while longer. There are so many places you haven't seen that I could show you. My wife and the kids are coming next week. I'd love for you to meet them."

"I can't. This experience has revealed to me the truth about everything I have ever needed to know, and it has changed the course of my life. I came to Japan feeling lost, depleted from the pain I accrued throughout my quest. I felt I was blind; I had no answers and believed I was wandering aimlessly. The dragon's gate showed me what I had unconsciously done was disarm my mind by trusting only in my instincts. Without being aware, I was taking each step with internalized faith. Standing under that power source, I re-engaged and cleared blockages I never knew I had. My full flow of chi has been restored as well as my access to the knowledge I need. My path is clear. I know what I must do and have to be on my way."

I stood up, "It's time for you to let me go and wish me well on my journey."

"Will, I ever see you again?"

"No."

"That seems harsh. Couldn't we stay in touch, email occasionally, maybe catch up for coffee when we're both back home? Why does it have to be so final?"

"Where I'm headed, none of this is going to be possible." I walked over to him. "Stand up and give me a cuddle."

Naruto stood, wrapped his arms around me, and squeezed tight. He took deep breaths and exhaled with a gentle wisp of a sigh as he guided our bodies to sway, "I'm never going to forget you, Harper."

"Nor I you."

* * * * *

I felt some small measure of reservation as I entered through the open gates of the Moto family home. Only recently, the Toyama streets were saturated with residents who walked with their heads down, living in fear. To return to see the front gates into homes unlocked, the air carrying the sounds of children playing in the laneways presented me with a resurgence of hope.

"Momma, momma, she's back," yelled Atsuko as she came running with her arms expanded while wearing the biggest smile. Latching herself to my waist with her head buried into my stomach, she muffled, "I missed you."

Reaching down, I placed my hands under her armpits to lift her. Atsuko happily put her spindly arms around my neck and clasped her hands. We walked into the front entrance as one.

"Harper san, you have returned," said Kimiko as she came over to greet me.

"Hai. I am here to say goodbye."

"You leaving Japan?"

"No, momma, she is staying with us," said Atsuko with confidence.

I laughed, "She gets that look from you."

Kimiko smiled, "Hai, so desu."

I bent down to release Atsuko. "Let go, little monkey."

"No."

I tickled her sides, "I don't want to drop you. Let go."

"No," she replied, wriggling about.

"Atsuko," said her mother in a sweet but stern tone.

She released my neck long enough for me to take the opportunity to stand up, then responded by quickly grabbing my right hand with a vice grip. I laughed. When Atsuko realized I wasn't going to protest, she readjusted her fingers to be intertwined with mine and began to swing our arms gently.

Kimiko smiled as she looked at both of us. "I sorry, she miss you. Ask for you every day."

"It's perfectly fine. How is Futoshi?"

"Hiro at school to bring Futoshi home. Come, I prepare supper."

I followed Kimiko into the kitchen. "Futoshi is at school?"

Her face lit up. "Yes. He and other children in special school."

"That's great. Is Okaasan here?"

"No. Go home," she paused to look at her fingers. Then held up two of them at me, "Come back."

"Two days."

"Hai, so desu. Two days."

"Ah, that's a shame. I would have liked to have seen her to say goodbye. Have you heard from Roman?"

"He no return."

Roman was still M.I.A. I'd asked my team to help trace his financial footprint, but he seemed to be intentionally off the radar. At least, I hoped that was the case. I had no way to confirm if he was okay, and I was running out of time to do anything more about it.

"Things seem to be better now in Toyama."

Kimiko was expertly using a sharp cleaver to chop a bunch of chives. "Yes. Better. Children home, no more secreto. Village come together. Protect, fight for children. Bad people must go."

"Has there been anyone caught or group blamed for what happened?"

Kimiko stopped chopping, "No. Children in Romania, take from family."

"Romania? Children were stolen in Romania. When?" Kimiko shrugged her shoulders.

"The same way?"

"Hai, I believe so. Masso grave, many, many children. People go. Here old story."

I released a sigh as I squeezed little Atsuko's hand. "Not good. I'm sorry to hear that. At least people around the world are aware and can help to seek the truth. This evil can't remain in hiding forever. Someone knows something."

"Kon'nichiwa Harper san," said Hiro with a welcoming smile.

"Hello Hiro san, Kon'nichiwa Futoshi chan, and this is?"

"Eiji."

"Kon'nichiwa Eiji chan." I said to the boy, who responded by correcting his posture to stand upright and firm in his frame.

"He's the boy from the woods. The one whose ankle I helped to mend."

Kimiko smiled and began to speak softly, "Hai. He no have family. We take care. Children happy together."

I gazed down at Atsuko, "Looks like you have another brother."

"We play lots of games," she said enthusiastically.

"Great."

"Please join for supper. I make bed. You to stay, no trouble."

"Thanks, Kimiko, but I need to get going. I just wanted to come and see how you all are before I leave the country."

"Stay for eat. I take after, after," offered Hiro.

"No, I've hired a driver to transport me to Tokyo, Narita airport. It's a six-hour drive, maybe seven. I've left just enough time to relax a little before my flight. I appreciate the gesture. Thank you."

Hiro bowed, "Okay."

"I wanted to check before I go if there is anything else you need? I can organize some financial support to help with Eiji's expenses."

Kimiko responded before Hiro could, "You do too much. Money no need. We okay."

"Please take no offense to my offering. I only want to help," I said, conscious that pride is an integral part of the culture.

"Berry kind. Good heart. Okay, no need money."

I smiled and nodded my head. "Well, I guess this is it. Thank you for helping me when I was not myself and trusting me to assist you with Futoshi."

"You honor us. Harper part of Moto family," said Hiro as he clasped his hands and bowed.

Bowing in response, I wanted to convey my thanks and let them know that the honor was all mine. "Meiyo wa watashi no mono desu. Dōmo arigatōgozaimashita," I completed my decisive tilt with a final nod of my head, then began to make my way toward the front gate with Atsuko still glued to my side. The rest of the clan followed closely behind.

Crouching down, I wrapped my hands around Atsuko's slender frame. "You are a very special girl. Please tell your grandmother that I am grateful to her for saving me, for believing in me."

Her head pressed down on my shoulder. With gentleness in my heart, I pried Atsuko slowly away so that we could see each other. Her cheeks were lined with wet trails from her tears. "I need to go. You keep an eye on your brothers and be good to your parents. Will you tell your grandmother goodbye from me?"

She inhaled deeply and shook her head, "I will."

Collecting a singular tear as it began its descent from her left eye, I whispered, "Thank you for everything, little one."

Returning to a stance, I stepped backward, out into the street while looking at all of them for one last time. They stood in silence. My heart was filled with love and absolute gratitude. Within seconds my driver, who had been waiting a few houses down, skillfully positioned the vehicle behind me. Before he could vacate his position, I swiftly turned, opened the door for myself, and entered the backseat. Rolling down the window, I placed my hand out and waved as the car pulled away.

I was ready to go.

* * * * *

As the wheels bounced from hitting the tarmac, I opened my weary eyes and stared out the window. Rarely did I dip into the riches I had accrued to indulge in luxury spoils with the exception of flying first class on this long-distance flight. I didn't care for the fancy champagne or food. It was all about reducing jet lag supported through creature comforts and the attractive prospect of gaining some sleep quality. My thirteen-hour flight passed by pleasurably. I'd not managed a solid rejuvenating slumber like this in a very long time.

The hostess opened the door to my private cabin.

"Good morning Ms. Perelle. We will be ready to escort you off the plane in approx. three minutes. Your bags will be delivered to the customs area on your behalf, so the driver will bypass the luggage carousels and take you straight there."

"Great, thanks." I released an unexpected yawn while stretching my arms.

She closed the door behind her.

I placed my carry-on bag on the table, reached in, and grabbed my phone to switch it on. One of the perks of flying out of Tokyo is the access to purchase the latest global technology. This high-end encryption device is guaranteed to be un-hackable, untraceable, and bulletproof. It wasn't cheap, but if the specs are accurate, then I didn't care. Some of the technology features were far in advance of what is known and available on the market. I had an inkling that I would be ultra-glad in my investment. Obtaining, activating, and carrying disposable phones was a painful process.

*Ping.*
*Ping.*
*Ping.*
*Ping.*
*Ping.*

Texts from my team were coming through.

*Message 1: The dossier on him is attached. We also found out his wife's name is Collette. We are tracking down the address of their place in central London.*

*Message 2: Top three routines: Runs locally around the park from 6 am to 7 am. Coffee shop by 8 am. Reads the paper for 30 mins. Every Thursday, he has an ongoing reservation for 7:30 pm at an Italian café called Il Solito Posto. It's the back corner booth on the window side overlooking the courtyard garden.*

*Message 3: We have secured a rental in their building for you to stay in. The landlord is expecting you today to collect the keys. The furniture rental company has delivered and decorated the space. The photos are attached. You're all set.*

*Message 4: As requested, I have emailed you an updated last will and testament. All the assets, stocks, and bonds are listed. Just fill in the blanks, get it notarized and lodge it.*

*Message 5: The invitations for drinks have been placed under the doors of the neighbors. The catering company will be arriving midday tomorrow to do the food prep and provide the complete service. The cocktail specialist will be there at 6 pm. The alcohol and mixers have been ordered and will be delivered to the catering company in the morning. Everything is set.*

The door opened.

"We are ready for you, Ms. Perelle," said the hostess.

"Thanks." I stood up, placed my phone inside my bag, and walked past the lady and down the narrow aisle toward the exit where I could see the flight captain and head hostess were waiting. The captain had an electric smile flashing his recently bleached teeth.

"Thank you for flying with us. I hoped you enjoyed the flight," he said as he oddly clicked the heels of his black highly polished shoes together.

The head hostess chimed in with a melodic, "Welcome to London." Slight marks on the inside of her shirt collar gave away the secret that her tan was derived from a synthetic source.

"Everything was great. Thanks a bunch."

I walked across the bridge and into the airport's main foyer, where a driver in a cart was waiting for me. As much as I would have appreciated the opportunity to stretch my legs, I equally wanted to get ahead of the other travelers.

"Hello, this is me," I said, pointing at the sign that had my name on it.

"Welcome to London, Ms. Perelle. Your bags are being collected and taken straight to customs. I'll take you there now."

"Thank you," I said, getting into the passenger side.

The driver clicked on a flashing light, looked over his right shoulder to confirm he was clear before putting his foot to the peddle and zooming off.

"This thing has some speed. I'm surprised your hat stays on," I said, impressed with how quickly we were moving.

The man grinned, "I'd like to go faster, but it's peak hour, so I can't show you what she can really do." He leaned forward and patted the console.

"For safety reasons, I wouldn't have thought it would be designed to go so quick."

"It's used for emergencies too. That's when I'm allowed to let her stretch her legs. She has a warning call similar to the sound of an ambulance that automatically engages when I go above a certain speed."

"Ah. Fair enough."

"We've arrived. Just head through those doors and to the priority counter. Your things will be there."

"It was nice meeting you. Thanks for the ride." I jumped out, and before I could turn to wave, he had already pulled out and whizzed off.

Through the doors, there were rows of counters with a winding cordoned trail to follow to get to them. The place was empty, with the exception of myself and the customs officers waiting at the booths. To the far right, there was a sign above a single booth marking it the priority lane. A length of red carpet led straight to the booth. I walked across to the counter.

"Please stand on the line and stare into the camera."

I looked down, stepped back to have my feet on the yellow line, then looked into the lens of the camera, trying not to be distracted by the flashing red indicator on the left.

"Okay, thank you. Please pass me your customs card, boarding pass, and passport."

I slid them across to her.

She opened the passport, looked at me, then the photo that had just been taken. Placing the passport down on a scanner, she started to type something on the screen.

"How long are you planning to stay in the United Kingdom, Ms. Perelle?"

"I'm not sure."

She stopped and looked directly at me.

"What is your reason for visiting?"

"I'm on holiday. I just spent a few months in Japan and decided that it would be nice to kick off my next leg of my travels with an English-speaking country before I head over to other parts of Europe. I don't have an itinerary."

"I can see you have listed your address for your accommodation. How long do you plan to stay there?"

Her eyes narrowed. She was looking for facial queues to detect whether I was nervous or lying.

"I've secured the apartment on a short-term lease agreement for a month. Traveling around Japan was nice, but being on the move all the time has worn out its novelty. I'm looking forward to the change of pace and being surrounded by some creature comforts."

"Is there a reason you don't have a flight booked to leave?"

"I'm not sure where I want to go next. That's the only reason I purchased a one-way ticket. I'd like to explore London, go to the theatre, museums and take some day trips to visit the English countryside. From here, I may go by train to explore Scotland and Ireland or maybe head straight to Paris. I'll see."

"Okay," she said as she stamped my passport and returned it to me. "Enjoy your stay."

I grabbed the passport smiled, and politely said, "Thanks."

A fellow with a white sash with the word customs written on it stepped forward.

"Ms. Perelle?"

"Yes."

"Follow me, please. We have your bags."

"Bags? No. I only have one bag checked in, singular, one bag."

The man didn't respond. He looked straight ahead as he walked me to the counter where two customs officers stood in front of two similar-looking bags.

"This is Ms. Perelle," said the man, who then walked back to his post situated behind the booth.

"Hello, Ms. Perelle. We would like to inspect your bags. Can you unlock them for us, please?"

"I only checked in one bag." I rummaged around my carry-on bag to locate the stub. "Here, look, it states right there one bag."

The two officers looked at each other, then the man on the right asked, "Which of these two bags are yours?"

I stepped forward, "May I touch them?"

"Yes."

I rolled over the first one, then did the same with the second. I stepped back, visually compared the cases to one another before lifting them at the same time so I could feel the weight.

"Neither of them are mine. They look similar. Both of these are far heavier than the bag I checked in. I was traveling light. See, the ticket says twelve kilos."

"Weigh them," commanded the man on the left.

The other officer pulled out a portable scale from under the bench. He placed the first bag on.

"Sixteen point three kilos."

He returned it to the bench in front of me. The other officer had a frozen expression on his face. I stared directly at him to increase the pressure of the situation he found himself in. I wanted him to know without a doubt that I knew this was an attempted set-up and that he was involved. He, in response, shifted the weight from his right leg to his left. I smiled as I acknowledged the change and detected a slight tremor of muscle spasm under his right eye.

"Fifteen point eight kilos. Ms. Perelle is right. Both of these bags are heavier than what the check-in stub says."

I released a sigh, "These bags have triple line stitching, whereas mine is cross-stitched. See, look at my carry-on bag. Cross-stitched."

In an attempt to revert the pressure, the guilty customs officer stepped forward and spoke in an aggressive tone, "Both these bags have your name on them. How do you explain that?"

"I don't need to. They aren't mine. You need to find the person who owns them. These aren't mine. I have one bag that looks an awful lot like these, that weighs twelve kilos and is cross-stitched on the seams."

The muscles along his cheekbones tightened as he clenched his jaw.

"What I find odd is that someone has gone to great lengths to make it look very similar to my luggage. Mine were custom pieces that I had designed so that I could easily spot them on a carousel. The probability that someone had an almost exacting match created is a curiosity."

The officer to the left spoke softly to his colleague, "There is something suspicious about all of this. Her bags are missing from the plane's cargo hold. Neither of these bags is a match to the weight listed on the check-in stub. We need to report this."

The customs officer to the right ignored him. "Ms. Perelle. Please open the bags and confirm if you recognize any of the contents."

I stepped away from the bench, and I shook my head, "I don't have a key to unlock them because they aren't my bags."

"Get the bolt cutters. We will open them so that you can inspect the contents of each."

"What? No way. These are not my bags. If the contents hold anything from my actual luggage that this officer has acknowledged are missing, then they have been planted, which is an elaborate set-up. In fact, the more you insist on pursuing this, the further reason I have to believe you might be involved. I want to speak to a lawyer and seek legal counsel before I say or do anything further. I further request this incident be documented and witnessed by a court-recognized representative that can testify to how I am being treated."

"Take her to an interview room," barked the agitated officer.

The other fellow was startled. He looked at him and then at me. "Please follow me, Ms. Perelle."

Once we were out of earshot from the other officer, I turned my head to look at my escort. "Can you please take the lead on this investigation? I don't trust the other officer. He was acting strange, and the tone he used when he tried to get me to open the two bags after I clearly said neither of them were mine is disconcerting. I feel like I am being set up."

"I apologize, Ms. Perelle. I cannot speak to you without a witness present." He stopped in front of a frosted glass window paned door. He turned the handle and pushed it open. "Please wait here. An officer will be here to take your statement and file a report."

I walked in and turned, "I'd like to make a call to arrange legal counsel."

"Someone will be with you in a few minutes," he said as he closed the door behind me. I heard the click as he locked the door. I felt trapped.

I sat down, put my bag between my legs, and lent my forehead down on top of the table. Knowing the room was likely monitored, I wanted the observers to think I was resting. Discreetly I pulled out my phone, typed a text to my team providing context about what had happened, and requested them to secure immediate specialized legal representation to come onsite with a court-recognized scribe. I switched the phone settings to stealth mode and connected to the satellite booster function, then pressed send on the text. As soon I received confirmation, I switched off the phone, placing it back into my bag. Instead of sitting up, I propped my left arm under my head and closed my eyes to rest.

An hour had passed, and then two. My legs jiggled as commanded by my bladder that was reaching total capacity. In contrast, my mouth was parched. It was getting increasingly more difficult to maintain decorum as my patience waned.

My head lifted when I heard the lock on the door being released.

A well-groomed fellow in a dark suit opened the door. "My apologies for keeping you waiting, Ms. Perelle. You are free to go."

"Did you find my bag?"

"No. It is still unaccounted for, but we have your details and will call you as soon as it is located. Here is the pink slip for your records. It has the number of the area that looks after missing luggage."

I accepted the piece of paper, glanced down at it to review the details then looked at the gentleman. "I don't understand. What's changed? I was under some form of suspicion, and now I'm free to go? Just like that?"

"Yes. We have spoken to your lawyer, and you are free to go. I'm sorry for the delay. I'll escort you out."

"What about those two bags. Did you locate the owner? Is there an explanation as to why my name was on them?"

"I am not at liberty to say. We will have to investigate it further and will contact you if we have further questions."

"No," I said, retaking a seat. "Can you bring my lawyer in? I'd like to have a full report documented on this incident."

He looked at me slightly confused, "You are free to go. There is no report required because there isn't any incident to report. There was confusion with the bags, and your luggage is missing. The pink slip is all you need."

I smiled, "With all due respect, I have been placed under suspicion, held in an interrogation room for hours with no water or opportunity to go to the toilet. When I requested to call my lawyer, no one offered me a phone call. My lawyer turns up, and all of a sudden, I am free to leave?"

The man looked around the room. "These walls have a special paint that is designed to block cell signals. How did you manage to make a call?"

I looked at him without blinking, "How is that even relevant?"

He readjusted his stance, "Clearly, there has been a mix-up, and for that, we apologize. There is nothing more to say on the matter. You are free to go. Please allow me to escort you out of the facility."

"Bring in my lawyer and the scribe. I'd like the two customs officers to be present so that a full independent account of this incident can be recorded."

The man shook his head, "I'll be back in a minute."

It dawned on me that I may be waiting a while. My bladder screamed in protest at the thought of being locked in the room again.

"Wait. I'll come out with you. I need to go to the toilet and would like to get a bottle of water. I'll meet you back here in a couple of minutes."

He looked at me, almost hesitating.

"You said I was free to go. What's the problem?"

His expression flash changed to showcase a level of agitation before he stepped aside, allowing me to go past.

"Where are the toilets?"

"Follow the arrows. You will see a sign on your right."

"Great, thanks." Focused on holding my bladder, I walked with laser precision toward the sign and straight into the bathroom's first cubicle. Quick as a whip, I dropped my pants and sat down in the nick of time. Lost in the blissful sensation of relieving myself, I hadn't noticed the pair of shoes that appeared to stand on the outside of my cubicle door.

"The next cubicle is free," I said, knowing that it was pretty obvious this one was occupied.

There was no response.

I finished up, flushed the toilet, and stood there for a moment. Instead of opening the door, I took a photo of the pointy-tipped black and white leather shoes and used the 'locate cells near me mode to get the person's phone number on the other side of the door. My caller ID, by default, was always set to block. I sent the picture to the cell.

*Ping.*

I smiled at the idea of creating a ruse and began without further thought.

"Yes, hello, airport security, please. Thanks"

"Hi, I'm in the E4 female toilet block near customs. There is an unstable person in here who is threatening to hurt the other occupants and me. Can you get someone here, please? We have locked ourselves in a cubicle. I'm trying to lock in a proximity tracer to their cell phone so that they can be identified. Yes, great, yep, thanks. Hurry, please."

I heard the rustle of material, then a click that I suspected was them checking their phone. The shoes stepped back from view; there was a momentary pause before the person made it obvious, they were walking away. I propped myself up on the toilet seat to look over the cubicle wall. They were gone. With my heart slightly elevated, I briskly walked out of the toilet block and into the main area. I glanced around at people's shoes, looking for a match, nothing. Dialing the number, I listened out for the ringtone. When I heard it, I hung up, walked toward where I believed it was coming from, and redialed to be sure it was coming from the number I called. As I got closer, I searched the bin and the area around it.

"Excuse me, are you looking for this?"

I turned to see a lady holding out a phone that was ringing.

"Yes, thank you. Where did you find it?"

"Just over there on the seat."

"Ah, of course. It must have fallen out of my pocket. Thank you," I said as she handed it to me.

"Enjoy your day."

"Yes, thanks, you too," I said as I headed back toward the interview room.

When I arrived, the room was empty with no one else in sight.

Glancing down at the mystery person's burner phone, I scrolled the history and rang the last number. Someone answered and remained silent. The call disconnected after approximately ten seconds. I waited a moment and called again. The service message stating the number I had dialed was not in use was playing in a loop. This only confirmed to me that interferons were upping their game. They wanted me to react and get distracted by the mayhem they create around me. Their pattern of coercion and misdirection was hyper clear to me now. I was more present to the feeling of looming fight or flight and was determined not to get swept up in it again. The hero complex they fed and I thrived on fulfilling was no longer a ploy they could use on me. With this thought in the forefront of my mind, I placed the cell in a free side pocket of my bag, then turned around and followed the exit signs. It was time to focus on what I came here to do.

* * * * *

The apartment was filled with stylish pieces of furniture and creature comforts that I had previously taken for granted. High thread count sheets, velvet duvet, and plush pullover blankets to wrap myself in were of particular note. It was amazing how these little things increased my material sense of improved quality of life. Waking up to the texture of the deep purple velvet pillowcase nurturing my head was delightful. A close second was utilizing two full-sized bath sheets after my shower last night, one to wrap my hair up and the other to cocoon my body. They were luxuries I most definitely appreciated a little more since my return from Japan.

'*Beep, Beep, Beep*'

I reached across to deactivate the alarm clock, then swiftly got up. My first stop was visiting the kitchen, where I switched the percolator from standby to brew. I then made a beeline to the bank of windows in the living area. The light from the sunrise was highlighting the thick film of dust on the outside of the glass. Through the window, I saw him leave for his routine jog. I wasn't sure if I should use this as part of my ploy to meet him. I wanted to find a way to become close enough, to be sure about them both. Instead of attempting to cross paths on the running track, I opted for the idea of waiting at the café where he was known to frequent on weekdays. This refinement to my plan now gave me an extra hour and a half up my sleeve before I had to leave my cozy apartment. I grabbed a throw, wrapped it around myself, and slumped onto the sofa to ponder my next steps.

Today was a critical opportunity for me to find a way 'in.' If I could make a subliminal impression this morning, then the party already organized to meet the neighbors this evening could help to bolster his sense of familiarity. It is a trick that calculated socially functioning psychopaths use to build rapport and trust with preselected victims. Given my time constraints, I needed to leverage any method possible. The dragon's gate unblocked my access to the knowledge of my past, present, and future. I knew it all. This gift of insight, along with its burdens were crucial leverage for me to expedite through my cycle of the seven sins and, most importantly, to be able to clear the path to unite with my twin flame, my counterpart soul key.

The legends foretold a final attempter is revealed in the time of the last battle. For all that I could see, I was still blindsided regarding any details of who this is. My arch nemesis Vernon Wreath was obliterated. One more attempter was still to come. When presented, I know I have to win that battle to destroy their kind permanently. Only then can the doors of Equanon be opened by the united soul keys. My twin flame and I are destined to be the ones who fulfill the prophecy. Understanding what we need to do was revealed to me. Prior to proceeding down my willed path, I want to complete my deep need to meet them. Understanding all the moving pieces of what is yet to come, I have a small window of time to deviate. This provides me with the only real opportunity to get to know them, and I'm selfishly going to take it.

* * * * *

I was greeted with a broad smile by the barista who watched me enter the coffee shop. Walking straight over to the counter, I reciprocated before looking down at a menu secured in place under a sheet of perspex.

"I'm going to order a long, strong black coffee, please."

"You're going to, or you are?" asked the barista with a playful tone and thick English accent.

"Hmmm. Good question. I'm going to…," I replied cheekily.

"You're welcome to sit down and wave to me when you are ready." He said, using air quotes to emphasize the word ready.

Amused by the linguistic play, I glanced at the menu and then at the clock. "How about I order a savory bagel toasted with avocado together with a long black coffee in a large takeaway cup. I'm eating in. I prefer a takeaway because I drink slow." I said, shrugging my shoulders.

"Anything else?"

"Actually, yes, that's the order part over with. As for when I'll be ready, if you can start making the order at 7:58 am, then call my name so I can pick it up. That would be ideal."

The barrister turned to look at the wall clock. "You want me to wait eight minutes before I start this order? Then call your name out so that you can pick it up rather than having it delivered to your seat?" He said, raising his right eyebrow remarkably high.

"Yes. All of that. Exactly." I scrunched my nose. "Is that weird? Am I too precise?"

He switched his position so he could lean forward to whisper, "Oh Hun, that doesn't even scratch the surface of the weird I've seen."

We both laughed.

He slid a pencil and scrap of paper toward me.

"Here, write your name down, and I'll call you when it's ready."

"Great, thanks," I said as I stepped aside to let the subsequent person order.

Once I finished writing my name, I pushed the paper closer to him and went to the first free booth to take a seat. I positioned myself with a clear view of the people coming in and out of the café. My senses were tingling in anticipation of him arriving any minute.

Several people entered the café, placed their order, collected and left. Only a tiny portion of the traffic chose to dine in. A portly older gentleman was located at a booth in front of the arched redwood framed front window. He had a classic long trench coat, unbuttoned and untied at the waist. His profile reminded me of Winston Churchill minus the receding hairline, a Romeo y Julieta cigar, and a black John Bull-style hat. The lady sitting opposite him was a woman who presented an air of frailty. Perhaps I had an association bias to the visual cues, such as her grey-colored skin that was akin to crepe paper. It felt as if a strong gust of wind could make her crumble into ash.

The music playing seemed to favor UK artists. Phil Collins, Elton John, and now a remix version of

Foreigners song I want to know what love is, was gently bouncing off every crevice of this old stone building.

"Harper, your food is ready."

I looked across at the barista who was waving to get my attention.

Shuffling across the bench seat, I tucked my bag under my jacket and left it there as I walked over to pick up my order.

"Thanks."

"Did I do a good job?" He said with a wink.

"Yes, it was perfect," I said while turning with the tray.

"Oops, I'm sorry I didn't see you there," I said to him.

He replied with a jolly smile, "No problems."

"Did you spill the coffee, Harper? Can I get you a rag and a top-up?" Enquired the barista.

"No, I'm good," I responded. "Apologies again for my clumsy waitressing skills," I said to him before heading to the booth.

My heart was racing like a child entering a classroom on the first day of school. He must have arrived just as I got to the counter. It's him. It's actually him. Being in such close proximity allowed me to interconnect and feel his presence. I was tempted to look across but didn't want to risk being caught. I placed the tray down, took a sip of my coffee, and then picked up one half of the bagel and took a big bite.

Our first encounter didn't go to plan as subtly as I wanted. However, I'm confident it did the trick. Almost bumping into him is enough of a memorable event. I released a sigh and continued to eat my delicious avocado-laden bagel with my eyes firmly planted down.

He typically stayed for thirty minutes, which means I have one more opportunity to imprint my presence into his subconscious mind. As quick as my stomach would allow, I scoffed down my food and washed it down in between bites with the coffee. The roasted blend they use is far weaker than what I would typically drink. Next time I would at least know to request a double, perhaps triple shot to compensate.

Finishing the last bite, I wiped my face with the paper napkin, placed it along with everything else on the tray. Once I was standing, I put my jacket on, grabbed my clutch and the tray then went over to the counter.

"That hit the spot. Thanks."

"You didn't eat the crisps?" replied the barista.

I shook my head, "No. I thought you put them on there by mistake. Chips for breakfast, really? It seems a bit much."

"Aside from your accent, referring to crisps as chips is a tell that you are from America."

I chuckled, "Correct. What do I owe you?"

"Twelve Pounds."

I pulled out twenty from my wallet and passed it across. "Keep the change. Do you know if there is a local picture frame shop around here?"

"Does it have to be specifically a picture frame shop?"

"I guess not. Anywhere that stocks frames will do."

"If you go left from here, walk three, possibly four blocks down, you will see a string of department stores on your right. Any of those will have a small selection available."

"Great, I'II start there. It was nice meeting you." I swiveled around and walked toward the door.

"See you, tomorrow Harper."

I laughed and waved as I called out from the street, "Definitely. See you tomorrow."

Consciously or not, he would have overheard that. How positively perfect.

* * * * *

The catering team transformed the entrance and living area of my apartment with some classy neo-baroque styling. They shifted all the furniture in a layout that followed the length of the back wall and supplemented it with a long white lacquered table and ultrawide dining chairs. The large plush black and white rug they placed down was now the centerpiece of the room. It depicted a classic baroque motif that complimented the black and white runner they placed in the hall. Candelabras were everywhere a hazard-free flat surface could be identified. The long thin candles had shavings collected at the base where some were jammed into the holder. Wax drippings have already begun gathering on the brightly polished silver trays placed there to catch them. Every little detail was spectacular, right down to the table setting being finished with eye-popping turquoise Fleur De Lis insignia napkin rings that were paired against plain black linen napkins.

Right at six in the evening, the guests began to arrive. The expressions on their faces provided a solid indication that the effort from the catering team was warranted. The wait staff were in both period costume and character. Extravagant white wigs paired perfectly with their over-the-top makeup. Frilled collars joined to rich fabrics covered their bodies. The detailing in the side panels of their thick tights invited the eye to gravitate down to where the stockings were neatly tucked into black brocade shoes. They were adorned in a bold purple satin bow, while pieces of intricate lace lined the sides to accentuate the baroque heels. The ensemble was stunning.

"Hello, I'm Harper," I said as I greeted the first couple who walked down the entrance toward where I was standing in the main room.

"I'm Hazel, and this is my husband, Grayson. We are so excited to be here. Thank you for inviting us to this event."

The waitress held out a tray for them to select from champagne, gin, or wine. Her husband reached out and grabbed himself a gin.

"Hello," said Grayson as he took a quick sip.

"I appreciate you accepting the invitation. I'll come around and chat some more once everyone has arrived. In the meantime, enjoy the drinks and find your allocated seat."

"Great, can I ask what you do for a living, Harper?"

"I plan to do a little intro speech to kick things off when everyone gets settled. Hopefully, that will reduce the aching repetition of the small talk that happens at times like these."

"Oh, yes, of course. That's smart. I can't wait," said Hazel, who looked genuinely excited. She took a glass of champagne and followed her husband around the table to see where they were to be seated.

I smiled at the waitress as I helped myself to a glass of gin.

"It would be a long night without a little help," I said, lifting my glass to my lips.

She simply smiled.

"Hello, this place is amazing. I feel like I've been transported to another time," said the fellow strutting in an overly flamboyant manner.

"Hi, I'm Harper."

He lent in and gave me an air kiss on either cheek. "I'm Karter, and this is all such a treat. What a wonderful way to make an 'I've just moved in' statement."

I laughed. "I'm glad you approve. Help yourself to a drink, find your name, and take a seat. I'll come chat later."

He pulled a funny face, "Ewe, I hope you didn't place me too close to the Hornsby's. They live two floors down, the way they carry on about the communal spaces you would they think they owned the building."

This amused me. "I'm sure if you are, we can work something out."

He tapped the side of his nose as he simultaneously winked and nodded. "Reshuffle," with that, he walked over to Hazel and Grayson.

"Hello, I'm Harper. Thanks for accepting my invitation."

"I assure you the pleasure is all ours. I'm Rachel."

"Greg."

"Michael."

"Dianne."

"Rachel, Greg, Michael, and Dianne, got it. Grab a drink find your seat. There are only a few more people to arrive. I'll be with you soon."

They, too, joined the rest of them, clinking glasses, whispering and laughing.

I gulped my gin just at the point when I saw him entering the front door with her. They were arm in arm. Unintentionally I found myself giving them a wave as they headed toward me. It was such an odd thing for me to do. I could feel the butterflies in my stomach.

"Hello, thanks for coming. I'm Harper."

"Harper, I know that name," he said with a puzzled look on his face.

"Of course, you do. It was on our invitation silly," she squeezed his arm to regain his attention.

He looked at her, "No, I meant to say, I saw her this morning at the coffee shop." He looked directly into my eyes, "You almost bumped into me, remember?"

"Oh, of course. Yes. What a small world."

"It is indeed. I'm Peter, and this is my wife Collette."

"Hello," said Collette. Her voice was lovely.

"I love your accent. Australia is one of those destinations on my bucket list of places to travel."

Collette blushed as she covered her mouth when she laughed. Her perfect skin was glowing from her application of a light sheen bronzer. "Thanks. You should go for a visit. It is an amazing country."

"As fate would have it, traveling there at some point is already on the cards." I pointed to the tray. "Grab a drink, find your name tag, and have a seat. There are a few more people coming in now. I won't be too long."

They joined the group, meanwhile, Karter came up from behind, pulled my hair away from my neck, and whispered in my ear, "I think we are in the clear. I can't see the Hornsby's names on any of the tags."

"I know. I only extended the invite to the people who live on this floor." I whispered back.

"Oooh, they are going to be super pissed when they realize they missed out on this soirée. I love your work."

I laughed.

"Oh, here come the boys," said Karter with a pseudo sneer.

"You got an invite, Karter?" Sporting a cheeky smile, he looked into my eyes, "It's an honest mistake we have all fell for. You invite him once, and forevermore he invites himself."

"Never gets old, Colton," said Karter as he returned to his seat.

He reached across, took my hand, and lightly kissed it. "I'm Colton. It's a pleasure to make your acquaintance Harper."

"Nice to meet you too, Colton."

"Hi, I'm Hunter."

"Cooper."

"Welcome, Gentleman, grab a drink, find your seat. I'll be with you in a minute."

They were the last of invitees. I went over to the waitress standing at the door. "That's it, twelve people, twelve seats. We can shut the door; I'm not expecting anyone else."

"As you wish," she said in a soft voice as she curtsied.

I walked back over to the living area, waved to everyone before disappearing into the kitchen.

"They are all here. Is there anything you need from me before I get seated?"

The chef replied, "Everything is in order. We will commence preparing the starters."

I released a big sigh, "It smells great. Wish me luck in there."

"The very best of luck, madam."

Returning from the kitchen to a captive audience of seated guests, I switched out my gin for a fresh glass, then stepped forward and raised it in the air. "Here's to getting to know new neighbors."

While they joined me in raising their glasses and taking a sip, I took my position at the head of the table. It didn't matter to me where they were all positioned. I had only set the allocation to have Peter and Collette situated to the left and right of me. Tonight was all about them.

"The chef is preparing the appetizers as we speak. Given none of us have to drive home tonight, we can let loose a little. I do have a selection of spirits available. Just ask one of the ladies to fix it for you. My only call out is to be mindful that you may not have to drive, but you do need to be capable of walking. Moderation is encouraged. I have a strictly no drama and no sleeping over policy."

"Damn," responded Colton with a cheeky grin.

They all laughed.

"Okay, I thought I'd start with a little mini blurb about myself so that when I switch seats to chat and get to know you all, I do not have to repeat the same general stuff over and over."

"She's so smart," whispered Hazel to her husband.

"My name is Harper Perelle. I was born and raised in the US and base myself in New York. My career was built off being a behavioral scientist who specialized in cognitive reasoning. I worked mainly within the criminal justice system and, in particular, spent a lot of time assessing convicts who were assigned the death penalty."

"Holy shit," Hunter raised his hand. "I've got questions. Lots and lots of questions."

Cooper piped up, "Me too. That's intense."

Karter leaned forward, placing his elbows on the table, "You have to be the most interesting neighbor we've had in a long time."

It was hard to contain my amusement, "Hold off on the questions for a minute. I'm retired from that vocation. It took its toll, so I've been on a sabbatical for a while, finding myself traveling, keeping a low profile, and enjoying a far simpler life. So that's me in a nutshell. I'm not sure how long I'm going to be staying here, so don't ask. Oh, I'm not married, never had children, happily single."

"Alright," said Cooper as he repositioned his body on more of an angle.

I laughed, "Appreciate the enthusiasm, Cooper. I'll qualify by saying I'm not looking to date, so once again, don't ask. My main reason for organizing this little gathering is because I thought it would be fun. I'm keen to collect some local knowledge on cool things to do, great places to eat. I'd like to make the most of my time here, however long that may be."

"Can I ask a question?" asked Hunter.

"Sure," I said, trying not to laugh at his need to place his hand in the air.

"What made you pick that as a career? I mean, how does someone even think to train for that? Is it even part of any curriculum?"

"I didn't know what I was getting myself into until I was in the thick of it. The career kind of picked me as much as I had it. I'd like to think that I didn't intentionally select that path. It all started because I found the study of criminology to be super interesting. I then specialized in applied cognitive science. The curriculum at the time I was studying was restricted; however, these days, anthropology, psychology, and psychiatry students also have access to modules that can be built into their degrees around behavioral science."

"What do you mean that it picked you?" Probed Hunter.

"Let's just say that I have a knack for observation and tend to identify behavioral queues that typically get undetected by most people. This became a useful trait that I leveraged, got known for, and eventually built a lucrative career from."

"Does that mean you can tell when someone is lying?" Asked Rachael as she glanced at her partner Michael.

"I can see this has the ability to lead down a path that could get ugly fast. You obviously have a situation in mind. Your question is loaded because it entails you requesting me to determine whether Michael lied to you about something. Yes?"

"Exactly," she said, folding her arms as she glared at him.

I looked at Michael. "Without providing me any context. Do you know what she is referring to? I only require a simple yes or no response."

He cleared his throat and shifted in his seat. "Yes."

"Before either of you react, listen to exactly what I am about to tell you. Okay?"

"Sure," said Michael with some hesitance.

"Rachael, agreed?" I asked.

"Yes, of course."

"I can tell you without knowing anything more, Michael lied."

Rachael almost leaped out of her seat, "I knew it."

"Hey, that's uncool. You agreed to listen, so listen." I paused for a moment to allow her to regain some composure. "Michael lied, but Rachael, you already knew he was. You have been playing a game of sorts by not being honest and upfront with Michael. Your actions are underpinned by very deceptive behavior. You tested him to see if he would lie. This has put you in a mindset where you feel you are justified in setting him up to be caught. I can say that it is highly probable that Michael has picked up subconscious cues from you. He can sense an escalating discomfort, perhaps a pattern he has experienced before, and opts to go toward the path of what he thinks is the least resistance. This leads him to convince himself that a little white lie won't hurt. It's a self-fulfilling prophecy that you both have a role in playing. So, you can unfold your arms, Rachael. You are being righteous and pushing Michael in a corner. Michael, you are only in a corner because you let yourself be placed there. Now's your opportunity to tell the truth, if you want to."

Michael turned to Rachael, "I wasn't at work. I went and played golf. Is she right? Did you already know that?"

Rachael took a sip from her champagne flute, "Yes. I knew. When I was speaking with Moira, she said that you were there with Bobby. That doesn't excuse the fact that you lied to me," she snapped.

"Doesn't it?" I asked with a shift in tone. "You weren't honest with him either. You never told him upfront that you knew he was playing golf. You asked him to test whether he would confess. When he chose to lie, you didn't use the opportunity to tell him you knew. Instead, you have been stewing about it. You were letting it dictate your mood. Michael has no idea that you know he lied and therefore has no idea why you are hyper moody and flying off the handle at him. He, in turn, gets annoyed and distant because he doesn't know how to deal with your behavior. In this scenario, who is making the situation far worse than it needs to be?"

Michael shrugged his shoulders, "I don't know. Me, I guess."

"That would be what I call a typical Michael response. I don't need to spend time with you both to know that Michael is the one who, more often than not, apologizes when you both get in a spat."

"Well, that's because he is usually wrong," she said in a jovial voice.

"Rachael, it's up to you to consider whether your approach is adding value to the quality of your relationship or whether it undermines what you want to achieve. Michael, consider why you feel compelled to lie about things. You likely apologize even when you don't mean it just to keep the peace. This is an indicator that you contribute and encourage the behaviors Racheal displays. You both cycle and feed each other's bad behavior. That's it. I'll leave it with you to both consider the observations. Continue as you have or utilize this as an opportunity to start altering your approach to seek a better outcome."

Karter started clapping, "Unbelievable. Teach me how to do this."

"Holy shit, that's impressive and super terrifying," said Colton, who flagged the waitress to bring across the drinks tray.

"Go, do a course, Karter," I replied, raising my glass at him and then taking a sip. "Colton, it might seem like a neat party trick, but providing an insight into this ability tends to place me in an awkward position. You are all now very self-conscious and will be wondering about what I am thinking. Reading people has a balance of pros and cons. On the other hand, cognitive reasoning is seeking the understanding of the thought processes used when an individual obtains information and applies the knowledge to make choices. An example is how the collection of perceived facts gathered are then used to make what is considered as an informed decision or conclusion."

Dianne grabbed her partner Greg's hand and squeezed it, "Can you give us an example?"

"Image a person who is raised in a family of Bigots and been taught to fear people of other races, creeds, and color. Then one day, this now fully-fledged bigot finds themself in a situation where there is a somewhat harmless altercation with a person who represents any one or all of those fears that have been ingrained in him. Words get exchanged, things get heated, and the bigot switches to a fight or flight adrenaline-fueled physical altercation. This bigot believes their life is being threatened, and in a moment's decision, the scenario escalates to an outcome that is fatal for the other party. What are they guilty of?"

"Murder, he killed the guy, right?" responded Greg.

"Yes, he killed the person. The bigot is arrested and charged with first-degree manslaughter."

"He needs to rot in jail for the rest of his life," said Karter.

Colton turned to Karter. "Really? Bigots raised him. He didn't go out of his way to intentionally kill the other person."

"Yeah, but he did kill him, and he needs to be punished," said Michael.

Grayson shook his head, "The whole situation is fucked up. The guy needs to be locked up for sure. It's the only way to keep everyone else safe. He's killed once, and he'll do it again."

"Cool. Firstly, every one of you assumed that it was a male rather than a female. That is an ingrained bias. Notice within you these opinions and bias were formed from my version of the story, instead of asking for more details to appreciate the entire situation. You all immediately applied emotion and used what I said to begin applying your judgments and morals. This stems from what you have conformed to and been conditioned by. It hopefully shows you how complex we humans are and how immersed in our own 'self' we have become. In behavioral science, the task is to establish who this person is, what they know and understand at the time of the incident, and how they use this information to make decisions. It's not about what I would do in the same situation or what I think the right thing to do is. I need to seek to understand the person's frame of mind, what they knew for certain, and how they used that information to make the decisions that led to that specific outcome."

"I must confess I thought it was a guy. I didn't even consider anything else. I associate bigots with men," Confessed Grayson.

"Was it a man or a woman?" Asked Collette.

I looked at her and smiled, "It was a man."

"I don't know how you separate yourself from it. A person died because he was discriminated against for the way he looked or his belief or whatever. How can you defend the bigot?" Asked Rachael.

"Who said I was defending him? My role is to be impartial. The job is to assess and understand what happened. My thoughts and feelings have no place in that assessment."

The waft of the entrée's followed the staff as they came out of the kitchen. My stomach grumbled as I watched the two ladies balance the trays partially on their shoulders with one hand poised underneath, leaving the other free to serve. A colorful ring of Ratatouille on a light mash was placed in front of each of us.

"Bon appetite," I said while picking up my fork to dig in.

The French Provençal stewed vegetable dish was tightly packed with thin slices of aubergine, squash, tomatoes, courgette, and bell peppers. It was garnished with basil leaves, a drizzle of fresh olive oil, and covered in juice from the stew. My mouth watered as I took my first bite.

The silence provided enough of a measure that the food was well-received except for Michael, who was picking out the aubergine pieces. Everyone else was making light work of the first course.

"How is it?" I asked.

"Marvelous," said Karter.

Collette replied, "Truly delicious."

"Not bad for a dish without meat," joked Hunter.

I turned to my left, "Peter, you seem to be rather quiet. How do you like the entrée?"

He looked at me, then back at his plate. He was blushing. "It's delicious."

Gently I leaned in and whispered, "There's something you want to ask me. What is it?"

Everyone immediately stopped mid-chew.

"Um, yeah, well, it might come across as a bit weird. I'm still trying to process it."

"Weird? There's no such thing. Tell me." I pretended as though I was oblivious.

He placed his knife down and pointed, "Where did you get that?"

Everyone turned to look at the framed Japanese calligraphy sitting on the mantle.

"Before arriving here, I had been traveling around Japan. I spent some time in a small fishing village in Suzu within the Ishikawa prefecture. There was a row of shops. One, in particular, had an array of things for sale. I found this calligraphy tucked inside a Polish magazine. I liked the quirkiness of discovery and purchased it as a keepsake. Why are you curious about it? Have you ever been to Japan?"

He nodded, "I was born in Japan. I believe that calligraphy was created by my father. It says my name in Japanese. He's Polish. The magazine you mentioned you found it in is likely one that was left behind when we returned to Europe."

There were gasps.

"What are the chances?" Exclaimed Rachael.

Karter shifted his chair to get a better view of the calligraphy. "Are you serious? So that is your name in Japanese?"

"Yes," confirmed Peter.

Karter shook his head, "How weird is that? What are the chances?"

"This night just gets better and better," said Colton rubbing his hands together.

"What's the back story to the calligraphy?" Asked Collette.

Peter looked at me, then at his wife. "It's a tradition called Oshichiya. On the seventh day of the birth of a child, the parents hold a dinner with the family and have the name and date displayed. It's a combination of welcoming the child and announcing their name. My father said he had practiced for days before he managed to produce one that was worthy of display. He thought he had lost the calligraphy when we moved back home."

"You are welcome to have it. Maybe surprise your father with it."

"No, I couldn't. It's yours."

I stood up and grabbed the frame. "Honestly, I insist. Please, take it. I'd like to think I was supposed to find it and return it to its' rightful owner."

He looked at Collette, who provided him an encouraging nod. "Take it."

Peter secured the edge of the frame in his hands. "Thank you. I'm not sure what to say. It all seems so impossibly odd." A flash of distinct furrow lines briefly appeared across his brow. "I'm finding it hard to explain how I'm feeling right now. This connection, it's a little overwhelming."

Collette reached over the table and touched his arm. "It's a happy coincidence." She looked at me with her kind eyes. "It is lovely of you to let us keep it."

"The truth is I couldn't make sense of why I bought it and carried it with me. Now I do. Perhaps this is a lovely reminder that there is still a little magic left in the world. We all have threads that bind."

The entrées were being cleared by one of the ladies while the other two walked in the opposite direction placing down the main course in front of us. The plate was decorated with Wild thyme-infused roasted cauliflower sitting on a bed of polenta with a generous serving of marinated whole swiss brown mushrooms. There were blanched French beans topped with salt-encrusted almond slivers and a splash of green peppercorn sauce on the side.

Karter dipped his head down and inhaled deeply before lifting his head. "This smells insane."

"It does smell pretty good," confirmed Hunter.

Inspired by the aroma, I grabbed my fork, loaded it up, and placed it in my mouth. I let the flavors infuse as I thoughtfully chewed.

"Hmm, it is delicious," I raised my glass as I looked at the others and then at Peter and Collette. "Here's to finding the threads that bind and celebrating the beauty of real connections. Cheers."

This was my time, and I planned to enjoy every last minute I could get with them.

# Élan Vital

Walking through the redwood forest felt incredibly cathartic. I had come full circle recognizing so much had come to pass since the owl guided me to the fateful tree. Standing before it, I wanted to pay homage to the innocuous journey. The foresight and genius it took to deliver me through the twists of reality. Locating the book intentionally opened dormant channels and altered the course of my life. The intricacy of every choice taken from that point onwards led me to return here once more.

"Are you here?" I whispered

"With you. Always." He responded.

The hairs on the back of my neck stood at attention as I felt the warmth of a presence standing ever so close. I closed my eyes to aid in enhancing this experience without distraction.

"I did it. I know the truth of everything. The books weren't just stories of other people's lives. They were mine. I wrote and left them for my future self to find to navigate this pivotal lifecycle. While under the Dragons Gate, I felt the presence of York and Patience holding hands, staring at me. Their energies were mine.

I surrendered to the truth of it all, and we merged into a state of completeness that amplified my connection to everything. All that was fractured is now rejoined with no scars left to heal. The Interferon's worst fears have come to fruition, for I can no longer be contained. And you, I know you and why I have ached and missed you so."

"Who am I?"

I gulped some air and steadied my hands as I tried not to respond to the overwhelming love I felt, "You are my soul."

"Yes."

I fell to my knees, placed my hands over my face, and began to bawl uncontrollably, "This has been so hard without you. All this time, I thought you were my twin flame, but I separated from you to protect us. It was the only way…"

"I've always been close." he said in a soothing tone.

"I knew something was missing. After the Dragons Gate when I understood what I had done…. Separating from you, denying access to this vessel to ensure they could not claim you made this journey impossibly lonely. The pain of absence was unbearable. I felt so lost."

"I know."

"I understand that is why I didn't immediately recognize my twin flame. He was there right in front of me, hidden in plain view, trapped for hundreds of years as a koi, waiting to be recognized, waiting to be found. When I felt him at the Dragons Gate, placed my hands on his broken body, the floodgates of dormant emotion opened to saturate us with the deepest exchange of love. I wanted to go with him so that we could be together. We have been apart for so long. The pain of losing him again is indescribable. The cycle of lives has been excruciatingly unkind to us. Moments gifted, lifetimes apart. A wealth of pain burdening our cloaked subconscious. Once revealed by the gate, I was released from the binds of torment. I was freed to channel what I truly am, love."

I felt the sun's warmth surround me as it broke through the clouds. I lifted my head to expose my face to the light. "He chose to sacrifice for the greater good, and now he is free from those binds too. Together we have one more life cycle to complete our journey. Is he safe?"

"Yes. He has passed through. It has begun."

"Then I guess it's time for me too. I met them. Knowing what laid ahead, I wanted to take the opportunity to spend some time with them."

"It is almost time. Are you ready?"

"Yes, more than ready. I ache to be united with you. I want to unite with my twin flame. I never want to feel alone again."

"You won't have to."

The faded outline of an energy mass began to appear before me. I watched as it formed the shape of a hand that reached out to me while the rest molded into an outline of a physique complete with massive wings that towered above its head. Fantastical ice blue eyes peered down at me. The features of a strong jawline, nose, and lips were the only stilled aspects. Everything else flecked as if the brush strokes of a Claude Monet painting had been blessed with movement. As I placed my hand in his instantaneously, our energy began merging.

"Look into my eyes and try not to fight it. Surrender your will so we can unite and propel."

I breathed in deep, tasting the sweetness of life coat my tongue and fill my lungs with the fragrance of wildflowers. I quietly smiled, maintaining focus on the ocean blue depth of his eyes. The limpness of my body was greeted with the expansion of my becoming, thrust into a darkened space that contained the energies of ocean swells. I tossed about mercilessly to the pull and push of the tides that captivated my essence. Surrounded by tepid waters, I heard the muffled screams. Voices were calling out unfamiliar names. The sting of the light hurt my eyes as I gasped for air and loudly cried in protest.

"Congratulations, Mr. and Mrs. Jacobs. It's a baby girl."

"Talia, her name is Talia," said Collette, exhausted and thrilled.

She looked at Peter, whose eyes were filled with tears.

He squeezed her hand and bent over to gently kiss her sweaty forehead. "Yes, Talia. Talia Temperance Jacobs. Our baby girl." He replied.